PAK POWER

Phssthpok was a Pak. That meant he had three stages of growth—Childhood, Breeder, and finally, Protector, the last achieved around the age of 45 Earth years. At that time, all being well, basic physiological changes would take place, and provided a Pak had access to proper food—his tree-of-life root—a Protector could be virtually immortal.

In this rigidly structured species, a Protector has only one genetically implanted objective—to Protect his bloodline. A Protector without progeny loses the will to live, ceases to be hungry, and so dies of starvation. *Unless* he can find a way to transfer his personal bloodline drive to a more generalized drive for survival of the species.

This prime drive, plus his superlative intelligence, his physical strength and structural simplicity, make him a most effective Protector—and a viciously formidable fighter. Since the Pak spend most of their time fighting one another in murderous planet-wide wars, they have never spread out to conquer the galaxy—

Until Phssthpok set out to find a lost group of Breeders . . .

Also by Larry Niven
Published by Ballantine Books:

ALL THE MYRIAD WAYS

CONVERGENT SERIES

FLIGHT OF THE HORSE

THE FLYING SORCERERS (with David Gerrold)

FOOTFALL (with Jerry Pournelle)

A GIFT FROM EARTH

A HOLE IN SPACE

THE INTEGRAL TREES

LIMITS

THE LONG *ARM* OF GIL HAMILTON

NEUTRON STAR

RINGWORLD

THE RINGWORLD ENGINEERS

TALES OF KNOWN SPACE: THE UNIVERSE OF
    LARRY NIVEN

WORLD OF PTAVVS

A WORLD OUT OF TIME

PROTECTOR

Larry Niven

A Del Rey Book

BALLANTINE BOOKS • NEW YORK

A Del Rey Book
Published by Ballantine Books

A shorter version of this novel appeared under the title, "The Adults," in *Galaxy* Magazine, June 1967. Copyright © 1967 Galaxy Publishing Corporation.

ISBN 0-345-33775-1

Manufactured in the United States of America

First Edition: September 1973
Thirteenth Printing: February 1986

Cover art by H. R. Van Dongen

PHSSTHPOK

Genesis, Chapter 3, King James version:

22 And the Lord God said, Behold, the man is become as one of *us*, to know good and evil: and now, lest he put forth his hand, and take also of the tree of life, and eat, and live forever:

23 Therefore the Lord God sent him forth from the garden of Eden, to till the ground from whence he was taken.

24 So he drove out the man; and he placed at the east of the Garden of Eden Chĕf-ū-bĭms, and a flaming sword which turned every way, to keep the way of the tree of life.

I

He sat before an eight-foot circle of clear twing, looking endlessly out on a view that was less than exciting.

Even a decade ago those stars had been a sprinkling of dull red dots in his wake. When he cleared the forward view, they would shine a hellish blue, bright enough to read by. To the side, the biggest had been visibly flattened. But now there were only stars, white points sparsely scattered across a sky that was mostly black. This was a lonely sky. Dust clouds hid the blazing glory of home.

The light in the center of the view was not a star. It was big as a sun, dark at the center, and bright enough to have burned holes in a man's retinae. It was the light of a Bussard ramjet, burning a bare eight miles away. Every few years Phssthpok spent some time watching the drive, just to be sure it was burning evenly. A long time ago he had caught a slow, periodic wavering in time to prevent his ship from becoming a tiny nova. But the blue-white light had not changed at all in the weeks he'd been watching it.

For most of a long, slow lifetime the heavens had been crawling past Phssthpok's porthole. Yet he remembered little of that voyage. The time of waiting had been too devoid of events to interest his memory. It is the way with the protector stage of the Pak species, that his leisure memories are of the past, when he was a child and, later, a breeder, when the world was new and bright and free of responsibilities. Only danger to himself or his children can rouse a protector from his normal dreamy

3

lassitude to a fighting fury unsurpassed among sentient beings.

Phssthpok sat dreaming in his disaster couch.

The cabin's attitude controls were beneath his left hand. When he was hungry, which happened once in ten hours, his knobby hand, like two fistfuls of black walnuts strung together, would reach into a slot on his right and emerge with a twisted, fleshy yellow root the size of a sweet potato. Terrestrial weeks had passed since Phssthpok last left his disaster couch. In that time he had moved nothing but his hands and his jaws. His eyes had not moved at all.

Before that there had been a period of furious exercise. It is a protector's duty to stay fit.

Even a protector with nobody to protect.

The drive was steady, or enough so to satisfy Phssthpok. The protector's knotted fingers moved, and the heavens spun about him. He watched the other bright light float into the porthole. When it was centered he stopped the rotation.

Already brighter than any star around it, his destination was still too dim to be more than a star. But it was brighter than Phssthpok had expected, and he knew that he had let time slip away from him. Too much dreaming! And no wonder. He'd spent most of twelve hundred years in that couch, staying immobile to conserve his food supply. It would have been thirty times that but for relativistic effects.

Despite what looked to be the most crippling case of arthritis in medical history, despite weeks spent like a paralytic, the knobby protector was instantly in motion. The drive flame went mushy; expanded; began to cool. Shutting down a Bussard ramjet is almost as tricky as starting one. At ramjet speeds the interstellar hydrogen comes on as gamma rays. It would have to be guided away by magnetic fields, even if it were not being burned as fuel.

He had reached the most likely region of space. Ahead was the most likely star. Phssthpok's moment of success was hard upon him. The ones he had come to help (if they existed at all; if they hadn't died out in all this time; if they circled this star and not one less likely) wouldn't be expecting him. Their minds were nearly animal. They might or might not use fire, but they certainly wouldn't have telescopes. Yet they were waiting for him. . .in a sense. If they were here at all, they had been waiting for two and a half million years.

He would not disappoint them.

He must not.

A protector without descendants is a being without purpose. Such an anomaly must find a purpose, and quickly, or die. Most die. In their minds or their glands a reflex twitches, and they cease to feel hunger. Sometimes such a one finds that he can adapt the entire Pak species as his progeny; but then he must find a way to serve that species. Phssthpok was one of the lucky few.

It would be terrible if he failed.

Nick Sohl was coming home.

The quiet of space was around him, now that his ears had learned to forget the hum of the ship's drive. Two weeks' worth of tightly coiled stubble covered his jaw and the shaved scalp on either side of his cottony Belter crest. If he concentrated he could smell himself. He had gone mining in Saturn's rings, with a singleship around him and a shovel in his hand (for the magnets used to pull monopoles from asteroidal iron did look remarkably like shovels). He would have stayed longer; but he liked to think that Belt civilization could survive without him for just about three weeks.

A century ago monopoles had been mere theory, and conflicting theory at that. Magnetic theory said that a north magnetic pole could not exist apart from a south magnetic pole, and vice-versa. Quantum theory implied that they might exist independently.

The first permanent settlements had been blooming among the biggest Belt asteroids when an exploring team found monopoles scattered through the nickel-iron core of an asteroid. Today they were not theory, but a thriving

Belt industry. A magnetic field generated by monopoles acts in an inverse linear relationship rather than an inverse square. In practical terms, a monopole-based motor or instrument will reach much further. Monopoles were valuable where weight was a factor, and in the Belt weight was always a factor. But monopole mining was still a one man operation.

Nick's luck had been poor. Saturn's rings were not a good region for monopoles anyway; too much ice, too little metal. The electromagnetic field around his cargo box probably held no more than two full shovelfuls of north magnetic poles. Not much of a catch for a couple of weeks backbreaking labor. . .but still worth good money at Ceres.

He'd have been satisfied to find nothing. Mining was an excuse the First Speaker for the Belt Political Section used to escape from his cramped office buried deep in the rock of Ceres, from the constant UN–Belt squabbles, from wife and children, friends and acquaintances, enemies and strangers. And next year, after frantic weeks spent catching up with current events, after the next ten months spent manipulating the politics of the solar system, he would be back.

Nick was building up speed for the trip to Ceres, with Saturn a fantastic bauble behind him, when he saw his mining magnet swing slowly away from the cargo box. Somewhere to his left was a new and powerful source of monopoles.

A grin split his face like lightning across a black sky. Better late than never! Too bad he hadn't found it on the way out; but he could sell it once he'd located it. . . which would take doing. The needle wavered between two attractions, one of which was his cargo box.

He invested twenty minutes focusing a com laser on Ceres. "This is Nick Sohl, repeating, Nicholas Brewster Sohl. I wish to register a claim for a monopole source in the general direction of—" He tried to guess how much his cargo was affecting the needle. "—of Sagittarius. I want to offer this source for sale to the Belt government. Details follow, half an hour."

He then turned off his fusion motor, climbed laboriously into suit and backpac, and left the ship carrying a telescope and his mining magnet.

The stars are far from eternal, but for man they might as well be. Nick floated among the eternal stars, motionless though falling toward the tiny sun at tens of thousands of miles per hour. *This* was why he went mining. The universe blazed like diamonds on black velvet, an unforgettable backdrop for golden Saturn. The Milky Way was a jeweled bracelet for all the universe. Nick loved the Belt from the carved-out rocks to the surface domes to the spinning inside-out bubble worlds; but most of all he loved space itself.

A mile from the ship he used 'scope and mining magnet to fix the location of the new source. He moved back to the ship to call in. A few hours from now he could take another fix and pin the source by triangulation.

When he reached the ship the communicator was alight. The gaunt fair face of Martin Shaeffer, Third Speaker, was talking to an empty acceleration couch.

"—Must call in at once, Nick. Don't wait to take your second fix. This is urgent Belt business. Repeating. Martin Shaeffer calling Nick Sohl aboard singleship *Hummingbird*—"

Nick refocused his laser. "Lit, I'm truly honored. A simple clerk would have sufficed to record my poor find. Repeating." He set the message to repeat, then started putting away tools. Ceres was light-minutes distant.

He did not try to guess what emergency might need his personal attention. But he was worried.

Presently the answer came. Lit Shaeffer's expression was strange, but his tone was bantering. "Nick, you're too modest about your poor find. A pity we're going to have to disallow it. One hundred and four miners have already called in to report your monopole source."

Nick gaped. One hundred and four? But he was in the outer system. . .and most miners preferred to work their own mines anyway. How many had *not* called in?

"They're all across the system," said Lit. "It's a hell of a big source. As a matter of fact, we've already located it by paralax. One source, forty AU out from the sun, which makes it somewhat further away than Pluto, and eighteen degrees off the plane of the solar system. Mitchikov says that there must be as big a mass of south magnetic monopoles in the source as we've mined in the past century."

Outsider! thought Nick. And: *Pity they'll disallow my claim.*

"Mitchikov says that big a source could power a really big Bussard ramjet—a manned ramrobot." Nick nodded at that. Ramrobots were robot probes to the nearby stars, and were one of the few sources of real UN–Belt co-operation. "We've been following the source for the past half-hour. It's moving into the solar system at just over four thousand miles per second, freely falling. That's well above even interstellar speeds. We're all convinced it's an Outsider.

"Any comments?

"Repeating—"

Nick switched it off and sat for a moment, letting himself get used to the idea. An Outsider!

Outsider was Belter slang for *alien;* but the word meant more than that. The Outsider would be the first sentient alien ever to contact the human race. It (singular) would contact the Belt instead of Earth, not only because the Belt held title to most of the solar system but because those humans who had colonized space were clearly more intelligent. There were many hidden assumptions in the word, and not every Belter believed them all.

And the emergency had caught Nick Sohl on vacation. Censored dammit! He'd have to work by message laser. "Nick Sohl calling Martin Shaeffer, Ceres Base. Yes, I've got comments. One, it sounds like your assumption is valid. Two, stop blasting the news all over the system. Some flatlander ship might pick up the fringes of a message beam. We'll have to bring them in on it sooner or later, but not just yet. Three, I'll be home in five days. Concentrate on getting more information. We won't have to make any crucial decisions for awhile." Not until the Outsider entered the solar system, or tried sending messages of its own. "Four—" Find out if the son of a bitch is decelerating! Find out where he'll stop! But he couldn't say any of that. Too specific for a message laser. Shaeffer would know what to do. "There is no four. Sohl out."

The solar system is big and, in the outer reaches, thin. In the main Belt, from slightly inside Mars's orbit to slightly outside Jupiter's, a determined man can examine a hundred rocks in a month. Further out, he's likely to spend a couple of weeks coming and going, just to look at something he hopes nobody else has noticed.

The main Belt is not mined out, though most of the big rocks are now private property. Most miners prefer to work the Belt. In the Belt they know they can reach civilization and civilization's byproducts: stored air and water, hydrogen fuel, women and other people, a new air regenerator, autodocs and therapeutic psychomimetic drugs.

Brennan didn't need drugs or company to keep him sane. He preferred the outer reaches. He was in Uranus's trailing Trojan point, following sixty degrees behind the ice giant in its orbit. Trojan points, being points of stable equilibrium, are dust collectors and collectors of larger objects. There was a good deal of dust here, for deep space, and a handful of rocks worth exploring.

Had he found nothing at all, Brennan would have moved on to the moons, then to the leading Trojan point. Then home for a short rest and a visit with Charlotte; and, because his funds would be low by then, a paid tour of duty on Mercury, which he would hate.

Had he found pitchblende he would have been in the point for months.

None of the rocks held enough radioactives to interest him. But something nearby showed the metallic gleam of an artifact. Brennan moved in on it, expecting to find some Belt miner's throwaway fuel tank, but looking anyway. Jack Brennan was a confirmed optimist.

The artifact was the shell of a solid fuel rocket motor. Part of the Mariner XX, from the lettering.

The Mariner XX, the ancient Pluto fly-by. Ages ago the ancient empty shell must have drifted back toward the distant sun, drifted into the thin Trojan-point dust and coasted to a stop. The hull was pitted with dust holes and was still rotating with the stabilizing impulse imparted three generations back.

As a collector's item the thing was nearly beyond price. Brennan took phototapes of it *in situ* before he moved in to attach himself to the flat nose and used his jet back-pac to stop the rotation. He strapped it to the fusion tube of his ship, below the lifesystem cabin. The gyros could compensate for the imbalance.

In another sense the bulk presented a problem.

He stood next to it on the slender metal shell of the fusion tube. The antique motor was half as big as his mining singleship, but very light, little more than a metal skin for its original shaped-core charge. If Brennan had found pitchblende the singleship would have been hung with cargo nets under the fuel ring, carrying its own weight in radioactive ore. He would have returned to the Belt at half a gee. But with the Mariner relic as his cargo he could accelerate at the one gee which was standard for empty singleships.

It might just give him the edge he'd need.

If he sold the tank through the Belt, the Belt would take thirty percent in income tax and agent's fees. But if he sold it on the Moon, Earth's Museum of Spaceflight would charge no tax at all.

Brennan was in a good position for smuggling. There were no goldskins out here. His velocity over most of his course would be tremendous. They couldn't begin to catch him until he approached the Moon. He wasn't haul-ing monopoles or radioactives; the magnetic and radia-tion detectors would look right through him. He could swing in over the plane of the system, avoiding rocks and other ships.

But if they did get him they'd take one hundred per-cent of his find. Everything.

Brennan smiled to himself. He'd risk it.

Phssthpok's mouth closed once, twice, three times. A yellow tree-of-life root separated into four chunks, raggedly, because the edges of Phssthpok's beak were not sharp. They were blunt and uneven, like the top of a molar. Phssthpok gulped four times.

He had hardly noticed the action. It was as if his hand, mouth and belly were on automatic, while Phssthpok watched the scope screen.

Under 10^4 magnification the screen showed three tiny violet points.

Looking around the edge of the scope screen Phssthpok could see only the bright yellow star he'd called GO Target #1. He'd been searching for planets. He'd found one, a beauty, the right size and approximate temperature, with a transparent water-bearing atmosphere and an oversized moon. But he'd also found myriads of violet points so small that at first he'd thought they were mere flashes in his retinae.

They were real, and they moved. Some moved no faster than planetary objects; others, hundreds of times faster than escape velocity for the system. They glowed intensely hot, the color of a neutron star in its fourth week of life, when its temperature is still in the millions of degrees.

Obviously they were spacecraft. At these speeds, natural objects would have been lost to interstellar space within months. Probably they used fusion drives. If so, and judging from their color, they burned hotter and more efficiently than Phssthpok's own.

They seemed to spend most of their time in space. At first he'd hoped they were some form of space-born life, perhaps related to the starseeds of the galactic core. But as he drew nearer the yellow sun he'd had to abandon the idea. All the sparks had destinations, from the myriad small orbiting rocks to the moons and planets of the inner system. One frequent target was the world with the water atmosphere, the one he'd classified as Pak-habitable. No lifeform native to space could have taken its gravity or its atmosphere.

That planet, GO Target #1-3, was the *biggest* such target, though the spacecraft touched many smaller bodies. Interesting. If the pilots of those fusion craft had developed on GO Target #1-3, they would naturally prefer lighter gravities to heavier.

But the ones he sought hadn't the minds to build such craft. Had something alien usurped their places?

Then he and his thousands had given their long lives to extract only a sterile vengeance.

Phssthpok felt fury building in him. He held it back. It needn't be the answer. GO Target #1 was not the only likely target. Probability was only twenty-eight percent. He could hope that the ones he had come to help circled another star.

But he'd have to check.

There is a minimum speed at which a Bussard ramjet will operate, and Phssthpok was not far above it. He had planned to coast through the system until he found something definite. Now he would have to use his reserve fuel. He had already found a bluewhite spark moving at high velocity toward the inner system. He should be able to match its course.

Nick landed *Hummingbird*, hurriedly issued orders for unloading and sale of his cargo, and went underground. His office was some two miles beneath the rocky bubble-dotted surface of Ceres, buried deep in the nickel-iron substrate.

He hung his suit and helmet in the vestibule of his office. There was a painting on the front of the suit, and he patted it affectionately before he went in. He always did that.

Most Belters decorated their suits. Why not? The interior of his suit was the only place many a Belter could call home, and the one possession he *had* to keep in perfect condition. But even in the Belt, Nick Sohl's suit was unique.

On an orange background was the painting of a girl. She was short; her head barely reached Nick's neck ring.

Her skin was a softly glowing green. Only her lovely back showed across the front of the suit. Her hair was streaming bonfire flames, flickering orange with touches of yellow and white, darkening into red-black smoke as it swept across the girl's left shoulder. She was nude. Her arms were wrapped around the suit's torso, her hands touching the air pac on its back; her legs embraced the suit's thighs, so that her heels touched the backs of the flexible metal knee joints. It was a very beautiful painting, so beautiful that it almost wasn't vulgar. A pity the suit's sanitary outlet wasn't somewhere else.

Lit lounged in one of the guest chairs in Nick's office, his long legs sprawling far across the rug. He was attenuated rather than big. Too much of his childhood had been spent in free fall. Now he could not fit into a standard pressure suit or spacecraft cabin; and wherever he sat, he looked like he was trying to take over.

Nick dropped into his own chair and closed his eyes for a moment, getting used to the feel of being First Speaker again. With his eyes still closed he said, "Okay, Lit. What's been happening?"

"Got it all here." Rustle of paper. "Yah. The monopole source is coming in over the plane of the solar system, aimed approximately at the sun. As of an hour ago it was two point two billion miles out. For a week after we spotted it it showed a steady acceleration of point nine two gee, largely lateral and braking thrust to warp its course around the sun. Now it's mainly deceleration, and the thrust has dropped to point one four gee. That aims it through Earth's orbit."

"Where will Earth be then?"

"We checked that. If he goes back to point nine two gee at—*this* point, he'll be at rest eight days from now. And that's where Earth will be." Lit looked grim. "All of this is more than somewhat approximate. All we really know is that he's aimed at the inner system."

"But Earth is the obvious target. Hardly fair. The Outsider's supposed to contact us, not them. What have you done about anything?"

"Mostly observations. We've got photos of what looks

like a drive flame. A fusion flame, somewhat cooler than ours."

"Less efficent, then. . .but if he's using a Bussard ramjet, he's getting his fuel free. I suppose he's below ramjet speeds now, though."

"Right."

"He must be huge. Could be a warship, Lit. Using that big a monopole source."

"Not necessarily. You know how a ramrobot works? A magnetic field picks up interstellar hydrogen plasma, guides it away from the cargo pod and constricts it so that the hydrogen undergoes fusion. The difference is that nobody can ride them because too much hydrogen gets through as radiation. In a manned ship you'd need enormously greater control of the plasma fields."

"*That* much more?"

"Mitchikov says yes, if he came from far enough away. The further he came, the faster he must have been going at peak velocity."

"Um."

"You're getting paranoid, Nick. Why would *any* species send *us* an interstellar warship?"

"Why would anyone send us a ship at all? I mean, if you're going to be humble about it. . .Can we contact that ship before it reaches Earth?"

"Oddly enough, I thought of that. Mitchikov has several courses plotted. Our best bet is to start a fleet from the trailing Jupiter Trojans sometime within the next six days."

"Not a fleet. We want the Outsider to see us as harmless. Do we have any big ships in the Trojans?"

"The *Blue Ox*. She was about to leave for Juno, but I commandeered her and had her cargo tank cleared."

"Good. Nice going." The *Blue Ox* was a mammoth fluid cargo carrier, as big as one of the Titan Hotel's luxury liners, though not as pretty. "We'll want a computer, a good one, not just a ship's autopilot. Also a tech to run it, and some spare senses for the machine. I want to use it as a translator, and the Outsider might talk by eye-blinks or radio or modulated current. Can we maybe fit a singleship into the *Ox's* cargo hold?"

enough. Third glance included a few instrument readings. Brennan was accelerating, but the stranger was decelerating, and still had enormous velocity. Either it had come from beyond Pluto's orbit, or its drive must generate tens of gees. Which gave the same answer.

The strange light was an Outsider.

How long had the Belt been waiting for him? Let any man spend some time between the stars, even a flatland moonship pilot, and someday he would realize just how *deep* the universe really was. Billions of light years deep, with room for anything at all. Beyond doubt the Outsider was out there somewhere; the first alien species to contact Man was going about its business beyond the reach of Belt telescopes.

Now the Outsider was here, matching courses with Jack Brennan.

And Brennan wasn't even surprised. Wary, yes. Even frightened. But not surprised, not even that the Outsider had chosen him. That was an accident of fate. They had both been heading into the inner system from roughly the same direction.

Call the Belt? The Belt must know by now. The Belt telescope net tracked every ship in the system; the odds were that it would find any wrong-colored dot moving at the wrong speed. Brennan had expected them to find his own ship, had gambled that they wouldn't find it soon enough. Certainly they'd found the Outsider. Certainly they were watching it; and by virtue of that fact they must be watching Brennan too. In any case Brennan couldn't laser Ceres. A flatland ship might pick up the beam. Brennan didn't know Belt policy on Earth–Outsider contacts.

The Belt must act without him.

Which left Brennan with two decisions of his own.

One was easy. He didn't have a snowman's chance of smuggling anything. He would have to alter course to reach one of the major asteroids, and call the Belt the first chance he had to advise them of his course and cargo.

But what of the Outsider?

Evasion tactics? Easy enough. Axiomatically, it is impossible to stop a hostile ship in space. A cop can match course with a smuggler, but he cannot make an arrest unless the smuggler cooperates—or runs out of fuel. He can blow the ship out of space, or even ram with a good autopilot; but how can he connect airlocks with a ship that keeps firing its drive in random bursts? Brennan could head anywhere, and all the Outsider could do was follow or destroy him.

Running would be sensible. Brennan did have a family to protect. Charlotte could take care of herself. She was an adult Belter, as competent to run her own life as Brennan himself, though she had never found enough ambition to earn her pilot's license. And Brennan had paid the customary fees in trust for Estelle and Jennifer. His daughters would be raised and educated.

But he could do more for them. Or he could become a father again. . .probably with Charlotte. There was money strapped to his hull. Money was power. Like electrical or political power, its uses could take many forms.

Contact the alien and he might never see Charlotte again. There were risks in being the first to meet an alien species.

And obvious honors.

Could history ever forget the man who met the Outsider?

Just for a moment he felt trapped. As if fate were playing games with his lifeline. . .but he couldn't turn this down. Let the Outsider come to him. Brennan held his course.

The Belt is a web of telescopes. Hundreds of thousands of them.

It has to be that way. Every ship carries a telescope. Every asteroid must be watched constantly, because asteroids can be perturbed from their orbits, and because a map of the solar system has to be up-to-date by seconds. The light of every fusion drive has to be watched. In crowded sectors ships can run through each other's exhausts if someone doesn't warn them away; and the exhaust from a fusion motor is deadly.

Nick Sohl kept glancing up at the screen, down at the stack of dossiers on his desk, up at the screen. . .The screen showed two blobs of violet-white light, one bigger than the other, and vaguer. Already they could both appear on the same screen, because the asteroid taking the pictures was almost in line with their course.

He had read the dossiers several times. Ten of them; and each might be the unknown Belter who was now approaching the Outsider. There had been a dozen dossiers. In the outer offices men were trying to locate and eliminate these ten as they had already found two, by phone calls and com lasers and dragnets.

Since the ship wasn't running, Nick had privately eliminated six of the dossiers. Two had never been caught smuggling: a mark of caution, whether he'd never smuggled or never been caught. One he knew; she was a xenophobe. Three were old-timers; you don't get to be an old-timer in the Belt by taking foolish chances. In the Belt the Finagle-Murphy Laws are only half a joke.

One of four miners had had the colossal arrogance to appoint himself humanity's ambassador to the universe. *Serve him right if he blows it,* thought Nick. *Which one?*

A million miles short of Jupiter's orbit, moving well above the plane of the solar system, Phssthpok matched velocities with the native ship and began to close in.

Of the thousands of sentient species in the galaxy, Phssthpok and Phssthpok's race had studied only their own. When they ran across other species, as in the mining of nearby systems for raw materials, they destroyed them as quickly and safely as possible. Aliens were dangerous, or might be, and Pak were not interested in anything but Pak. A protector's intelligence was high; but intelligence is a tool to be used toward a goal, and goals are not always chosen intelligently.

Phssthpok was working strictly from ignorance. All he could do was guess.

At a guess, then, and assuming that the oval scratch in the native ship's hull was really a door, the native would be not much taller and not much shorter than Phssthpok. Say, three to seven feet tall, depending on how much elbow room it needed. Of course the oval might not be designed for the native's longest length, as for the biped Phssthpok. But the ship was small; it wouldn't hold something too much larger than Phssthpok.

One look at the native would tell him. If it was not Pak, he would need to ask it questions. If it was—

There would still be questions, many of them. But his search would be over. A few ship's days to reach GO Target #1-3, a short time to learn their language and explain how to use what he'd brought, and he could stop eating.

It showed no awareness of Phssthpok's ship. A few minutes and he would be alongside, yet the stranger made no move—cancel. The native had turned off its drive. Phssthpok was being invited to match courses.

Phssthpok did. He wasted neither motion nor fuel; he might have spent his whole life practicing for this one maneuver. His lifesystem pod coasted alongside the native ship, and stopped.

His pressure suit was on, but he made no move. Phssthpok dared not risk his own person, not when he was so close to victory. If the native would only step out on the hull . . .

Brennan watched the ship come alongside.

Three sections, spaced eight miles apart. He saw no cable joining them. At this distance it might be invisibly thin. The biggest, most massive section must be the drive: a cylinder with three small cones jutting at angles from the tail. Big as it was, the cylinder must be too small to hold fuel for an interstellar voyage. Either the Outsider had dropped expendable tanks along the way, or. . .a manned ramrobot?

Section two was a sphere some sixty feet across. When

the ship finally stopped moving, this section was immediately opposite Brennan. A large circular window stared out of the sphere, so that the sphere looked like a great eyeball. It turned to follow Brennan as it moved past. Brennan found it difficult to return that uncanny stare.

He was having second thoughts. Surely the Belt government could have organized a better meeting than this. . .

The trailing pod—he'd had a good look as it eased past. It was egg shaped, perhaps sixty feet long by forty feet through. The big end, facing away from the drive section, was so uniformly pitted with dust grains that it looked sandblasted. The small end was pointed and smooth, almost shiny. Brennan nodded to himself. A ramscoop field would have protected the forward end from micro-meteoroids during acceleration. During deceleration its training position would have done the same.

There were no breaks in the egg.

There was motion within the bulging iris of the center section. Brennan strained, trying to see more. . .but nothing more happened.

It was a peculiar way to build a ship, he thought. The center pod must be the life support system, if only because it had a porthole and the trailing pod did not. And the drive was dangerously radioactive; otherwise why string the ship out like this? But that meant that the life-system was positioned to protect the trailing pod from the drive radiation. Whatever was in that trailing pod must be more important than the pilot, *in the opinion of the pilot.*

Either that, or the pilot and the designer had both been inept or insane.

The Outsider ship was motionless now, its drive going cold, its lifesystem section a few hundred feet away. Brennan waited.

I'm being chauvinistic, he told himself. *I can't judge an alien's sanity by Belt standards, can I?*

His lip curled. *Sure I can. That ship is badly designed.* The alien stepped out onto its hull.

Every muscle in Brennan jerked as he saw it. The

alien was a biped; it looked human enough from here. But it had stepped *through* the porthole. It stood on its own hull, motionless, waiting.

It had two arms, one head, two legs. It used a pressure suit. It carried a weapon—or a reaction pistol; there was no way to tell. But Brennan saw no backpac. A reaction pistol takes a deal more skill than a jet backpac. Who would use one in open space?

What the Finagle was it waiting for?

Of course. For Brennan.

For a wild moment he considered starting the drive *now,* get out of here before it was too late! Cursing his fear, Brennan moved deliberately to the door. The men who built singleships built as cheaply as possible. His ship had no airlock; there was just the door, and pumps to evacuate the lifesystem. Brennan's suit was tight. All he had to do was open the door.

He stepped outside on sandal magnets.

The seconds stretched away as Brennan and the Outsider examined each other. *It looks human enough,* Brennan thought. *Biped. Head on top. But if it's human, and if it's been in space long enough to build a starship, it can't be as inept as this ship says it is.*

Have to find out what it's carrying. Maybe it's right. Maybe its cargo is worth more than its life.

The Outsider jumped.

It fell toward him like a falcon diving. Brennan stood his ground, frightened, but admiring the alien's skill. The alien didn't use its reaction pistol. Its jump had been perfect. It would land right next to Brennan.

The Outsider hit the hull on springy limbs, absorbing its momentum like any Belter. It was smaller than Brennan: no more than five feet tall. Brennan saw dimly through its faceplate. He recoiled, a long step backward. The thing was hideously ugly. Chauvinism be damned: the Outsider's face would stop a computer.

The one backward step didn't save him.

The Outsider was too close. It reached out, wrapped a pressurized mitten around Brennan's wrist, and jumped.

Brennan gasped and, too late, tried to jerk away. The Outsider's grip was like spring steel inside its glove. They were spinning away through space toward the eyeball-shaped life support system, and not a thing Brennan could do about it.

"Nick," said the intercom.

"Here," said Nick. He'd left it open.

"The dossier you want is labeled 'Jack Brennan.' "

"How do you know?"

"We called his woman. He has only one, a Charlotte Wiggs, and two kids. We convinced her it was urgent. She finally told us he was off searching the Uranus Trojan-points."

"Uranus. . .that sounds right. Cutter, do me a favor."

"Sure. Official?"

"Yes. See to it that *Hummingbird* is fueled and provisioned and kept that way until further notice. Fit it with strap-on boosters. Then get a com laser focused on ARM Headquarters, New York, and keep it there. You'll need three, of course." For relays as the Earth rotated.

"Okay. No message yet?"

"No, just hold a laser ready in case we need it."

The situation was so damn fluid. If he needed help from Earth he'd need it quickly and badly. The surest way to convince the flatlanders would be to go himself. No First Speaker had ever touched Earth. . .and he didn't expect to now; but *The Perversity of the Universe Tends Toward a Maximum*.

Nick began to skim Brennan's dossier. Too bad the man had children.

Phssthpok's first clear memories dated from the day he woke to the fact that he was a protector. He could conjure blurred memories from before: of pain, fighting, discovering new foods, experiences in sex and affection and hate and tree climbing in the valley of Pitchok; watching curiously, half a dozen times, as various female breeders bore children he could smell were his. But his mind had been vague then.

As a protector he thought sharply and clearly. At first it had been unpleasant. He had had to get used to it. There had been others to help him, teachers and such.

There was a war, and he had graduated into it. Because he had had to develop the habit of asking questions, it had been years before he understood its history:

Three hundred years earlier several hundred major Pak families had allied to refertilize a wide desert area of the Pak world. Erosion and overgrazing had produced that desert, not war, though there were mildly radioactive patches all across it. No place on the Pak world was entirely free from war.

The heartbreakingly difficult task of reforesting had been completed a generation ago. Immediately and predictably the alliance had split into several smaller alliances, each determined to secure the land for its own descendants. By now most of the earlier alliances were gone. A number of families had been exterminated, and the surviving groups changed sides whenever expedient to protect their blood lines. Phssthpok's blood line now held with South Coast.

Phssthpok enjoyed war. Not because of the fighting. As a breeder he'd had fights, and war was less a matter of fighting than of outwitting the enemy. At its start it had been a fusion bomb war. Many of the families had died during that phase, and part of the reclaimed desert was desert once more. Then South Coast had found a damper field to prevent fissionables from fissioning. Others had swiftly copied it. Since then the war had been artillery, poison gas, bacteria, psychology, infantry, even freelance assassination. It was a war of wits. Could South Coast counteract propaganda designed to split off the Meteor Bay region? If Eastersea Alliance had an antidote to river poison Iota, would it be easier to steal it from them or invent our own? If Circle Mountains should find an innoculation for bacterial strain Zeta-Three, how likely was it that they'd turn a mutated strain against us? Should we stick with South Coast, or could we do better with Eastersea? It was fun.

As Phssthpok learned more the game grew more complex. His own Virus QQ would kill all but eight percent of breeders but would leave their protectors unharmed . . .unharmed and fighting with doubled fury to salvage a smaller and less vulnerable group of strain-resistant hostages. He agreed to suppress it. Aak(pop) Family had too many breeders for the local food supply; he rejected their offer of alliance but blocked their path toward Eastersea.

Then Eastersea Alliance built a pinch field generator which could set off a fusion reaction without previous fission.

Phssthpok had been a protector for twenty-six years.

The war ended within a week. Eastersea had the recultivated desert, the part that wasn't bare and sterile from seventy years of war. And there had been a mighty flash over the Valley of Pitchok.

The infants and breeders of Phssthpok's line had lived in the Valley of Pitchok for unremembered generations. He had seen that awful light on the horizon and known that all his descendants were dead or sterile, that he had no blood line left to protect, that all he could do was to stop eating until he was dead.

He hadn't felt that way since. Not until now.

But even then, thirteen centuries ago in biological time, he hadn't felt this awful confusion. What *was* this pressure-suited thing at the end of his arm? Its faceplate was darkened against sunlight. It looked like a breeder, as far as he could tell from the shape of the suit. But *they* couldn't have built spacecraft or pressure suits.

Phssthpok's sense of mission had held steady for more than twelve centuries. Now it was drowning in pure confusion. Now he could regret that the Pak knew nothing of other intelligent species. The biped form might not be unique to Pak. Why should it be? Phssthpok's shape was good designing. If he could see this native without his suit. . .if he could smell it! That would tell the tale.

They landed next to the porthole. The Outsider's aim was inhumanly accurate. Brennan didn't try to fight as the Outsider reached through the curved surface, grasped something, and pulled them both inside. The transparent material resisted movement, like invisible taffy.

In quick, jerky movements, the alien stripped off its pressure suit. The suit was flexible fabric, including the transparent bubble. There were drawstrings at the joints. With its suit off, but still maintaining its iron grip on Brennan, the alien turned to look at him.

Brennan wanted to scream.

The thing was all knobs. Its arms were longer than human, with a single elbow joint in something like the right place; but the elbow was a ball seven inches across. The hands were like strings of walnuts. The shoulders and the knees and the hips bulged like cantaloupes. The head was a tilted melon on a nonexistent neck. Brennan could find no forehead, no chin. The alien's mouth was a flat black beak, hard but not shiny, which faded into wrinkled skin halfway between mouth and eyes. Two slits in the beak were the nose. Two human looking eyes were protected by not at all human looking masses of deeply convoluted skin, and by a projecting shelf of brow. From the beak the head sloped backward as if streamlined. A bony ridge rose from the swelling skull, adding to the impression of streamlining.

It wore nothing more than a vest with big pockets, a human-seeming garment as inappropriate as a snap-brim Fedora on Frankenstein's monster. The swollen joints on its five-fingered hand felt like a score of ball bearings pressing into Brennan's arm.

Thus, the Outsider. Not merely an obvious alien. A dolphin was an obvious alien, but a dolphin was not horrible. The Outsider was horrible. It looked like a cross between human and. . .something else. Man's monsters

have always been that. Grendel. The Minotaur. Mermaids
were once considered horrors: all lovely enticing woman
above, all scaly monster below. And that fitted too, for
the Outsider was apparently sexless, with nothing but
folds of armor-like skin between its legs.

The inset eyes, human as an octopus eye, looked deep
into Brennan's own.

Abruptly, before Brennan could make a move to fight
back, the Outsider took two handfuls of Brennan's rub-
berized suit and pulled them apart. The suit held,
stretched, then ripped from crotch to chin. Air puffed.
Brennan felt his ears pop.

No point in holding his breath. Several hundred feet of
vacuum separated him from his own ship's breathing-air.
Brennan sniffed cautiously.

The air was thin, and it carried a strange scent.

"You son of a bitch," said Brennan. "I could have
died."

The Outsider didn't answer. It stripped off Brennan's
suit like peeling an orange, without unnecessary rough-
ness but without excessive care. Brennan fought. One
wrist was still manacled by the alien's grip, but Brennan
bruised his free fist against the alien's face without causing it to do more than blink. Its skin was like leather
armor. It finished stripping away the suit and held Brennan out for inspection. Brennan kicked it where its groin
ought to be. The alien noticed and looked down, watched
as Brennan kicked twice more, then returned to its inspection.

Its gaze moved over Brennan, head to feet, feet to
head, insultingly familiar. In regions of the Belt where air
and temperature were controlled, the Belters practiced
nudity all their lives. Never before had Brennan felt
naked. Not nude; naked. Defenseless. Alien fingers
reached to probe his scalp along the sides of the Belter
crest; massaged the knuckles of his hand, testing the
joints beneath the skin. At first Brennan continued to
fight. He couldn't even distract the alien's attention.

Then he waited, limp with embarrassment, enduring the examination.

Abruptly it was over. The knobby alien jumped across the room, dug briefly into a bin along one wall, came up with a folded rectangle of clear plastic. Brennan thought of escape; but his suit was in ribbons. The alien shook the thing open, ran fingers along one edge. The bag popped open as if he'd used a zipper.

The alien jumped at Brennan, and Brennan jumped away. It bought him a few seconds of relative freedom. Then knobby steel fingers closed on him and pushed him into the sack.

Brennan found that he couldn't open it from inside. "I'll suffocate!" he screamed. The alien made no response. It wouldn't have understood him anyway. It was climbing back into its suit.

Oh, no. Brennan struggled to rip the sack.

The alien tucked him under an arm and moved out through the porthole. Brennan felt the clear plastic puff out around him, thinning the air inside even further. He felt ice-picks in his ears. He stopped struggling instantly. He waited with the fatalism of despair while the alien moved through vacuum, around the eyeball-shaped hull to where an inch-thick tow line stretched away toward the trailing pod.

There are few big cargo ships in the Belt. Most miners prefer to haul their own ore. The ships that haul large cargoes from asteroid to asteroid are not large; rather, they are furnished with a great many attachments. The crew string their payload out on spars and rigging, in nets or on lightweight grids. They spray foam plastic to protect fragile items, spread reflective foil underneath to ward off hot backlighting from the drive flame, and take off on low power.

The *Blue Ox* was a special case. She carried fluids and fine dusts; refined quicksilver and mined water, grain, seeds, impure tin scooped molten from lakes on dayside Mercury, mixed and dangerous chemicals from Jupiter's atmosphere. Such loads were not always available for hauling. So the *Ox* was a huge tank with a small three-man lifesystem and a fusion tube running through her long axis; but, since her tank must sometimes become a cargo hold for bulky objects, it had been designed with mooring gear and a big lid.

Einar Nilsson stood at the rim of the hold, looking in. He was seven feet tall, and overweight for a Belter; and that was overweight for anyone, for the fat had gone into his belly and the great round curve of second chin. He was all curves; there were no sharp edges on him anywhere. It had been a long time since he rode a singleship. He did not like the high gravity.

The device on his suit was a Viking ship with snarling dragon prow, floating half-submerged in the bright, milky swirl of a spiral galaxy.

Nilsson's own small, ancient mining ship had become the *Ox's* lifeboat. The slender length of its fusion tube, flared at the end, stretched almost the length of the hold. There was an Adzhubei 4-4 computer, almost new; there were machines intended to serve as the computer's senses and speakers, radar and radio and sonics and monochromatic lights and hi-fi equipment. Each item was tethered separately, half a dozen ways, to hooks on the inner wall.

Nilsson nodded, satisfied, his graying blond Belter crest brushing the crown of his helmet. "Go ahead, Nate."

Nathan La Pan began spraying fluid into the tank. In thirty seconds the tank was filled with foam which was already hardening.

"Close 'er up."

Perhaps the foam crunched as the great lid swung down. The sound did not carry. Patroclus Port was in vacuum, open beneath the black sky.

"How much time we got, Nate?"

"Another twenty minutes to catch the optimum course," said the young voice.

"Okay, get aboard. You too, Tina."

"Sold." The voice clicked off. Nathan was young, but he had already learned not to waste words over a phone.

Einar had taken him on at the request of his father, an old friend.

The computer programmer was something else again. Einar watched her slender figure arcing toward the *Ox*'s airlock. Not a bad jump. Perhaps a touch too much muscle?

Tina Jordan was an expatriate flatlander. She was thirty-four years old, old enough to know what she was doing, and she loved ships. Probably she had sense enough to stay out of the way. But she had never flown a single-ship. Einar tended to distrust people who did not trust themselves enough to fly alone. Well, there was no help for it; nobody else at Patroclus Base could run an Adz-hubei 4-4.

The *Ox* would make a lateral run to put her in the path of the alien ship, then curve inward toward the sun. Einar looked away into diamond-studded darkness, in a direction almost opposite the sun. The sparse, dim points of the Trailing Trojans did not block his view. He did not expect to see the Outsider, and he didn't. But it was there, falling to meet the *Ox*'s J-shaped orbit.

Three blobs in a line, a fourth hanging nearby. Nick stared at the screen, his eyes squinched almost shut so that strain lines showed like webs around his eyelids. Whatever had happened, it had happened now.

Other matters begged for the First Speaker's attention. Dickerings with Earth on the funding of ramrobots and on apportionment of ramrobot cargoes among the four interstellar colonies. Trade matters regarding Mercurian tin. The extradition problem. He was spending too much time on this. . .but something kept telling him that it could be the most important event in human history.

Cutter's voice burst jarringly from a speaker. "Nick? The *Blue Ox* wants to take off."

"Fine," said Nick.

"Okay. But I notice they aren't armed."

"They've got a fusion drive, don't they? And over-sized attitude jets to aim it. If they need more than that we've got a war on our hands." Nick clicked off.

And sat wondering. Was he right? Even an H-bomb would be less effective as a weapon than the directed exhaust of a fusion drive. And an H-bomb was an obvious weapon, an insult to a peace-loving Outsider. Still. . .

Nick went back to Brennan's dossier. It was thin. Belters would not accept a government that kept more than minimal tabs on them.

John Fitzgerald Brennan was very much the average Belter. Forty-five years of age. Two daughters—Estelle and Jennifer—by the same woman, Charlotte Leigh Wiggs, a professional farming machine repairwoman in Confinement. Brennan had the beginnings of a nice retirement fund, though he'd drained it twice for trust funds for his children. He had twice lost loads of radioactive ore to the goldskins. Once would have been typical. Belters laugh at inept smugglers, but a man who has never been caught may be suspected of never having tried. No guts.

Suit design: *The Madonna of Port Lligat.* Dali. Nick frowned. Miners sometimes lost their grip on reality, out there. But Brennan was alive and fairly well-off on his own earnings, and he'd never had an accident.

Twenty years ago he'd worked with a crew mining molten tin on Mercury. Mercury was rich with valuable nonferrous elements, though the sun's magnetic field made special ships necessary; a solar storm could pick up a metal ship and drop it miles away. Brennan had been competent, and he'd made good money, but he'd quit after ten months and never worked with a crew again. Apparently he didn't like working with others.

Why had he let the Outsider catch him?

Hell, Nick would have done the same. The Outsider was here in the system; somebody had to meet him. Running would have been an admission that Brennan couldn't handle such a meeting.

His family wouldn't have stopped him. They were Belters; they could take care of themselves.

But I wish he'd run, Nick thought. His fingers beat a nervous tattoo on his desk.

Brennan was all alone in a small space.

It had been a hairy, scary ride. The Outsider had
jumped into space with a balloonful of Brennan, balanced
itself against his mass and used its reaction pistol. They
had coasted for twenty minutes. Brennan had been near
suffocation before they reached the trailing pod.

He remembered the alien touching a flat-nosed tool to
the hull, then pulling them both through a viscous surface
that looked like metal from both sides. The alien had
unzipped the balloon, turned and jumped and vanished
through the wall while Brennan was still tumbling help-
lessly in air.

The air tasted like the cabin air, though the peculiar
scent was much stronger. Brennan drew it in in great
rarefied gasps. The Outsider had left the balloon behind.
It floated toward him like a translucent ghost, menacing
and inviting, and Brennan began to laugh, a painful
sound, almost like sobbing.

He began to look around him.

The light was greener than the sunlight tubes he was
used to. The only clear space was the space he floated in,
as roomy as the lifesystem of his singleship. On his right
were a number of squarish crates whose material was
almost wood, certainly a plant of some kind. To his left,
a massive rectangular solid with a lid, almost like a big
deep freeze. Above and around him, the curved wall.

So he'd been right. This was a cargo hold. But half of
the space in this teardrop-shaped hold was still locked
off from him.

And all through the air, a peculiar scent, like an unfamiliar perfume. The smell in the lifesystem had been
an animal smell, the smell of the Outsider. This was different.

Below him, behind a net of coarse weave, were things
that looked like yellow roots. They occupied most of what
Brennan could see of the cargo hold. Brennan jumped
down at them, wrapped his fingers in the net to bring
his eyes closer.

The smell became hugely more intense. He'd never
smelled, imagined, dreamed anything like it.

They still looked like pale yellow roots: a cross between a sweet potato and a peeled piece of the root of a small tree. They were squat and wide and fibrous, pointed at one end and knife-flattened at the other. Brennan reached through the net, got a two-finger grip on one, tried to pull it through the net and couldn't.

He'd had breakfast just before the Outsider pulled alongside. Yet, with no warning grumblings in his belly, suddenly he was ravenously hungry. His lips skinned back from teeth and gums. He stabbed his fingers through the net, grasped for the roots. For minutes he tried to pull one through holes that were just too small. He tore at the net, raging. The net was stronger than human flesh; it would not tear, though fingernails did. He screamed his frustration. The scream brought him to his senses.

Suppose he did get one out? What then?

EAT IT! His mouth ran saliva.

It would kill him. An alien plant from an alien world, a plant that an alien species probably saw as food. He should be thinking of a way out of here!

Yet his fingers were still tearing at the net. Brennan kicked himself away. He was *hungry*. The fragments of his suit were gone, left behind in the Outsider's cabin, including the water and food-syrup nipples in his helmet. Was there water in here? Could he trust it? Would the Outsider guess that he had a use for partially burnt hydrogen?

What would he do for food?

He had to get out of here.

The plastic bag. He fielded it from the air and examined it. He found out how to seal and unseal it—from the outside. Wonderful. Wait—yes! He could turn the bag inside out, seal it from the inside. Then what?

He couldn't move around in that plastic bag. No hands. Even in his own suit it would have been risky, jumping across eight miles of space without a backpac. He couldn't get through the wall anyway.

He had to distract his stomach somehow.

So. Why were the contents of this hold so valuable?

How could they be worth more than the pilot, who was needed to get them to where they were going?

Might as well see what else is here.

The rectangular solid was a glossy, temperatureless material. Brennan found the handle easily enough, but he couldn't budge it. Then the smell of the roots made a concerted attack on his hunger, and he yelled and pulled with all the strength of killing rage. The handle jarred open. It was built for Outsider strength.

The box was filled with seeds, large seeds like almonds, frozen in a matrix of frost, bitterly cold. He wrenched one loose with numbing fingers. The air about him was turning the color of cigarette smoke when he closed the lid.

He put the seed in his mouth, warmed it with saliva. It had no taste; it was merely cold, and then not even that. He spit it out.

So. Green light and strange, rich-smelling air. But not too thin, not too strange; and the light was cool and refreshing.

If Brennan liked the Outsider's lifesystem, the Outsider would like Earth. He had brought a crop to plant, too. Seeds, roots, and. . .what?

Brennan kicked across the clear space to the stack of crates. Not all the strength of his back and legs would tear a crate loose from the wall. Contact cement? But a lid came up with great reluctance and a creaking noise. Sure enough, it had been glued down; the wood itself had torn away. Brennan wondered what strange plant had produced it.

Inside was a sealed plastic bag. Plastic? It looked and felt like a strong commercial sandwich wrap gone crinkly with age. What was inside felt like fine dust packed nearly solid. It was dark through the plastic.

Brennan floated near the crates, one hand gripping the torn lid. He wondered. . .

An autopilot, of course. The Outsider was only a backup for the autopilot: it didn't matter what happened to him, he was only a safety device. The autopilot would get this crop to where it was going.

To Earth? But a crop meant other Outsiders, following.

He had to warn Earth.

Right. Good thinking. *How?*

Brennan laughed at himself. Was ever a man so completely trapped? The Outsider had him. Brennan, a Belter and a free man, had allowed himself to become property. His laughter died into despair.

Despair was a mistake. The smell of the roots had been waiting to pounce.

. . .It was the pain that brought him out of it. His hands were bleeding from cuts and abrasions. There were sprains and blisters and bruises. His left little finger screamed its agony at him; it stuck out at a strange angle, and it swelled as he watched. Dislocated or broken. But he'd torn a hole in the net, and his right hand gripped a fibrous root.

He threw it as hard as he could and instantly curled in upon himself, hugging his knees as if to surround his pain and smother it. He was angry, he was scared. Why, that damnable smell had turned off his mind as if he were no more than a child's toy robot!

He floated through the cargo space like a football, hugging his knees and crying. He was hungry and angry and humiliated and scared. The Outsider had seared his mind with his own unimportance. But this was worse.

Why? What did the Outsider want with him?

Something smacked him across the back of the head. In one fluid motion Brennan snatched the missile out of the air and bit into it. The root had returned to him on a ricochet orbit. It was tough and fibrous between his teeth. Its taste was as indescribable and as delicious as its scent.

In a last lucid moment Brennan wondered how long he would take to die. He didn't much care. He bit again, and swallowed.

Phssthpok tracked a chain of answers with dogged persistence; but behind every answer there were more questions. His native captive smelled wrong: strange, animalistic. He was not of those Phssthpok had come seeking. Where were they, then?

They had not come here. The natives of GO Target #1-3 would have offered little resistance to colonists, judging by this one sample. But protectors would have exterminated them anyway, as a precaution. Some other star, then. Where?

The natives might have astronomical knowledge enough to tell him. With ships like these they might even have reached nearby stars.

In pursuit of answers, Phssthpok poised and leapt toward the native's vehicle. It was an hour's jump, but Phssthpok was not hurried. With his superb reflexes he did not even need the reaction pistol.

His captive would keep. Presently Phssthpok would have to learn his language, to question him. Meanwhile he would not hurt anything. He was too terrified, and too puny. Bigger but weaker than a breeder.

The captive ship was small. Phssthpok found little more than a cramped life support system, a long drive tube, a ring-shaped liquid hydrogen tank with a cooling motor. The toroidal fuel tank was detachable, with room for several more along the slender length of the drive tube. Around the rim of the cylindrical life support system were attachments for cargo, booms and folded fine-mesh nets and retractable hooks.

Several hooks now secured a lightweight metal cylinder which showed signs of erosion. Phssthpok examined it, dismissed it without knowing its purpose. Obviously it was not needed for the ship to function.

Phssthpok found no weaponry.

He did find inspection panels in the drive tube. Within an hour he could have built his own crystal-zinc fusion tube, had he the materials. He was impressed. The natives might be more intelligent than he had guessed, or luckier. He moved up to the lifesystem and through the oval door.

The cabin included an acceleration couch, banks of controls surrounding it in a horseshoe, a space behind the couch big enough to move around in, an automatic kitchen that was part of the horseshoe, and attachments to mechanical senses of types frequently used in Pak warfare. But this was no warship. The natives' senses must be less acute than Pak senses. Behind the cabin were machinery and tanks of fluid, which Phssthpok examined with great interest.

If these machines were well designed, then GO Target #1-3 was habitable. Very. A bit heavy, both in air and in gravity. But—to a people who had been travelling for five hundred thousand years, it would have looked irresistible.

Had they reached here, they would have stopped.

That cut Phssthpok's region of search in half. His target must be inward from here, back toward the galactic core. They simply had not got this far.

The life support system was most puzzling to Phssthpok. He found things he flatly didn't understand, that he would never understand.

The kitchen, for instance. Weight was important in space. Surely the natives could have provided a lightweight food, synthetic if necessary, capable of keeping the pilot fed and healthy indefinitely. The saving in effort and fuel consumption would have been enormous when multiplied by the number of ships he'd seen. Instead they preferred to carry a variety of prepackaged foods, and a complex machine to select and prepare them. They had chosen to cool these foods against decomposition rather than reduce them to a powder. Why?

Pictures, for instance. Phssthpok understood photographs, and he understood graphs and maps. But the three works of art on the back wall were neither. They were charcoal sketches. One showed the head of a native like Phssthpok's captive, but with longer crest of hair and with odd pigmentation around eyes and mouth; the others must have been younger editions of the same uncomfortably Pak-like species. Only heads and shoulders were shown. What was their purpose?

Under other circumstances the design on Brennan's spacesuit might have provided a clue.

Phssthpok had noticed that design and understood in part. For members of a cooperative, space-going subgroup, it would be useful to code spacesuits in bright colors. Others would recognize the pattern at great distances. The native's design seemed overcomplex, but not enough so to rouse Phssthpok's curiosity.

For Phssthpok would never understand art or luxury.

Luxury? A Pak breeder might appreciate luxury, but was too stupid to make it for himself. A protector hadn't the motivation. A protector's desires were all connected to the need to protect his blood line.

Art? There had been maps and drawings among the Pak since before Pak history. But they were for war. You didn't recognize your loved ones by sight anyway. They smelled right.

Reproduce the smell of a loved one?

Phssthpok might have thought of that, had the painting on Brennan's chest been anything else. *That* would have been a concept! A method of keeping a protector alive and functioning long after his line was dead. It could have changed Pak history. If only Phssthpok had been led to understand representational art. . .

But what could he make of Brennan's suit?

Its chest was a copy in fluorescent dyes of Salvador Dali's *Madonna of Port Lligat*. There were mountains floating above a soft blue sea, resisting gravity, their undersides flat and smooth. There were a woman and child, supernaturally beautiful, with windows through them. There was nothing for Phssthpok.

One thing he understood immediately.

He was being very careful with the instrument panel. He didn't want to wreck anything before he found out how to pull astronomical data from the ship's computer. When he opened the solar storm warning to ascertain its purpose, he found it surprisingly small. Curious, he investigated further. The thing was made with magnetic monopoles.

In one kangaroo leap Phssthpok was crossing interplanetary space. He fired half the gas charge in his reaction pistol, then composed himself to wait out the fifteen minutes of fall.

He'd jumped toward the cargo pod. It would be necessary to tie the native down against acceleration. Already a cursory inspection of the native's ship had cut his search area in half. . .and now he must abandon it. The native might have knowledge even more valuable. Even so, Phssthpok bitterly regretted the need to protect his captive; for the time involved could cost him his mission and his life.

The natives used monopoles. They must have means to detect them. Phssthpok had captured a native—a hostile act. And Phssthpok's unarmed ship used a bigger mass of south poles than were to be found in this solar system.

Probably they were after him now.

They couldn't catch him in any reasonable time. Their drives would be more powerful; gravity on GO Target #1-3 was about one point zero nine. But they wouldn't have ramjet fields. Before their bigger drives could make a difference they'd be out of fuel. . .provided he started in time.

He braked to meet the cargo section, used his softener and oozed through the opaque twing hull. He reached for a handhold without looking, knowing where it would be, his eyes searching for the native.

He missed the handhold. He floated across the empty space while his muscles turned to jelly and melted.

The native had broken through the net and was burrowing feebly among the roots. His belly had become a hard, distended bulge. There was no sentience in his eyes.

With a kind of bewildered fury, Phssthpok thought: *How can I get anything done if they keep changing the rules?*

Stop that. I'm thinking like a breeder. One step at a time. . .

Phssthpok reached for a handhold and pushed himself down to Brennan. Brennan was limp now, his eyes half closed with the whites showing under the lids, his hand still clutching half of a root. Phssthpok set him rotating to make an examination.

All right.

Phssthpok climbed through the hull into vacuum and made his way around to the small end of the egg. There he crawled back inside, emerging in a cubicle just big enough to hold him.

Now he must find a hiding place.

No question now of leaving this solar system. He would have to abandon the rest of his ship. Let them chase the monopoles in his empty drive section.

It would be like hiding all his children in the same cave, but there was no help for that. It could have been worse. Though the instruments in the cargo pod were designed only to drop that section from orbit around some planet, the motor itself—the gravity polarizer—would take him anywhere he wanted to go within GO Target #1's gravity well. Except that he would have to do everything right the first time. Except that he could only land once. As a ship's drive, the gravity polarizer had many of the virtues and faults of a paraglider. He could aim it anywhere he wanted to go, even after he'd killed his velocity, provided that he wanted to go *down*. The polarizer would not lift him against gravity.

Compared to the fusion drive controls, the controls around him were fiercely complicated. Phssthpok began doing things to them. The line at the small end of the egg separated in a puff of flame. The twing around him became transparent . . . and slightly porous; in a century it would have lost a dangerous amount of air. Phssthpok's manlike eyes took on a glassy look. The next moves would take intense concentration. He hadn't dared tie the captive down; or otherwise restrict him. To avoid crushing him, he would have to keep the internal and external gravities exactly balanced. The hull, which carried the polarizing field, might melt at these accelerations.

The rest of his ship floated in Phssthpok's rear screen. He twisted two knobs hard over, and it was gone.

Where to now?

He'd need weeks to hide. He couldn't hope to hide on GO Target #1-3, given their technology.

But space was too open to hide in.

He could only land once. Where he came down, he'd have to stay, unless he could rig some kind of launching or signaling device.

Phssthpok began to search the sky for planets. His eyes were good, and planets were big and dim, easy to spot. The ringed gas giant would have been a good one —easy to hide in the rings—except that it was behind him. A gas giant ahead of him, with moons—too far ahead. He'd have to coast for days to reach it. The natives must be after him now. Without a telescope he'd never see them until too late.

That one. He'd studied it when he had a telescope. Small, with low gravity and a trace of atmosphere. Asteroids all around it, and too much atmosphere for vacuum cementing. With luck, it should make for deep dust pools.

He should have studied it before. There might be mining industries, or even colonies. Too late now. He had no choice; he had had no real choice in quite some time. That planet was his target. When the time came to leave he would have to hope the native could signal his kind. He didn't like it much.

II

The robot was a four-foot upright cylinder floating placidly in one corner of the Struldbrugs' Club reading room. Its muted two tone brown blended with the walls, making it almost invisible. Externally the robot was motionless. In its flared base, fans whirred silently, holding it two inches off the floor, and inside the featureless dome that was its head, scanners revolved endlessly, watching every corner of the room.

Without taking his eyes off the reading screen, Lucas Garner reached for his glass. He found it with careful fingertips, picked it up and tried to drink. It was empty. He held it aloft, wiggled it and, still without looking up, said, "Irish coffee."

The robot was at his elbow. It made no move to take the double-walled glass. Instead, it chimed softly. Garner looked up at last, scowling. A line of lighted print flowed across the robot's chest.

"Terribly sorry, Mr. Garner. You have exceeded your maximum daily alcohol content."

"Cancel, then," said Luke. "Go on, beat it."

The robot scooted for its corner. Luke sighed—it was partly his own fault—and went back to reading. The tape was a new medical tome on "The Aging Process in Man."

Last year he had voted with the rest to let the Club autodoc monitor the Club serving robots. He couldn't regret it. Not a single Struldbrug was less than one hundred and fifty-four years of age, by Club law, and the age requirement went up one year for every two that passed. They needed the best and most rigid of medical protection.

Luke was a prime example. He was approaching, with little enthusiasm, his one hundred and eighty-fifth birthday. He had used a travel chair constantly for twenty years. Luke was a paraplegic, not because of any accident to his spine, but because his spinal nerves were dying of old age. Central nervous tissue never replaces itself. The disproportion between his thin unused legs and his massive shoulders and arms and huge hands made him look a little ape-like. Luke was aware of this, and rather enjoyed it.

His attention was wholly on the tape he was speed-reading when he was disturbed again. A barely audible murmur of voices filled the reading room with a formless, swelling whisper. Regretfully Luke turned to look.

Someone was walking in his direction, using a purposeful stride which could not have been matched by any Struldbrug. The man had the long, narrow frame of one who has spent some years on a stretch rack. His arms and the skin below his larynx were negro dark; but his hands and his heavily lined face were the black of a starless night, a true space black. His hair was a cockatoo's crest, an inch-wide strip of snow-white rug from the crown of his head to the nape of his neck.

A Belter had invaded the Struldbrugs' Club. No wonder they whispered!

He stopped before Luke's chair. "Lucas Garner?" His voice and manner were grave and formal.

"Right," said Luke.

The man lowered his voice. "I'm Nicholas Sohl, First Speaker for the Belt Political Section. Is there someplace we can talk?"

"Follow me," said Luke. He touched controls in the arm of his chair, and the chair rose on an air cushion and moved across the room.

He settled them in an alcove off the main hall. He said, "You really caused an uproar in there."

"Oh? Why?" The First Speaker sprawled limp and boneless in a masseur chair, letting the tiny motors knead him into new shapes. His voice was still quick and crisp with the well known Belt accent.

Luke couldn't decide whether he was joking. "Why? For one thing, you're nowhere near admission age."

"The guard didn't say anything. He just sort of stared."

"I can imagine."

"Do you know what brought me to Earth?"

"I heard. There's an alien in the system."

"It was supposed to be secret."

"I used to be an ARM, a member of the United Nations Police. They didn't retire me until two years ago. I've still got contacts."

"That's what Lit Shaeffer told me." Nick opened his eyes. "Excuse me if I'm being rude. I can stand your silly gravity lying in a ship's couch, but I don't like walking through it."

"Relax then."

"Thanks. Garner, nobody at the UN seems to realize how urgent this is. There's an alien in the system. He's performed a hostile act, kidnapped a Belter. He's abandoned his interstellar drive, and we can both guess what *that* means."

"He's planning to stay. Tell me about that, will you?"

"Simple enough. You know the Outsider ship came in three easy-to-assemble parts?"

"I found out that much."

"The trailing section must have been a re-entry capsule. We might have guessed there'd be one. Two and a half hours after Brennan and the Outsider made contact, that section disappeared."

"Teleport?"

"No, thank Finagle. We've got one film panel that shows a blurred streak. The acceleration was huge."

"I see. Why come to us?"

"Huh? Garner, this is humanity's business!"

"I don't like that game, Nick. The Outsider was humanity's business the second you spotted him. You didn't come to us until he pulled his disappearing act. Why not?

Because you thought the aliens would think better of humanity if they met Belters first?"

"No comment."

"Why tell us now? If the Belt scopes can't find him, nobody can."

Nick turned off his massage chair and sat up to study the old man. Garner's face was the face of Time, a loose mask covering ancient evil. Only the eyes and teeth seemed young; and the teeth were new, white and sharp and incongruous.

But he talked like a Belter, in straight lines. He didn't waste words and he didn't play games.

"Lit said you were bright. That's the trouble, Garner. We've found him."

"I still don't see the problem."

"He went through a smuggler trap near the end of his flight. We were looking for a bird who has the habit of coasting through populated regions with his drive off. A heat sensor found the Outsider, and a camera caught a section of his course and stayed on him long enough to give us velocity, position, acceleration. Acceleration was huge, tens of gees. It's near certain he was on his way to Mars."

"Mars?"

"Mars, or a Mars orbit, or the moons. If it was an orbit we'd have found him by now. Ditto for the moons; they both have observation stations. Except that they belong to the UN—"

Luke began to laugh. Nick closed his eyes with a pained expression.

Mars was the junkheap of the system. In truth there were few useful planets in the solar system; Earth and Mercury and Jupiter's atmosphere just filled the list. It was the asteroids that were important. But Mars had proved the bitterest disappointment. A nearly airless desert, covered with craters and with seas of ultrafine dust, the atmosphere almost too thin to be considered poisonous. Somewhere in Lacis Solis was an abandoned base, the remains of Man's third and last attempt on the rusty planet. Nobody wanted Mars.

When the Free Belt Charter was signed, after the Belt had proven by embargo and propaganda that Earth needed the Belt more than the Belt needed Earth, the UN had been allowed to keep Earth, the Moon, Titan, rights in Saturn's rings, mining and exploratory rights on Mercury, Mars and its moons.

Mars was just a token. Mars hadn't counted until now.

"You see the problem," said Nick. He'd turned the massage unit on again. Little muscles all over his body were giving up under Earth's unaccustomed strain, stridently proclaiming their existence for the first time in Nick's life. The massage helped.

Luke nodded. "Considering the way the Belt is constantly telling us to stay off their property, you can't blame the UN for trying to get a little of its own back. We must have a couple of hundred complaints on file."

"You exaggerate. Since the Free Belt Charter was signed we've registered some sixty violations, most of which were allowed and paid for by the UN."

"What is it you want the UN to do that they aren't doing?"

"We want access to Earth's records on the study of Mars. Hell, Garner, the Phobos cameras might already show where the Outsider came down! We want permission to search Mars from close orbit. We went permission to land."

"What have you got so far?"

Nick snorted. "There's only two things they can agree on. We can search all we want to—from space. For letting us examine their silly records they want to charge us a flat million marks!"

"Pay it."

"It's robbery."

"A Belter says that? Why don't *you* have records on Mars?"

"We were never interested. What for?"

"What about abstract knowledge?"

"Another word for useless."

"Then what makes you want useless knowledge enough to pay a million marks for it?"

Slowly Nick matched his grin. "It's still robbery. How in Finagle's name did Earth know they'd need to know about Mars?"

"That's the secret of abstract knowledge. You get in the habit of finding out everything you can about everything. Most of it gets used sooner or later. We've spent *billions* exploring Mars."

"I'll authorize payment of a million marks to the UN Universal Library. Now how do we land?" Nick turned off the chair.

"I. . .have an idea on that."

A ridiculous idea. Luke would not have considered it for a moment. . .except for his surroundings. The Struldbrugs' Club was luxurious and quiet, soundproofed everywhere, rich with draperies. His own jarring laughter had been swallowed the instant it left his lips. People seldom laughed or shouted here. The Club was a place to rest, after a lifetime of. . .not resting?

"Can you fly a two-man ship, Starfire make?"

"Sure. There's no difference in the control panels. Belt ships use drives bought from Rolls-Royce, England."

"You're hired as my pilot at a dollar a year. I can get a ship ready in six hours."

"You've flipped."

"Not I. Look, Nick. Every so-called diplomat in the UN knows how important it is to find the Outsider. But they can't get moving. It's not because they're getting their own back with the Belt. That's only part of it. It's inertia. The UN is a world government. It's unwieldy by its very nature, having to rule the lives of eighteen billion people. Worse than that, the UN is made up of individual nations. The nations aren't very powerful nowadays. Someday not too soon, even their names will be forgotten; and I'm not sure that's a good idea. . .but today national prestige can get in the way. You'd be weeks getting them to agree on anything.

"Whereas there's no law against a UN citizen going anywhere he wants to in terrestrial space, or hiring anyone he wants to. A number of our round-the-Moon pilots are Belters."

Nick shook his head as if to clear it. "Garner, I don't get you. You can't think we can find the Outsider in a two man ship. Even I know about the Martian dust. He's hidden in one of the dust seas, dissecting Jack Brennan, and there's no way to get at him without searching the deserts inch by inch with deep-radar."

"Right. But when the politicians realize that you've started searching Mars, what do you think they'll do? You being hired as a pilot is a technicality, obvious to anyone. Suppose we did find the Outsider? The Belt would get the credit."

Nick closed his eyes and tried to think. He wasn't used to such circular logic. But it looked like Garner was right. If they thought he was going to Mars, with or without a flatlander for company. . . Nick Sohl, First Speaker for the Belt, empowered to make treaties. Ominous. They'd send a fleet to start searching first.

"So I need a flatlander to hire me as pilot. Why you?"

"I can get a ship *now*. I've got contacts."

"Okay. Get the ship, then get a tough explorer-type flatlander. Sell him the ship. Then he hires me as his pilot, right?"

"Right. But I won't do it."

"Why?" Nick looked at him. "You aren't seriously thinking of coming along?"

Luke nodded.

Nick laughed. "How old are you?"

"Too old to waste my remaining years sitting in the Struldbrugs' Club waiting to die. Shake hands, Nick."

"Mph? Sure, but—Yipe! All right, dammit, so you've got strong hands. All you flatlanders are overmuscled anyway."

"Hey, now, I didn't mean to push any buttons. I'm sorry. I wanted to demonstrate that I haven't gone feeble."

"Stipulated. Not in the hands, anyway."

"And we won't be using our legs. We'd be riding everywhere we went."

"You're crazy. Suppose your heart gave out on me?"

"It's likely to survive *me* for a good long time. It's prosthetic."

"You're crazy. All of you. It comes from living at the bottom of a gravity well. The gravity pulls the blood from your brains."

"I'll show you to a telephone. You'll have to pay in your million marks before the UN catches on where we're going."

Phssthpok dreamed.

He had hidden the cargo pod deep beneath the fluid dust of the Lacis Solis region. It showed as an ochre wall beyond the twing hull. They would be safe here for as long as the life support system held out: a long, long time.

Phssthpok stayed in the cargo hold where he could watch his captive. After landing he had disassembled every machine in the cargo pod to make what repairs and adjustments were needed. Now he only watched his captive.

The native required little care. He was developing almost normally. He would be a monster, but perhaps not a cripple.

Phssthpok rested on his pile of roots and dreamed.

In a few weeks he would have completed his long, long task. . .or failed. In any case he could stop eating. He had been alive long enough to suit him. Soon he would end as he had nearly ended thirteen hundred shiptime years ago, at the core of the galaxy. . .

He had seen light flare over the Valley of Pitchok, and known that he was doomed.

Phssthpok had been a protector for twenty-six years. His remaining children in the radiation-blasted valley were twenty-six to thirty-five years of age; their own children were of all ages up to twenty-four or so. Now his lifespan would depend on who had survived the bomb. He had returned immediately to the valley to find out.

Not many breeders were left in the valley, but such

as were still alive had to be protected. Phssthpok and the rest of the Pitchok families made peace, the terms being that they and their sterile breeders should have the valley until their deaths, at which time the valley would revert to Eastersea Alliance. There were ways to partially neutralize radioactive fallout. The Pitchok families used them. Then, leaving their valley and its survivors in the hands of one of their number, they had scattered.

Of the several surviving breeders, all had been tested and all had been found essentially sterile. "Essentially" being taken to mean that if they did have children, the children would be mutants. They would smell wrong. With no protector to look after their interests, they would quickly die.

To Phssthpok, the most important of his surviving descendants was the youngest, Ttuss, a female of two years.

He was on a time limit. In thirty-two years Ttuss would reach the age of change. She would become an intelligent being, and a heavily armored one, with skin that would turn a copper knife and strength to lift ten times her own weight. She would be ideally designed for the purpose of fighting, but she would have nothing to fight for.

She would stop eating. She would die, and Phssthpok would stop eating. Ttuss's lifespan was his own.

But sometimes a protector could adopt the entire Pak species as his descendants. At least he would have every opportunity to find a purpose in life. There was always truce for a childless protector, for such had no reason to fight. And there was a place he could go.

The Library was as old as the radioactive desert which surrounded it. That desert would never be recultivated; it was reseeded every thousand years with radiocobalt so that no protector could covet it. Protectors could cross that desert; they had no gonadal genes to be smashed by subatomic particles. Breeders could not.

How old was the Library? Phssthpok never knew, and never wondered. But the section on space travel was three million years old.

He came to the Library with a number of—not friends, but associates in misery, childless former members of the Pitchok families. The Library was huge and rambling, a composite of at least three million years of Pak knowledge, crossfiled into sections according to subject. Naturally the same book often appeared in several sections. The associates divided at the entrance, and Phssthpok didn't see any of them again for thirty-two years.

He spent that time in one vast room, a floor-to-ceiling labyrinth of bookshelves. At scattered corners there were bins of tree-of-life root kept constantly filled by attendants. There were other foodstuffs brought at seeming random: meats, vegetables, fruits, whatever was available to childless protectors who had chosen to serve the Library rather than die. Tree-of-life root was the perfect food for a protector, but he could eat nearly anything.

And there were books.

They were nearly indestructible, those books. They would have emerged like fluttering meteors from the heart of a hydrogen fusion explosion. All were written more or less in the present language, and all were constantly being recopied by librarians as the language changed. In this room the books all dealt with space and space travel.

There were treatises on the philosophy of space travel. They all seemed to make a fundamental assumption: someday the Pak race must find a new home; hence any contribution to the techniques of spaceflight contributed to the immortality of the species. Phssthpok could discount that assumption, knowing that a protector who did not believe it would never write a book on the subject. There were records of interstellar and interplanetary flights, tens of thousands of them, starting with a fantastic trip some group had made almost three million years ago, riding a hollowed-out asteroidal rock into the galactic arms in search of yellow dwarf suns. There were technical texts on anything that could possibly bear on space: spacecraft, astrogation, ecology, miniaturization, nuclear and subnuclear physics, plastics, gravity and how to use it, astronomy, astrophysics, records of the mining of worlds

in this and nearby systems, diagrams for a hypothetical
Bussard ramjet (in an unfinished work by a protector
who had lost his appetite halfway through), ion drive
diagrams, plasma theory, light-sails. . .

He started at the left and began working his way
around.

He'd chosen the section on space travel more or less at
random; it had looked less crowded than the others. The
romance of space was not in Phssthpok's soul. He kept
with it rather than start over elsewhere. He might need
every minute of his thirty-four years of grace no matter
where he chose to work. In twenty-eight years he read
every book in the Astronautics section, and still he had
found nothing that drastically needed doing.

Start a migration project? It simply wasn't that urgent.
The Pak sun had at least hundreds of millions of years
to live. . .longer than the Pak species, probably, given
the constant state of war. And the chance of disaster
would be high. Yellow suns were scarce in the galactic
core; they would have to travel far. . .with the protector
crew constantly fighting for control of the ship. Come to
that, the cores of galaxies could sometimes explode in a
chain reaction of supernovae. A migration project really
should travel into the arms.

The first expedition to try that had met a horrible fate.

So. Join the Library staff? He'd thought of it many
times, but the answer always came out the same. No
matter what phase of the Library he concerned himself
with, his life would depend on others. To retain his will
to live he would need to know that all Pak would benefit
from his aspect of Library work. Let there be a dry spell
in new discoveries, let his faith flag, and he would find
himself no longer hungry.

It was frightening not to be hungry. During the last
few decades it had happened several times. Each time he
would force himself to reread the communications from
the Valley of Pitchok. The latest communication always
told him that Ttuss had been alive when it was sent. Gradually his appetite would come back. Without Ttuss he
would be dead.

He had investigated the librarians. Their lives were usually short. Joining the staff was no answer.

Find a way to keep Ttuss alive? If he could do that he would have used the method on himself.

Study theoretical astronomy? He had some ideas, but they would not help the Pak species. The Pak did not seek abstract knowledge. Mine the asteroids? The asteroids of this and nearby stars were as thoroughly mined out as the surface of the planet had often been, with the difference that convection currents in the planet's interior eventually replaced worked-out mines. He should have gone in for metal reclamation. Now it was too late to change studies. Put plastic-bubble cities in orbit to provide more living room for breeders? Nonsense: too vulnerable to capture or accidental destruction.

One day Phssthpok's appetite was gone. The letters from the Valley of Pitchok did not help; he didn't believe them. He thought of returning to the valley, but he knew he would starve to death on the way. When he was sure, he sat down against a wall, the last in a line of protectors who also did not eat, who were waiting to die.

A week passed. The librarians found that two at the head of the line were dead. They picked them up, a pair of skeletons clothed in dry, wrinkled leather armor, and carried them away.

Phssthpok remembered a book.

He still had the strength to reach it.

He read carefully, with the book in one hand and a root in the other. Presently he ate the root. . .

The ship had been a roughly cylindrical asteroid, reasonably pure nickel-iron with stony strata running through it, about six miles long and four through. A group of childless protectors had carved it out with solar mirrors and built into it a small life-support and controls system, a larger frozen-sleep chamber, a breeder atomic pile and generator, a dirigible ion drive, and an enormous cesium tank. They had found it necessary to exterminate the protectors of a large family in order to get control of a thousand breeders. With two protectors as pilots and seventy more in frozen sleep with the thousand breeders, with a careful selection of the beneficial lifeforms of the Pak world, they set out into one arm of the galaxy.

Though their knowledge was three million years scantier than Phssthpok's, they had good reason for choosing the galaxy's outer reaches. They'd have a better chance of finding yellow suns out there, and a better chance to find a double planet at the right distance. Perturbations from stars an average of half a light year apart made double planets scarce in the galactic core; and there was reason to think that only an oversized moon could give any world an atmosphere capable of supporting Pak-like life.

An ion drive and a certain amount of cesium. . . They expected to move slowly, and they did. At twelve thousand miles per second relative to the Pak sun, they coasted. They fired a laser message back at the Pak sun to tell the Library that the ion drive had worked. The blueprints were somewhere in the Library, with a list of suggested design changes.

Phssthpok was not interested. He moved on to the last section, which was nearly half a million years more recent.

It was a record of a laser message that had come plowing through the Pak system, torn and attenuated and garbled by dust clouds and distance, in a language no longer spoken. The librarians had translated it and filed it here. It must have been retranslated hundreds of times since then. Hundreds of searchers like Phssthpok must have read it, and wondered about the part of the story they could never know, and passed on. . .

But Phssthpok read it very carefully.

They had traveled deep into the galactic arms. Half the protectors had been gone at journey's end, dying not of starvation or violence but of age. This was so unusual that a detailed medical description had been included as part of the message. They had passed yellow suns with no planets, others whose worlds were all gas giants. Yellow suns had gone by carrying worlds that might have been habitable; but all were too far off course to be reached on the maneuvering reserve of cesium. Galactic dust and the galaxy's gravity had slowed their strange craft, increasing their maneuver reserve. The sky had darkened around them as suns became rare.

They had found a planet.

They had braked the ship. They had transferred what was left of the plutonium to the motors of landing craft, and gone down. The decision was not final; but if the planet failed to measure up they would have to work for decades to make their rockship spaceworthy again.

It had life. Some was inimical, but none that could not be handled. There was soil. The remaining protectors woke the breeders and turned them loose in the forests to be fruitful and multiply. They planted crops, dug mines, made machines to dig more mines, made machines to tend crops. . .

The black, nearly starless night sky bothered some, but they got used to it. The frequent rains bothered others, but did not hurt the breeders, so that was all right. There was room for all; the protectors did not even fight. None stopped eating. There were predators and bacteria to exterminate, there was a civilization to build, there was much to do.

With spring and summer came crops—and disaster. There was something wrong with the tree-of-life.

The colonists themselves did not understand what had gone wrong with the crop. Something had come up. It looked and tasted like tree-of-life, though the smell was wrong, somehow. But for all its effect on breeders and protectors alike, they might as well have been eating weeds.

They could not return to space. Their scant remaining store of roots represented an inflexible number of protector work-hours. They might refuel their cesium tanks, they might even build a plutonium-producing technology in the time they had left, but to find and reach another Pak-like world—no. And if they reached it, what guarantee had they that it would grow tree-of-life?

They had spent their last years building a laser beam

powerful enough to pierce the dust clouds that hid them from the galactic core. They did not know that they had succeeded. They did not know what was wrong with the crop; they suspected the sparsity of a particular wavelength of starlight, or of starlight in general, though their experiments along those lines had produced nothing. They gave detailed information on the blood lines of their breeder passengers, in the hope that some of the lines might survive. And they asked for help.

Two and a half million years ago.

Phssthpok sat by the root bin, eating and reading. He would have smiled if his face had been built that way. Already he could see that his mission would involve every childless protector in the world.

For two and a half million years those breeders had been living without tree-of-life. Without any way to make the change to the protector stage. Dumb animals.

And Phssthpok alone knew how to find them.

You're flying from New York, USA, to Piquetsburg, North Africa. Suddenly you become aware that New York is flying in one direction, Piquetsburg in another, and a hurricane wind is blowing your plane off course in still a third. . .

Nightmare? Well, yes. But travel in the solar system is different from travel on a planet. Each individual rock moves at its own pace, like flecks of butter in a churn.

Mars moved in a nearly circular path. Asteroids moved nearby in orbits more elliptical, catching up to the red planet or falling behind. Some carried telescopes. Their operators would report to Ceres if they saw purposeful action on the surface.

The abandoned Bussard ramjet crossed over the sun and curved inward, following a shallow hyperbola which would take it through the plane of the planets.

The *Blue Ox* followed an accelerating higher-order curve, a J whose upright would eventually match the *Ox's* velocity and position to the Outsider's.

U Thant rose from Earth on a ram-and-wing rented

from Death Valley Port. There was a lovely scenic ride
up and out over the Pacific. One hundred and fifty miles
up and orbiting, as required by law, Nick switched to
fusion power and headed outward. He left the ram-and-
wing to find its own way home.

The Earth wrapped itself around itself and dropped
away. It was four days to Mars at one gee, with Ceres to
tell them which asteroids to dodge.

Nick put the ship on autopilot. He was not entirely dis-
pleased with the *U Thant*. It was a flatlander navy job,
its functions compromised by streamlining; but the equipment seemed adequate and the controls were elegantly
simple. And the kitchen was excellent.

Luke said, "Okay to smoke?"

"Why not? You *can't* be worried about dying young."

"Does the UN have its money yet?"

"Sure. They must have got it transferred hours ago."

"Fine. Call them, identify yourself, and ask for everything they've got on Mars. Tell them to put it on the
screen, and you'll pay for the laser. That'll kill two birds
with one stone."

"How?"

"It'll tell them where we're going."

"Right. . .Luke, do you really think this will get them
moving? I know how unwieldy the UN is. There was the
Müller case."

"Look at it from another direction, Nick. How did you
come to represent the Belt?"

"Aptitude tests said I had a high IQ and liked order-
ing people around. From there I worked my way up."

"We go by the vote."

"Popularity contests."

"It works. But it does have drawbacks. What government doesn't?" Garner shrugged. "Every speaker in the
UN represents one nation—one section of the world. He
thinks it's the best section, filled with the best people. Otherwise he wouldn't have been elected. So maybe twenty
representatives each think they know just what to do about
the Outsider, and no one of them will knuckle down to
the others. Prestige. Eventually they'd work out a com-

promise. But if they get the idea that a civilian and a
Belter could beat them to the Outsider, they'll get off
their thumbs faster. See?"

"No."

"Oh, make your call."

A message beam found them some time later. They
began to skim Earth's stored information on Mars.

There was quite a lot of it. It covered centuries. At
one point Nick said, "I'm ready for summer vacation. Why
do we have to watch all this? According to you we're just
running a bluff."

"According to me we're running a search, unless you
have something better to do. The best time to bluff is
with four aces."

Nick switched off the screen. The lecture was on tape
now; they wouldn't miss anything. "Come, let us reason
together. I paid a million marks in Belt funds for this
stuff, plus additional charges for the message beam.
Thrifty Sohl that I am, I feel almost compelled to use it.
But we've been studying the Müller case for the past hour,
and it all came out of Belt files!"

Eleven years ago a Belt miner named Müller had tried
to use the mass of Mars to make a drastic course change.
He had come too close; had been forced to land. There
would have been no problem. The goldskin cops would
have picked him up as soon as they had clearance from
the UN. No hurry. . .until Müller was murdered by
martians.

Martians had been a myth until then. Müller must have
been amazed. But, strangling in near-vacuum, he had
managed to kill half a dozen of them, using a water tank
to spray death in all directions.

"Not all of it. We were the ones who studied the martian corpses you recovered," said Garner. "We may need
that information. I'm still wondering why the Outsider
picked Mars. Maybe he knows about martians. Maybe he
wants to contact them."

"Much good may it do him."

"They use spears. By me that makes them intelligent.
We don't know how intelligent, because nobody's ever

tried to talk to a martian. They could have any kind of civilization you can imagine, down there under the dust."

"A civilized people, are they?" Nick's voice turned savage. "They slashed Müller's tent! They let his air out!" In the Belt there is no worse crime.

"I didn't say they were friendly."

The *Blue Ox* coasted. Behind her the alien ship was naked-eye visible and closing. It made Tina nervous to be unable to watch it. But that could work two ways; and this was the Outsider's blind side, where three Belters worked to free Einar Nilsson's singleship from its vast metal uterus.

"Clamps free back here," said Tina. She was sweating. She felt the breeze on her face, as the air system worked to keep her faceplate from fogging.

Nate's voice spoke behind her ear. "Good, Tina."

Einar's said, "We could have carried a fourth crewman in the singleship's lifesystem. Damn! I wish I'd thought of it. There'd be two of us to meet the Outsider."

"It probably won't matter. The Outsider's gone. That's a dead ship." Nonetheless Nate sounded uneasy.

"And how many crew got left behind? I never much believed the Outsider would come riding between the stars alone in a singleship. Too poetic. Never mind. Tina, give us five seconds of thrust under the fusion tube."

Tina set her shoulders and fired her backpac jets. Other flames sprouted forward under the lifesystem hull. The old singleship drifted slowly up between the great doors.

"Okay, Nate, get aboard fast. Make sure you keep the *Ox* between you and the Outsider at all times. We'll have to assume he doesn't have deep-radar."

There was no way either of them could see Tina's puzzled frown.

Belter women averaged around six feet tall; but Belter women tended to be willowy, slender. Tina Jordan was six feet tall and built to scale: flatlander scale. She was in good trim and proud of it. She found it annoying that Belters still took her for a flatlander.

She had left Earth at twenty-one. She had been fourteen years in the Belt, on Ceres, Juno, Mercury, at Hera Station in close orbit around Jupiter, and in the Trailing Trojans. She regarded the Belt and the solar system as her home. It did not bother her that she had never flown a singleship. Many Belters had not. The singleship miners were only one aspect of Belt industry, which included chemists, nuclear physicists, astrophysicists, politicians, astronomers, file clerks, merchants. . .and computer programmers.

She had heard, long ago, that there was no prejudice against women in the Belt. And it was true! On Earth women still held lower-paying jobs. Employers claimed that physical strength was needed for certain jobs, or that a woman would quit to get married at the most crucial time, or even that her family suffered when a woman worked. Things were different in the Belt; and Tina had been more surprised than elated. She had expected to be disappointed.

And now a woman and a computer programmer was the most crucial *Ox's* personnel. Fear and delight. The fear was for Nate, who was too young to take such a risk; for one Belter had already met the Outsider, and nothing had been heard of him since.

But what was Nate doing aboard the singleship?

She helped Einar out of his suit—he was a mountain of flesh; he could never have lifted himself against Earth's gravity—then let him do the same for her. She said, "I thought Nate would be the one to board the Outsider."

Einar looked surprised. "What? No. You."

"But—" She searched for words, and found them, to her horror. *But I'm a girl.* She said nothing.

"Think it through," Einar said with forced patience. "The ship might not be empty. Boarding it could be dangerous."

"Right." With emphasis.

"So we give whoever boards it all the protection we've got. The *Ox* is part of that protection. I'll keep the drive warm; it should vaporize the bastard if he tries anything, and the com laser should punch holes in him at this range. But there's a chance the *Ox* will be blasted too."

"So the singleship stands guard." Tina made a dismissing gesture. "I worked it out that far. I thought *I'd*—"

"No, don't be silly. You've never flown a singleship in your life. I don't have much free choice here. I thought of leaving Nate to fly the *Ox*, but hell, she's my ship, and he knows singleships. I couldn't put you in either job."

"I suppose not." She was outwardly calm, but a cold lump of fear grew in her belly.

"You'd be the best choice anyway. You're the one who will make contact with the Outsider, try to learn his language. Aside from that, you're a flatlander. You're physically the strongest of us."

Tina nodded jerkily.

"You could have stayed behind, you know."

"Oh, it's not *that*. I hope you don't think I was trying to chicken out. I just—hadn't—"

"No, you just hadn't bothered to think it through. You'll get used to doing that, living in the Belt," Einar said kindly. Damn him.

The dust of Mars is unique.

Its uniqueness is the result of vacuum cementing. Once vacuum cementing was the bugaboo of the space industries. Small space probe components which would slide easily over one another in air would weld solidly in vacuum, just as soon as the gas adsorbed by their surfaces could evaporate away. Vacuum cementing fused parts in the first American satellites and in the first Soviet interplanetary probes. Vacuum cementing keeps the Moon from being fathoms deep in meteor dust. The particles weld into crunchy rock, into natural cement, under the same molecular attraction that fuses Johanssen blocks and turns the mud of sea bottoms to sedimentary rock.

But on Mars there is just enough atmosphere to stop that process, and not nearly enough to stop a meteor. Meteor dust covers most of the planet. Meteors can fuse the dust into craters, but it does not cement, though it is fine enough to flow like viscous oil.

"That dust is going to be our biggest problem," said Luke. "The Outsider didn't even have to dig a hole for himself. He could have sunk anywhere on Mars."

Nick turned off the laser transmitter. It was hot from two days of use in blasting a locator beam at Earth. "He could have hidden anywhere in the system, but he picked Mars. He must have had a reason. Maybe it's something he couldn't do under the dust. That puts him in a crater or on a hill."

"He'd have been spotted." Luke keyed a photograph from the autopilot memory. It was one of a group from the smuggler trap. It showed a dimly shining metal egg with the small end pointed. The egg moved big-end first, and it moved as if rocket-propelled. But there was no exhaust, at least none that any instrument could detect.

"It's big enough to see from space," said Luke, "and easy to recognize, with that silver hull."

"Yah. All right, he's under the dust. It'll take a lot of ships with deep-radar to find him, and even then there's no guarantee." Nick ran his hands back along his depilated scalp. "We could quit now. Your flatlander government has finally picked up its feet and sent us some ships. I got the impression they aren't too happy about us joining their search." His tone was noncommittal.

"I'd like to go on. How do you feel?"

"I'm game. Hunting strange things is what I do on my vacation."

"Where would you start looking?"

"I don't know. The deepest dust on the planet is in Tractus Albus."

"He'd have been stupid to pick the deepest. He'd have picked his place at random."

"You've got other ideas?"

"Lacis Solis."

"—Oh. The old flatlander base. That's good thinking. He might need a life support system for Brennan."

"I wasn't even thinking that. If he needs anything there —human technology, water, *anything*—there's only one place on the planet he can go. If he's not there we can at least pick up some dustboats—"

"*Blue Ox* calling *U Thant*. This is *Blue Ox* calling *U Thant* out of Death Valley Port."

There would be a directional signal in that message. Nick set the autopilot to aiming his own com laser. "It'll take a few minutes," he said. Then, "I wonder what's happening to Brennan."

"Can we take the deep-radar out of this heap?"

"Let's hope. I don't know what else we can use for a finder."

"A metal detector. There must be one aboard."

"This is Nicholas Brewster Sohl aboard *U Thant* calling any or all aboard *Blue Ox*. What's new? Repeating. This is Nicholas—"

Einar flicked to transmit. "Einar Nilsson commanding *Blue Ox*. We have matched with the Outsider ship. Tina Jordan is preparing to board. I will switch you to Tina." He did.

And settled back to wait.

He liked Tina. He was half certain she would find a way to get herself killed. Nate had protested mightily, but Einar's own arguments had no holes to crawl through. He sat watching the picture transmitted from Tina's helmet camera.

The Outsider ship looked deserted, with its attitude skewed and its tow lines slack and beginning to loop. Tina could see no motion in the lens of the big eyeball. She brought herself to a stop several yards from the port, and was pleased to note that her hands were steady on the jet firing keys.

"Tina speaking. I am outside what seems to be a control module. I can see an acceleration couch through the glass—if it's glass—and controls around it. The Outsider must be roughly hominid.

"The drive module is too hot to get near. The control module is a smooth sphere with a big porthole and cables trailing off in both directions. You should be able to see all this, *U Thant*."

She did a slow loop around the big eyeball. Taking her time. Belters only hurried when there was need. "I can find no sign of an airlock. I'll have to burn my way through."

"Through the porthole. You don't want to burn through anything explosive," said Einar's voice behind her ear.

The transparent stuff had a two-thousand Kelvin melting point, and a laser was obviously out of the question. Tina used a hot point, tracing a circle over and over. Gradually she wore it down. "I'm getting fog through the cracks," she reported. "Ah, I'm through."

A three-foot transparent disc puffed away on the last of the air, with a breath of white mist playing around it. Tina caught it and sent it gliding toward the *Ox* for later recovery.

Einar's voice crackled. "Don't try to enter yet!"

"I wasn't." She waited for the edges to cool. Fifteen minutes, while nothing happened. They must be getting restless aboard *U Thant,* she thought. Still no sign of motion inside. They had found nothing when they probed this module with the deep-radar; but the walls were thick, and something as tenuous as water, for instance, might not have shown up.

Time enough. She ducked through the hole.

"I'm in a small control cabin," she said, and turned at the waist to give the camera a full view. Tendrils of icy fog drifted toward the hole in the porthole. "Very small. The control bank is almost primitively complex, so complex that I'm inclined to think the Outsider had no autopilot. No man could handle all these controls and adjustments. I see no more that one couch, and no aliens present but me.

"There's a bin full of sweet potatoes, it looks like, right beside the control couch. It's the only sign of kitchen facilities in this section. I think I'll move on." She tried to open the door in the back of the control room. Pressure forced it shut. She used her hot point. The door cut easily, must more so than the porthole material. She waited while the room filled with thick fog, then pushed her way in. More fog.

"This room is about as big as the control room. Sorry about the view. The place seems to be a free-fall gymnasium." She swept her camera around the room, then crossed to one of the machines and tried to work it. It looked as though you were supposed to stand up inside it against the force of springs. Tina couldn't budge it.

She dismounted the camera and fixed it to a wall, aimed at the exercise machine. She tried it again. "Either I'm doing this wrong," she told her audience, "or the Outsider could pick his teeth with me. Let's see what else there is." She looked around. "That's funny," she said presently.

There was nothing else. Only the door to the control room.

A two hour search by Tina and Nate La Pan only confirmed her find. The lifesystem consisted of:

One control room the size of a singleship control room.

One free-fall gymnasium, same size.

A bin of roots.

An enormous air tank. There were no safeties to stop the flow in case of puncture. The tank was empty. It must have been nearly empty when the ship reached the solar system.

Vastly complex air cleaning machinery, apparently designed to remove even the faintest, rarest trace of biochemical waste. It had all been many times repaired.

Equally complex equipment for conversion of fluid and solid waste.

It was incredible. The single Outsider had apparently spent his time in two small rooms, eating just one kind of food, with no ship's library to keep him entertained, and no computer-autopilot to keep him pointed right and guard his fuel supply and steer him clear of meteors. Yet the trip had taken decades, at least. In view of the complexity of the cleaning and renewal plant, the huge air tank must have been included solely to replace air lost by osmosis through the walls!

"That's it," Einar said finally. "Come on back, you two. We'll take a break, and I'll ask *U Thant* for instructions. Nate, put some of those roots in a pressure bag. We can analyze them."

"Search the ship again," Nick told them. "You may find a simplified autopilot: not a computer, just a widget for keeping the ship on course. Could you have overlooked a bolthole of some kind, anyplace where an Outsider could have hidden? In particular, try to get into the air tank. It might make a very nice emergency bolthole." He turned the volume down and faced Luke. "They won't find anything, of course. Can you think of anything else?"

"I'd like to see them analyze the air. Have they got the facilities?"

"Yah."

"And the porthole glass, and the chemistry of that root."

"They'll finish with the root by the time this reaches them." He turned up the volume. "After you finish analyzing what you've got, you might start thinking about how to tow that ship home. Stay with the ship, and keep your drive warm. If an emergency comes up, use the fusion flame immediately. Sohl out."

He looked at the screen for some time after it had gone dark. Presently he said, "A super-singleship. Finagle's Eyes! I wouldn't have believed it."

"Flown by a kind of super-Belter," said Luke. "Solitary. Doesn't need entertainment. Doesn't care what he eats. Strong as King Kong. Roughly humanoid."

Nick smiled. "Wouldn't that make him a superior species?"

"I wouldn't deny it. And I'm deadly serious on that. We'll have to wait and see."

Brennan shifted.

He hadn't moved in hours. He lay on his back in the root bin, his eyes closed, his body folded into near-foetal position around his swollen belly, his fists clenched. But now he moved one arm, and Phssthpok came suddenly alert.

Brennan reached for a root, put it in his mouth, bit and swallowed. Bit and swallowed. Bit and swallowed, under Phssthpok's watchful eye. His own eyes stayed closed.

Brennan's hand released the last inch or so of root, and he turned over and stopped moving.

Phssthpok relaxed. Presently he dreamed.

Days ago he had stopped eating. He told himself it was too early, but his belly didn't believe it. He would live just long enough. Meanwhile, he dreamed.

. . .He sat on the floor of the Library with a piece of root in his jaws and an ancient book balanced on one cantaloupe knee and a map spread before him on the floor. It was a map of the galaxy, but it was graded for time. The Core stars showed in positions three million years old, but the outer arms were half a million years younger. The Library staff had spent most of a year preparing it for him.

Assume they went a distance X, he told himself. *Their average velocity must have been .06748 lightspeed, considering dust friction and the galaxy's gravitational and electromagnetic fields. Their laser returned at lightspeed; figure for space curvature. Give them a century to build the laser; they'd use all the time they had for that. Then X = 33,210 light years.*

Phssthpok set his compass and drew an arc, using the Pak sun as a center. Margin of error: .001, thirty light years. *They're on that arc!*

Now assume they went straight outward from the galactic hub. It was a good assumption: there were stars in that direction, and the Pak sun was well off-center from the hub. Phssthpok drew a radial line. *Greater margin of error here. Original error, course alterations. . .* And the straight line would have curved by now, while the galaxy turned like curdled milk. *They would have stayed flat in the galactic plane. And they're near this point. I've found them. . .*

Phssthpok's minions pouring like army ants through the

Library. Every protector in reach had joined his quest. *It's in the Astronautics section, Phwee. Find it! We need those ramscoop diagrams. Ttuss, I need to know what happens when a protector gets old, and when it happens, and any contributing factors. There's probably a copy of that report in the Medical section. It may have been added to. Hratchp, we have to learn what could stop a tree-of-life from growing right in the galactic arms. You need agronomists, medical researchers, chemists, astrophysicists. Use the Valley of Pitchok for your experiments, and re-member the environment was habitable. Try experiment-ing with the soil, reduced starlight, reduced radiation. You of the Physics and Engineering sections: I need a fusion drive for insystem maneuvers. I need launching vehicles for everything we build. Design them!* Every childless protector on the planet was looking for a purpose in liv-ing, a Cause. And Phssthpok gave it to them...

...The ship, finally completed, standing in three parts on the sand not far from the Library. Phssthpok's army assembling. *We need monopoles, we need tree-of-life roots and seeds, we need enormous quantities of hydrogen fuel. The scoop won't work below a certain speed. Meteor Bay has everything we need. We can take them!* For the first time in twenty thousand years, the childless protec-tors of Pak assembled for war...

...His own Virus QQ used on breeders, with mop-up squads to hunt the survivors. Newly childless protec-tors switching sides, joining his army. Hratchp reporting in with the strange, complex secret of the tree-of-life root...

Something thumped three times on the hull.

For an instant he thought it was a memory. He was that far gone. Then he was on his feet, staring up at a point high on the curved wall of the hold. His mind racing.

He had known that there was some kind of non-organic photosynthetic process going on on the surface of the dust. Now his mind extrapolated: currents in the dust, photosynthesis going on on the top, currents bringing food down to larger forms of life. He should have guessed before, and checked. He was far gone, was Phssthpok. Age and dwindling motivation were switching him off too early.

Three measured thumps came from almost beneath his feet.

He crossed the hold in one leap, landed softly, silently. Picked up the flat-nosed softener key. Waited.

Hypothesis: something intelligent was sounding the cargo hold for echoes. Size: unknown. Intelligence: unknown. Sophistication: probably low due to their environment. They would be blind down here, if they had eyes at all. A feel for sound could compensate. The echoes from this thumping could tell them a good deal about what was inside. And then?

They would try to break in. Intelligent beings were curious.

Twing was tough, but not invulnerable.

Phssthpok leapt straight upward, through the hatch and into the control cubby. He hated to leave the captive, but there was no choice. He closed the door to the cargo hold, tested it to be sure it was locked. He climbed rapidly into his pressure suit.

Three measured thumps from somewhere below him. Pause.

Something thumped next to his right arm. Phssthpok applied the softener key to the twing. *Thump*—and a foot of crude glass rod slammed through the twing. Phssthpok yanked hard on it, reached through the wall and had something softer. He pulled.

He had something roughly Pak-shaped, both smaller and denser than a Pak. It was clutching a reversed spear. Phssthpok hit it savagely where its head joined its shoulders. Something broke, and it went limp. Phssthpok probed its body for soft spots. There was a spot in the middle of its body where bone did not protect. Phssthpok pushed hard into it and clutched with his fingers until he felt something give. Presumably it was dead.

It began to smoke.

Phssthpok watched.

Something in the pod's atmosphere was causing it to give off fumes. That seemed promising. The spear did not speak for a high civilization. Probably they would have nothing that could penetrate twing. He did not like to risk it—but the alternative was to leak his own breathing-air into the surrounding dust, to poison it.

He opened his helmet for a moment and sniffed. Closed it fast. But he'd smelled chemicals he was familiar with. . .

He got a squeeze of water, trickled it on the alien's leg. The result was a fireball. Phssthpok leapt away. From across the room he watched the alien burn.

That seemed straightforward enough.

He went to work rigging a hose from the pod's water supply to the hull. His last moves he made in haste: using the softener key, running the hose through the hull, removing the key to harden the twing, then running water. There was frantic thumping from all over the hull. It stopped rather suddenly.

He ran most of his reserve of water out into the dust.

He waited several hours, until the whine of the air system dropped to normal. Then he doffed his pressure suit and rejoined Brennan. The captive had noticed nothing.

The water should hold off the natives for awhile. But Phssthpok's reserves were dwindling almost ludicrously. His ship was abandoned, his remaining drive system was useless, his environment bordered by a spherical shell of dust. Now his water reserve was gone. His life story was almost visibly coming to a close.

Presently he dreamed.

The *Blue Ox* had circled the sun and was now on the other side of the system, headed for interstellar space. Between *Ox* and *U Thant* there was a communications gap of thirty minutes. Sohl and Garner waited, knowing that any information would be half-an-hour late.

Mars was three-quarters full and impressively large in their rear view camera.

They had asked all the questions, made guesses at the

answers, mapped out their search pattern of the Lacis Solis region. Luke was bored. He missed the conveniences built into his travel chair. He thought Nick was bored too, but he was wrong. In space Nick was silent by habit.

The screen flashed on: a woman's face. The radio cleared its throat and spoke.

"U Thant, this is Tina Jordan aboard *Blue Ox."* Luke sensed the woman's barely repressed panic. Tina caught on her own voice, then blurted, "We're in trouble. We were testing that alien root in the lab and Einar took a bite out of it! The damn thing was like asbestos from vacuum exposure, but he chewed a piece off and swallowed if before we could stop him. I can't understand why he did it. It smelled awful!

"Einar's sick, very sick. He tried to kill me when I took the root away from him. Now he's gone into coma. We've hooked him into the ship's 'doc. The 'doc says Insufficient Data." They heard a ragged intake of breath. Luke thought he could see bruises beginning to form on the woman's throat. "We'd like permission to get him to a human doctor."

Nick cursed and keyed *Transmit.* "Nick Sohl speaking. Pick a route and get on it. Then finish analyzing that root. Did the smell remind you of anything? Sohl over." He turned it off. "What the blazes got into him?"

Luke shrugged. "He was hungry?"

"Einar Nilsson, for Finagle's sake! He was my boss for a year before he quit politics. Why would he try a suicidal trick like that? He's not stupid." Nick drummed on the arm of his chair, then began looking for Ceres with the com laser.

In the half hour that passed before the *Blue Ox* called again, he got dossiers on all three of her crew. "Tina Jordan's a flatlander. That explains why they waited for orders," he said.

"Does that need an explanation?"

"Most Belters would have turned around the moment Einar came down sick. The Outsider ship's empty, and there's no problem tracking it. No real point in staying.

But Jordan's still a flatlander, still used to being told when to breathe, and La Pan probably didn't trust his own judgment enough to overide her."

"Age," said Luke. "Nilsson was the oldest."

"What would that have to do with it?"

"I don't know. He was also the biggest. Maybe he *was* after a new taste thrill. . .no, dammit, I don't believe it either—"

"Blue Ox calling *U Thant.* We're on our way home. Course plotted for Vesta. The root analyzes almost normal. High in carbohydrates, including right-hand sugars. The proteins look ordinary. No vitamins at all. We found two compounds Nate says are brand new. One resembles a hormone, testosterone, but it definitely isn't testosterone.

"The root doesn't smell like anything I can name, except possibly sour milk or sour cream. The air in the Outsider ship was thin, with an adequate partial pressure of oxygen, no poisonous compounds, at least two percent helium. We spectroanalyzed the porthole material, and—" She listed a spectrum of elements, high in silicone. "The 'doc still reports Einar's illness as Insufficient Data, but now there's an emergency light. Whatever it is, it's not good. Any further questions?"

"Not at the moment," said Nick. "Don't call back, because we're going to be too busy landing." He signed off. He sat drumming on the console with long, tapering fingers. "Helium. That ought to tell us something."

"A small world with no moon," Luke speculated. "Big moons tend to skim away a planet's atmosphere. The Earth would look like Venus without her oversized moon. The helium would be the first to go, wouldn't it?"

"Maybe. It would also be the first to leave a small planet. Think about the Outsider's strength. It was no small planet he came from."

Nick and Luke were men who would stop to think before speaking. Conversation aboard *U Thant* would lapse for minutes, then take up just where it had left off.

"What then?"

"From somewhere in a gas cloud, with lots of helium.

The galactic core is in the direction he came from. Plenty of gas clouds and dust clouds in that direction."

"But that's an unholy distance away. Will you stop that drumming?"

"It helps me think. Like your smoking."

"Drum then."

"There's no limit to how far he could have come. The faster a Bussard ramjet ship moves, the more fuel it would pick up."

"There has to be a limit at which the exhaust velocity equals the velocity at which the gas hits the ramscoop field."

"Possible. But it must be way the Finagle up there. That air tank was *huge*. The Outsider is a long way from home."

The autodoc was built into the back wall, set over one of the three disaster couches. Einar was in that couch. His arm was in the 'doc almost to the shoulder.

Tina watched his face. He had been getting progressively worse. It did not look like sickness; it looked like age. Einar had aged decades in the past hour. He urgently needed a human doctor. . .but a higher thrust than the *Ox's* would have killed him, and the *Ox* was all they had.

Could they have stopped him? If she'd yelled at once —but then Einar had his hands on her throat, and it was too late. Where had Einar got such strength? He would have killed her.

His chest stopped moving.

Tina looked up at the dial faces on the 'doc. Usually a panel covered those dials; a spaceship has enough gadgets to watch without added distractions. Tina had been looking at those dials every five minutes, for hours. This time they all showed red.

"He's dead," she said. She heard the surprise in her voice, and wondered at it. The cabin walls began to blur and recede.

Nate squirmed out of the control couch and bent over Einar. "And you just noticed! He must have been dead for an hour!"

"No, I swear. . ." Tina gulped against the rising anaesthesia in her veins. Her body was water. She was going to faint.

"Look at his face and tell me that!"

Tina climbed onto watery legs. She looked down at the ravaged face. Einar, dead, looked hundreds of years old. In sorrow and guilt and repugnance, she reached to touch the dead cheek.

"He's still warm."

"Warm?" Nate touched the corpse. "He's on fire. Fever. Must have been alive seconds ago. Sorry, Tina, I jumped at conclusions. Hey! Are you all right?"

"How dangerous are these approaches?"

"Get that brave little quiver out of your voice," said Nick. It was pure slander; Luke was nothing but interested. "I've made a couple of hundred of these in my life. For sheer thrills I've never found anything to beat letting you fly me to Death Valley Port."

"You *said* you were in a hurry."

"So I did. Luke, I'd like to request an admiring silence for the next few minutes."

"Aha! Ah HA!"

The red planet reached for them, unfolding like a war-god's fist. Nick's bantering mood drained away. His face took on a set, stony look. He had not been quite candid with Luke. He had made several hundred powered approaches in his life; true. But those had been asteroid approaches, with gravity negligible or nearly so.

Diemos went by in the direction technically known as "ship's upward." Nick inched a lever toward him. Mars was flattening out and simultaneously sliding away as they moved north.

"The base should be there," said Luke. "At the north edge of that arc. Ah, that must be it, that little crater."

"Use the scope."

"Mmmmm. . .dammit. Ah. There it is. Deflated, of course. See it, Nick?"

"Yah."

It looked like the abandoned shred of a sky-blue toy balloon.

Dust rose in churning clouds to meet their drive flame. Nick swore viciously and increased thrust. By now Luke had caught on to Nick's vagaries in blasphemy. When he swore by Finagle it was for humor or emphasis. When he blasphemed in Christian fashion, he meant it.

U Thant slowed and hovered. She was above the dust, then in the dust, and gradually the ochre clouds thinned and backed away. A ring shaped sandstorm receded toward three hundred and sixty degrees of horizon. The bedrock lay exposed for the first time in millennia. It was lumpy and brown and worn. In the light of the drive the rounded rock blazed white, with sharp black shadows. Where the drive flame touched it melted.

Nick said, "I'll have to land in the crater. That dust will flow back in as soon as I turn off the motor." He angled the ship left and killed the drive. The bottom dropped out. They fell.

They fell all the way on attitude jets, and touched with hardly a bounce.

"Beautiful," said Luke.

"I do that all the time. I'm going to search the base. You monitor me on helmet camera."

The ring wall rose above him in worn, rounded, volcanic-looking stone. Dust dripped back from the rim, ran like molasses down the shallow slope to collect in a pool around the ship's shock legs. The crater was half a mile across. In the approximate center was the dome, surrounded by a lapping sea of dust.

Nick looked about him, frowning. There seemed no way to reach the dome without crossing the dust, which might not be as shallow as it looked. The crater was ancient; it looked just younger than the planet itself. But it was criss-crossed with younger cracks. Some of the edges were almost sharp; the air and dust were too thin to erode things quickly. There would be bad footing.

He started around the base of the ring wall, walking with care. Dust concealed some of the cracks.

A small, intense sun hung above the crater rim, in a deep purple sky.

On the far side of the dome a narrow path of laser-fused dust led from the dome to the ring wall. It must have been made with the base's communications laser. The boats were there, moored along the path. Nick did not pause to study them.

There must have been dozens of slits in the dome material. Nick found twelve dried bodies within. Martians had murdered the base personnel over a century ago. They had killed Müller the same way, after Müller had re-inflated the dome.

Nick searched each of the small buildings in turn. At some places he had to crawl beneath the transparent folds of the dome. There was no Outsider to meet him. There was no sign of tampering since Müller's forced visit.

"Dead end," he reported. "Next step?"

"You'll have to carry me piggyback until we can find a sand boat."

Dust had settled over the boats, leaving only flat, wide shapes the color of everything else. For twelve years they had waited for another wave of explorers—explorers who had lost interest and gone home.

It was like seeing ghosts. An Egyptian pharaoh might find such ghosts waiting for him in the afterworld: rank on rank of dumb, faithful retainers, gone before him, and waiting, waiting.

"From here they look good," said Luke. He settled himself more comfortably on Nick's shoulders. "We're in luck, Sinbad."

"Don't count your money yet." Nick started across the dust pond toward the dome. Luke was light on his shoulders, and his own body was light here; but together they were top-heavy. "If I start falling I'll try to fall sideways. That dust won't hurt either of us."

"Don't fall."

"The UN fleet will probably be coming here too. To get the boats."

"They're days behind us. Come on."

"The path's slippery. Dust all over it."

The boats, three of them, were lined along the west side. Each had four seats and a pair of fans at the stern, below the dust line, caged for protection against submerged rocks. The boats were so flat that any ocean ripple would have sunk them; but in the heavy dust they rode high.

Nick settled his burden not too gently into one of the seats. "See if she'll start, Luke. I'm going to the dome for fuel."

"It'll be hydrazine, with compressed martian air as oxidizer."

"I'll just look for something labeled *Fuel*."

Luke was able to start the compressor, but the motor wouldn't fire. *Probably drained the tanks,* he decided, and turned everything off. He found a bubble dome collapsed in the back. After making sure it was meant to be worked manually, he wrestled it into place and sealed it down, holding himself in place with a seat belt to get leverage. His long arms and wide hands had never lost an arm wrestling match. The edges of the bubble would probably leak, he decided, but not seriously. He found the inspection hatch that hid an air converter for changing the nitric oxides outside into breathable nitrogen and oxygen.

Nick returned with a green tank balanced on one shoulder. He fueled the boat through an injector nozzle. Luke tried the starter again. It worked. The boat tried to take off without Nick. Luke found the neutral setting, then reverse. Nick waited while he backed up.

"How do I get through the bubble?"

"I guess you don't." Luke collapsed the bubble, unsealed one side for Nick, then sealed it after him. The bubble began to fill, slowly. "Best keep our suits on," said Luke. "It may be an hour before we can breathe in here."

"You can collapse it then. We've got to get provisions from the ship."

It was two hours before they raised the bubble and started for the opening in the ring wall.

The dark sandstone cliffs that framed the opening were sharp and clear, clearly dynamite-blasted, as artificial as the glassy path between dome and ring wall. Nick was settled comfortably in one of the passenger chairs, his feet propped on another, his eyes on the screen of the dismounted deep-radar.

"Seems deep enough now," he said.

"Then I'll open her up," said Luke. The fans spun; the stern dipped far down, then righted. They skimmed across the dust at ten knots, leaving two straight, shallow, regular swells as a wake.

The deep-radar screen registered a density pattern in three dimensions. It showed a smooth bottom, regular swells and dips from which millions of years had eliminated all sharp lines and points. There was little volcanic activity on Mars.

The desert was as flat as a mirror. Rounded dun rocks poked through its surface, incongruous, Daliesque. Craters sat on the dust like badly made clay ash trays. Some were a few inches across. Some were so large that they had to be seen from orbit. The horizon was straight and close and razor sharp, glowing yellow below and artery red above. Nick turned his head to watch the crater recede.

His eyes widened, then squinted. Something?

"Damn't. Hold it!" he shouted. "Turn around! Turn hard left!"

"Back toward the crater?"

"Yes!"

Luke cut the power in one motor. The boat turned its prow to the left but continued to skid sideways across the dust. Then the right fan bit in, and the boat curved around.

"I see it," said Luke.

It was little more than a dot at that distance, but it showed clearly against the calm monochrome sea around it. And it moved. It jerked, it paused to rest, it jerked again, rolling sideways. It was several hundred yards from the crater wall.

As they approached, it grew clearer. It was cylindrical, the shape of a short caterpillar, and translucent; and soft, for they saw it bend as it moved. It was trying to reach the opening in the ring wall.

Luke throttled down. The dustboat slowed and settled deeper. As they pulled alongside Luke saw that Nick had armed himself with a signal gun.

"It's him," said Nick. He sounded awed. He leaned over the side, gun at the ready.

The caterpillar was a transparent, inflated sack. Inside was something that rolled over and over, slowly, painfully, trying to get closer to the side of the boat. It was as clearly alien as anything created in the days of flat television.

It was humanoid, as much so as a stick-figure drawing is humanoid. It was all knobs. Elbows, knees, shoulders, cheekbones, they stuck out like marbles or grapefruit or bowling balls. The bald head swelled and rose behind like hydrocephalus.

It stopped trying to roll when it bumped against the boat.

"It looks helpless enough," Nick said dubiously.

"Well, here goes our air again." Luke deflated the bubble. The two men reached over the side, picked up the pressurized sack and dropped it in the bottom of the boat. The alien's expression did not change, and probably could not. That face looked *hard*. But it did a strange thing. With thumb and forefinger of a hand like a score of black walnuts strung together, it made a circle.

Nick said, "It must have learned that from Brennan."

"Look at the bones, Nick. The bones correspond to a human skeleton."

"Its arms are too long for human. And its back slopes more."

"Yah. Well, we can't take him back to the ship, and

we can't talk to him the way he is now. We'll have to
wait out here while the bubble inflates."

"We seem to spend most of our time waiting," said
Luke.

Nick nodded. His fingers drummed against the back of
a chair. For twenty minutes the boat's small converter
had been straining to fill the bubble, using and changing
the thin, poisonous mixture outside.

But the alien hadn't moved at all. Luke had been
watching. The alien lay in its inflated bag in the bottom
of the boat, and it waited. Its human eyes watched them
from inside pits of tough, leathery wrinkles. Just so, with
just such patience, might a dead man wait for Judgment Day.

"At least we have it at a disadvantage," said Nick. "It
won't be kidnapping us."

"I think he must be insane."

"Insane? Its motives may be a little strange—"

"Look at the evidence. He came plowing into the system in a ship just adequate to get him here. His air tank
was on its last gasp. There was no evidence of failsafe
devices anywhere aboard. He made no attempt to contact anyone, as far as we can tell. He killed or kidnapped
Brennan. He then proceeded to abandon his interstellar
drive and run for Mars, presumably to hide. Now he's
abandoned his reentry vehicle, and whatever's left of Brennan too; he's rolled across a martian desert in a sandwich bag to reach the first place any exploring ship would
land! He's a nut. He's escaped from some interstellar mental institution."

"You keep saying *him*. It's an *it*. Think of it as an *it*
and you'll be ready for it to act peculiar."

"That's a cop-out. The universe is rational. In order to
survive, this thing has to be rational too, he, she, or it."

"Another couple of minutes and we can—"

The alien moved. Its hand slashed down the length
of the sack. Instantly Nick raised the signal gun. Instantly. . .but the alien reached through a long gap in the

sack and took the gun out of Nick's hand before Nick could react. There was no sign of haste. It placed the gun in the back of the boat and sat up.

It spoke. Its speech was full of clickings and rustlings and poppings. The flat, hard beak must have been a handicap. But it could be understood.

It said, "Take me to your leader."

Nick recovered first. He straightened his shoulders, cleared his throat and said, "That will involve a trip of several days. Meanwhile, we welcome you to human space."

"I'm afraid not," said the monster. "I hate to ruin your day. My name's Jack Brennan, and I'm a Belter. Aren't you Nick Sohl?"

III

The awful silence erupted in the sound of Luke's laughter. "You think of it as an alien and you'll be ready for s-strange—h-hahaha. . ."

Nick felt panic close around his throat. "You. You're Brennan?"

"Yah. And you're Nick Sohl. I saw you once in Confinement. But I don't recognize your friend."

"Lucas Garner." Luke had himself under control. "Your photographs don't do you justice, Brennan."

"I did something stupid," said the Brennan-monster. Its voice was no more human, its appearance no less intimidating. "I went to meet the Outsider. You were trying to do the same, weren't you?"

"Yes." There was a sardonic amusement in Luke's eyes and Luke's voice. Whether or not he believed the Brennan-monster, he was enjoying the situation. "Was there really an Outsider, Brennan?"

"Unless you want to quibble about definitions."

Sohl broke in. "For God's sake, Brennan! What *happened* to you?"

"That's a long story. Are we pressed for time? Of course not, you'd have started the motor. All right, I'd like to tell this my own way, so please maintain a respectful silence, remembering that if I hadn't gotten in the way you'd look just like this, and serve you right, too." He looked hard at the two men. "I'm wrong. You wouldn't. You're both past the age.

"Well, bear with me. There exists a race of bipeds that live near the edge of the globe of close-packed suns at the core of the galaxy. . .

82

"The most important thing about them is that they live in three stages of maturity. There is childhood, which is self-explanatory. There is the breeder stage, a biped just short of intelligence, whose purpose is to create more children. And there is the protector.

"At around age forty-two, our time, the breeder stage gets the urge to eat the root of a certain bush. Up to then he stayed away from it, because its smell was repugnant to him. Suddenly it smells delicious. The bush grows all over the planet; there's no real chance that the root won't be available to any breeder who lives long enough to want it.

"The root initiates certain changes, both physiological and emotional. Before I go into detail, I'll let you in on the big secret. The race I speak of calls itself—" The Brennan-monster clicked its horny beak sharply together. *Pak.* "But we call it *Homo habilis.*"

"What?" Nick seemed forced into the position of straight man, and he didn't like it. But Luke sat hugging his useless legs to his chest, grinning with huge enjoyment.

"There was an expedition that landed on Earth some two and a half million years ago. The bush they brought wouldn't grow right, so there haven't been any protector stage Pak on Earth. I'll get to that.

"When a breeder eats the root, these changes take place. His or her gonads and obvious sexual characteristics disappear. His skull softens and his brain begins to grow, until it is comfortably larger and more complex than yours, gentlemen. The skull then hardens and develops a bony crest. The teeth fall out, whatever teeth are left; the gums and lips grow together and form a hard, almost flat beak. My face is *too* flat; it works better with *Homo habilis.* All hair disappears. Some joints swell enormously, to supply much greater leverage to the muscle. The moment arm increases, you follow? The skin hardens and wrinkles to form a kind of armor. Fingernails become claws, retractile, so that a protector's fingertips are actually more sensitive than before, and better toolmakers. A simple two-chamber heart forms where the two veins from the legs, whatever the hell they're called, join to approach the heart. Notice that my skin is thicker there? Well, there are less dramatic changes, but they all contribute to make the protector a powerful, intelligent fighting machine. Garner, you no longer seem amused."

"It all sounds awfully familiar."

"I wondered if you'd spot that. . . The emotional changes are drastic. A protector who has bred true feels no urge except the urge to protect those of his blood line. He recognizes them by smell. His increased intelligence does him no good here, because his hormones rule his motives. Nick, has it occurred to you that all of these changes are a kind of exaggeration of what happens to men and women as they get older? Garner saw it right away."

"Yes, but—"

"The extra heart," Luke broke in. "What about that?"

"Like the expanded brain, it doesn't form without tree-of-life. After fifty, without modern medical care, a normal human heart becomes inadequate. Eventually it stops."

"Ah."

"Do you two find this convincing?"

Luke was reserving judgment. "Why do you ask?"

"I'm really more interested in convincing Nick. My Belt citizenship depends on my convincing you I'm Brennan. Not to mention my bank account and my ship and cargo. Nick, I've got an abandoned fuel tank from the Mariner XX attached to my ship, which I last left falling across the solar system at high speed."

"It's still doing that," said Nick. "Likewise the Outsider ship. We ought to be doing something about recovering it."

"Finagle's eyes, *yes!* It's not that good a design, I could improve it blindfold, but you could buy Ceres with the monopoles!"

"First things first," Garner said mildly.

"That ship is receding, Garner. Oh, I see what you mean; you're afraid to put an alien monster near a working spacecraft." The Brennan-monster glanced back at the

flare gun, flickeringly, then apparently abandoned the idea
of hijacking the dustboat. "We'll stay out here until you're
convinced. Is that a deal? Could you get a better deal
anywhere?"

"Not from a Belter. Brennan, there is considerable evidence that man is related to the other primates of Earth."

"I don't doubt it. I've got some theories."

"Say on."

"About that lost colony. A big ship arrived here, and
four landing craft went down with some thirty protectors
and a lot of breeders. A year later the protectors knew
they'd picked the wrong planet. The bush they needed
grew wrong. They sent a message for help, by laser, and
then they died. Starvation is a normal death for a protector, but it's usually voluntary. These starved against
their will." There was no emotion in the Brennan-monster's voice or mask-like face.

"They died. The breeders were breeding without check.
There was endless room, and the protectors must have
wiped out any dangerous life forms. What happened next
has to be speculation. The protectors were dead, but the
breeders were used to their helping out, and they stayed
around the ships."

"And?"

"And the piles got hot without the protectors to keep
them balanced. They had to be fission piles, given the state
of the art. Maybe they exploded. Maybe not. The radiation caused mutations resulting in everything from lemurs
to apes and chimpanzees to ancient and modern man."

"That's one theory," said the Brennan-monster. "Another is that the protectors deliberately started breeding
mutations, so that breeders would have a chance to survive in some form until help came. The results would be
the same."

"I don't believe it," said Nick.

"You will. You should now. There's enough evidence,
particularly in religions and folk tales. What percentage of
humanity genuinely expects to live forever? Why do so
many religions include a race of immortal beings who are

constantly battling one another? What's the justification for ancestor worship? You know what happens to a man without modern geriatrics: as he ages his brain cells start to die. Yet people tend to respect him, to listen to him. Where do guardian angels come from?"

"Race memory?"

"Probably. It's hard to believe a tradition could survive that long."

"South Africa," said Luke. "They must have landed in South Africa, somewhere near Olduvai Gorge National Park. All the primates are there."

"Not quite. Maybe one ship landed in Australia, for the metals. You know, the protectors may have just scattered radioactive dust around and left it at that. The breeders would breed like rabbits without natural enemies, and the radiation would help them change. With all the protectors dead, they'd have to develop new shticks. Some got strength, some got agility, some got intelligence. Most got dead, of course. Mutations do."

"I seem to remember," said Luke, "that the aging process in man can be compared to the program running out in a space probe. Once the probe has done its work it doesn't matter what happens to it. Similarly, once we pass the age at which we can have children—"

"—Evolution is through with you. You're moving on inertia only, following your course with no corrective mechanisms." The Brennan-monster nodded. "Of course the root supplies the program for the third stage. Good comparison."

Nick said, "Any idea what went wrong with the root?"

"Oh, that's no mystery. Though it had the protectors of Pak going crazy for awhile. No wonder a small colony couldn't solve it. There's a virus that lives in the root. It carries the genes for the change from breeder to protector. It can't live outside the root, so a protector has to eat more root every so often. If there's no thalium in the soil, the root still grows, but it won't support the virus."

"That sounds pretty complicated."

"Ever work with a hydroponics garden? The relationships in a stable ecology can be complicated. There was no problem on the Pak world. Thalium is a rare earth, but it must be common enough among all those Population II stars. And the root grows everywhere."

Nick said, "Where does the Outsider come in?"

A hiss and snap of beak: *Phssth-pok*. "Phssthpok found old records, including the call for help. He was the first protector in two and a half million years to realize that there was a way to find Sol, or at least to narrow the search. And he had no children, so he had to find a Cause quick, before the urge to eat left him. That's what happens to a protector when his blood line is dead. More lack of programming. Incidentally, you might note the heavy protection against mutation in the Pak species. A mutation doesn't smell right. That could be important in the galactic core, where radiation is heavy."

"So he came barreling out here with a hold full of seeds?"

"And bags of thalium oxide. The oxide was easiest to carry. I wondered about the construction of his ship, but you can see why he trailed his cargo section behind his lifesystem. Radiation doesn't bother him, in small amounts. He can't have children."

"Where is he now?"

"I had to kill him."

"What?" Garner was shocked. "Did he attack you?"

"No."

"Then—I don't understand."

The Brennan-monster seemed to hesitate. It said, "Garner, Sohl, listen to me. Twelve miles from here, some fifty feet under the sand, is part of an alien spacecraft filled with roots and seeds and bags of thalium oxide. The roots I can grow from those seeds can make a man nearly immortal. Now what? What are we going to do with them?"

The two men looked at each other. Luke seemed about to speak, closed his mouth.

"That's a tough one, right? But you can guess what Phssthpok expected, can't you?"

Phssthpok dreamed.

He knew to within a day just how long it would take for Brennan to wake up. He could have been wrong, of course. But if he were, then Brennan's kind would have mutated too far from the Pak form.

Knowing how long he had, Phssthpok could time his dreaming. The martians were no threat now, though something would have to be done about them eventually. Dreaming was a fine art to a protector. He had about ten days. For a week he dreamed the past, up until the day he left the Pak planet. Sensory stimulation had been skimpy during the voyage. He moved on into the future.

Phssthpok dreamed. . .

It would begin when his captive woke. From the looks of him, the captive's brain would be larger than Phssthpok's; there was that frontal bulge, ruining the slope of the face. He would learn fast. Phssthpok would teach him how to be a protector, and what to do with the roots and seeds of tree-of-life.

Did the breeder have children? If so, he would take the secret for his own, using tree-of-life to make protectors of his own descendants. That was all right. If he had sense enough to spread his family around, avoiding inbreeding, his blood line should reach out to include most of this system's Pak race.

Probably he would kill Phssthpok to keep the secret. That was all right too.

There was a nightmare tinge to Phssthpok's dreaming. For the captive didn't look right. His fingernails were developing wrong. His head was certainly not the right shape. That frontal bulge. . .and his beak was as flat as his face had been. His back wasn't arched, his legs were wrong, his arms were too short. His kind had had too much time to mutate.

But he'd reacted correctly to the roots.

The future was uncertain. . .except for Phssthpok. Let the captive learn what he needed to know, if he could; let him carry on the work, if he could. There would come a day when Earth was a second Pak world. Phssthpok had done his best. He would teach, and die.

Brennan stirred. He unfolded his curled body, stretched wide and opened his eyes. He stared unwinking at Phssthpok, stared as if he were reading the protector's mind. All new protectors did that: orienting themselves through memories they were only now beginning to understand.

"I wonder if I can make you understand how fast it all was," said the Brennan-monster. He gazed at the two old men, one twice the age of the other but both past the transition age, and wondered that they should be his judges.

"In two days we learned each other's language. His is much faster than mine and fits my mouth better, so we used it. He told me his life story. We discussed the martians, working out the most efficient way to exterminate them—"

"What?"

"To exterminate them, Garner. Hell they've killed thirteen men already! We talked practically nonstop, with Phssthpok doing most of the talking, and all the time we were hard at work: calisthenics to build me up, fins for Phssthpok's suit so he could swim the dust, widgets to get every atom of air and water out of the life support system and take it to the base. I've never seen the base; we had to extrapolate the design so we'd know how to re-inflate it and protect it.

"The third day he told me how to get a tree-of-life crop growing. He had the box open and was telling me how to unfreeze the seeds safely. He was giving me orders just as if I were a voice-box computer. I was about to ask, 'Don't I get any choices at all?' And I *didn't*."

"I don't follow," said Garner.

"I didn't get any choices. I was too intelligent. It's been that way ever since I woke up. I get answers before I can finish formulating the question. If I always see the best answer, then where's my choice? Where's my free will? You can't believe how fast this all was. I saw the whole chain of logic in one flash. I slammed Phssthpok's head hard against the edge of the freezer. It stunned him long enough so that I could break his throat against the edge. Then I jumped back in case he attacked. I figured I could hold him off until he strangled. But he didn't attack. He hadn't figured it out, not yet."

"It sounds like murder, Brennan. He didn't want to kill you?"

"Not yet. I was his shining hope. He couldn't even defend himself for fear of bruising me. He was older than me, and he knew how to fight. He could have killed me if he'd wanted to, but he couldn't want to. It took him thirty-two thousand years of real time to bring us those roots. I was supposed to finish the job.

"I think he died believing he'd succeeded. He half-expected me to kill him."

"Brennan. *Why?*"

The Brennan-monster shrugged cantaloupe shoulders. "He was wrong. I killed him because he would have tried to wipe out humanity when he learned the truth." He reached into the slit balloon that had brought him across twelve miles of fluid dust. He pulled out a jury-rigged something that hummed softly—his air renewal setup, made from parts of Phssthpok's control board—and dropped it in the boat. Next he pulled out half of a yellow root like a raw sweet potato. He held it under Garner's nose. "Smell."

Luke sniffed. "Pleasant enough. Like a liqueur."

"Sohl?"

"Nice. How's it taste?"

"If you knew it would turn you into something like me, would you take a bite of it? Garner?"

"This instant. I'd like to live forever, and I'm afraid of going senile."

"Sohl?"

"NO. I'm not ready to give up sex yet."

"How old are you?"

"Seventy-four. Birthday two months from now."

"You're already too old. You were too old at fifty; it would have killed you. Would you have volunteered at forty-five?"

Sohl laughed. "Not likely."

"Well, that's half the answer. From Phssthpok's point of view we're a failure. The other half is that no sane man would turn the root loose on Earth or Belt or anywhere else."

"I should hope not. But let's hear *your* reasons."

"War. The Pak world has never been free from war at any time in its history. Naturally not, with every protector acting to expand and protect his blood line at the expense of all the others. Knowledge keeps getting lost. The race can't cooperate for a minute beyond the point where one protector sees an advantage in betraying the others. They can't make any kind of progress because of that continual state of war.

"And I'm to turn that loose on Earth? Can you imagine a thousand protectors deciding their grandchildren need more room? Your eighteen billion flatlanders live too close to the edge already; you can't afford the resources.

"Besides which, we don't really need tree-of-life. Garner, when were you born? Nineteen forty or thereabouts?"

" 'Thirty-nine."

"Geriatrics is getting so good so fast that my kids could live a thousand years. We'll get longevity without tree-of-life, without sacrificing anything at all.

"Now look at it from Phssthpok's viewpoint," the Brennan-monster continued. "We're a mutation. We've settled the solar system and started some interstellar colonies. We will and must refuse the root, and even when it's forced on us, the resulting mutated protectors are atypical. Phssthpok thought in terms of the long view. We're not Pak, we're no use to the Pak, and it's conceivable that someday we'll reach the core suns. The Pak will attack us the moment they see us, and we'll fight back." He shrugged. "And we'll win. The Pak don't unite effectively. We do. We'll have a better technology than theirs."

"We will?"

"I told you, they can't keep their technology. Whatever can't be used immediately, gets lost until someone files it in the Library. Military knowledge never gets filed; the families keep it a deep, dark secret. And the only ones to use the Library are childless protectors.

There aren't many of them, and they aren't highly motivated."

"Couldn't you have tried to talk to him?"

"Garner, I'm not getting through to you. He'd have killed me the moment he figured it out! He was trained to fight protectors. I wouldn't have had a chance. Then he'd have tried to wipe out the human species. We'd have been much worse to him than hostile aliens. We're a corruption of the Pak form itself."

"But he couldn't do it. He was all alone."

"I've thought of half a dozen things he could have tried. None of them sure things, but I couldn't risk it."

"Name one."

"Plant tree-of-life all through Congo National Park. Organize the monkey and chimpanzee protectors."

"He was marooned here."

"He could have commandeered your ship. He'd have had your silly flare gun as fast as I did. Gentlemen, may I point out that it's near sunset? I don't think we want to navigate the ring wall in darkness."

Luke started the motor.

"This is Martin Shaeffer at Ceres calling Nick Sohl aboard *U Thant*. Nick, I don't know how your hunting goes, but Phobos reports that you've landed safely at Olympus Base, and they're tracking your dustboat wake. Presumably you'll find this on tape when you get back.

"We've sent the *Blue Ox* to meet you, on the theory that you may need the computer package as a translating device. Eisaku Ikeda commanding. The *Ox* should reach Olympus Base a day behind the UN fleet.

"Einar Nilsson is dead. We'll have an autopsy report shortly.

"We've sent fuel ships and construction facilities to rendezvous with the Outsider ship. There are two single-ships falling alongside already, and the Outsider ship has a tested tow line of its own. We may be able to rig the singleships for towing. Still, it's all going to be very sticky and time consuming. We may not get it home to the Belt for a couple of years.

"Nick, when the *Ox* gets there, be careful of Tina Jordan. Don't shake her up. She's had a bad shock. I think she blames herself for what happened to Einar.

"Repeating. . ."

Luke docked the dustboat in near-darkness. He said, "You'll have to wait in the boat, Brennan. Nick can't carry us both."

"I'll roll," said the Brennan-monster.

Nick's walk down the path and around the rim of the dust pool was made in unseemly haste. "Take it easy," Luke complained. "You can't *trot* in this light. You'll fall and crack both our helmets."

"He's going to beat us to the ship," Nick said edgily.

Brennan was taking the short cut, rolling directly across the dust.

"Slow down. You can't beat him, and he can't get up the ladder."

"Maybe *he's* thought of a way. If he does. . .oh, hell." Nick slowed down. Brennan had rolled uphill to the foot of *U Thant's* ladder. He waited for them there like a translucent sausage.

"Nick? Do you trust him?"

It was seconds before he answered. "I think his story's straight. He's a Belter. Or an ex-Belter."

"He swore by damn instead of by Finagle."

"So do I. And he recognized me. No, I'll tell you what really convinced me. He didn't ask about his wife, because she can take care of herself. He asked about his cargo. He's a Belter."

"We accept his story, then. Anthropology and all. Wow."

"His story, yes. Luke, I'll take you up, then come back for Brennan. But I won't come down until you're talking to Ceres. I want all of this on record before I let him in the ship. I'm still wondering about his motives."

"Ah."

"He said it himself. Motives change for a protector."

Garner was already signing off when Brennan climbed out of his zippered balloon. Brennan made no mention of the delay. He said, "If you're worried about accommodations, I can get along without an acceleration couch. In fact, I can ride outside in a cargo net if you'll give me a radio link. If my patchwork air plant breaks down I'd want to get inside fast."

"That won't be necessary. It'll be cramped, but not that cramped," said Nick. He squeezed past Brennan, wincing inside himself from the dry leathery touch, and into the control chair. "We seem to have a message."

They listened in silence to the recorded voice of Lit Shaeffer.

"Too bad about Nilsson," Brennan said afterward. "There wasn't much chance they'd let him eat enough of the root, even if he wasn't past the age."

Nobody answered.

"Shaeffer's right, you know. Doing it that way, it'll take you a couple of years to drag Phssthpok's ship home."

"Have you got a better idea?"

"Of course I've got a better idea, Nick, you idiot. I can fly that ship home myself."

"You?" Nick stared. "When did the Outsider ever let you operate the controls?"

"He never did. But I saw them, and they didn't look cryptic. Just complicated. I'm sure I can figure out how to fly it. All you've got to do is fuel the ship and fly me to it."

"Uh huh. What do we do about the cargo pod? Leave it where it is?"

"No. There's a gravity polarizer in that pod."

"Oh?"

"Not to mention the supply of roots, which I need, even if you don't. The seeds count too. Gentlemen, when you have finally grasped the extent of my magnificent intelligence, you'll see what those seeds represent. They're a failsafe for the human race. If we ever really need a leader, we can make one. Just pick a forty-two-year-old childless volunteer and turn him or her loose in the tree-of-life patch."

"I'm not sure how well I like that," said Garner.

"Well, the gravity polarizer's important enough. You and the UN fleet can retrieve it while Nick and I go after Phssthpok's ship—"

Nick said, "Just a—"

"—You won't have to worry about the martians for awhile. I dumped Phssthpok's share of the water into the dust, just before I left. *Don't let anyone into the pod without a pressure suit.* Need I elaborate?"

"No," said Garner. He felt like an amateur on skis. Somewhere he had lost control, and now events were moving too fast.

Nick spoke with a certain amount of anger. "Hold it, What makes you think we'd trust you to fly the Outsider ship?"

"Take your time. Think it through," said Brennan. "You'll have my supply of root for hostage. And where would I go with a Bussard ramjet? Where would I sell it? Where would I hide, with my face?"

Nick's face wore a trapped look. Where was his own free will?

"It's probably the most valuable artifact in human space," said Brennan. "It's falling outward at several hundred miles per second. Each minute you take to make up your mind now is going to cost us a couple of hours hauling it back from interstellar space. You'll pay for that in extra fuel and provisions and man-hours and delays. But take your time. Think it through."

The Brennan-monster had the ability to relax. Sometime in the future there would be periods of furious activity...

They left Lucas Garner on Phobos, refueled there, and took off. Garner did not see Nick again for seven months. He did not see Brennan ever again.

For the rest of his life he remembered that cramped conversation. Brennan—on his back with his knees up, in a position of acute discomfort—was a blurred half-alien voice behind his control couch. Brennan had trouble with his V's and W's, but he could be understood. His voice was full of clickings.

An indefinite tension went out of Nick once they were in free fall. Mars converged slowly on itself, a bright varied landscape reddening as it lost detail.

"Children. You've got children," Luke remembered suddenly.

"I'm aware of that. But fear not. I don't intend to hover over them. They'll have a better chance for happiness without that."

"The hormone changes didn't work?"

"I'm as neuter as a bumblebee. They must have worked to some extent. I think most of a protector's urge to die after his blood line is dead must be cultural. Training. I don't have that training, that conviction that a breeder can't be happy or safe without his ancestors constantly telling him what to do. Nick, can you give it out that the Outsider killed me?"

"What? What for?"

"Best for the children. I couldn't keep seeing them without affecting their lives. Best for Charlotte too. I don't intend to rejoin society as such. There's nothing there for me."

"The Belt doesn't look down on cripples, Brennan."

"No," Brennan said with finality. "Give me an asteroid I can bubble-form and I'll raise tree-of-life. Set me up a monthly liaison with Ceres so I can keep abreast of current developments. I'll be able to pay for all this with new inventions. I think I can design a manned ramrobot. Better than Phssthpok's."

Garner said, "You called it tree-of-life?"

"It's a good name. You remember that Adam and Eve ate from the Tree of Knowledge of Good and Evil. According to Genesis, the reason they were kicked out was that they might also have eaten from the Tree of Life, to live forever. 'And be as one of us'—it would have made them equivalent to angels. Now it looks like both trees were the same."

Luke found a cigarette. "I don't know that I like the idea of you producing tree-of-life crops."

"I don't much like the idea of a State secret," said Nick. "The Belt has never had State secrets."

"I hope I can convince you. I can't protect my children, but I can try to protect the human race. If I was needed, I'd be there. If more were needed, there would be the root."

"The cure would be worse than the disease, most likely." Luke used his lighter. "Wha—" A knotted hand had reached around the crash couch and taken the cigarette from his mouth and stubbed it out against the hull.

It had been a shock. He remembered it with a shiver as he traversed the double airlocks at the axis of Farmer's Asteroid.

Long ago, Farmer's Asteroid had been an approximate cylinder of nickel-iron orbiting between Mars and Jupiter. Then Belt industry had bubble-formed it: set it rotating, heated the metal nearly to melting and inflated it, via exploding bags of water, into a cylindrical bubble five miles in radius. Its rotation produced half a gravity. Much of the Belt's food supply was grown here.

Luke had been in Farmer's Asteroid once before. He enjoyed the landscaped interior, the wedding-ring lake, the checkered farmlands that rolled out and away and up and over, to where tiny tractors plowed furrows ten miles overhead.

The airlock let him out at the axis. It was cold here behind the sunshield, where the rays of the axial fusion tube never fell. Icebergs condensed out of the air here; and eventually broke loose and slid downslope, and melted into rivers that flowed in carved beds to the wedding-ring lake that girdled Farmer's Asteroid. Nick Sohl met him here, and helped him tow himself downslope to where a travel chair waited.

"I can guess why you're here," Nick told him.

"Officially, I'm here at the request of the Joint Interstellar Colony Authority. They got your request to send a warning message to Wunderland. They weren't at all clear on what the situation was, and I couldn't give them much help."

"You had my report," Nick said a bit stiffly.

"It wasn't much of a report, Nick."

After a bit Nick nodded. "My fault. I just didn't want to talk about it—and don't now, for the matter of that —and it was too bloody late. We didn't just give up, you know. We've been tracking him."

"What happened, Nick?"

"They'd done considerable work when I got there with Brennan. The idea was to rig two singleships together with their drive tubes aimed about ten degrees apart, then moor the framework to the cable from the Pak ship. There was eight miles of it behind the lifesystem section. We could have hauled them home at low thrust. But Brennan said that the Pak drive section would produce ten times the thrust.

"So we boarded the Pak lifesystem sphere and Brennan played around with the controls. I spent a couple of days in there watching him. It turns out you can make the whole hull transparent, or just part of it, the way it was when we found it. We widened the hole Tina Jordan left and fitted an airlock into it.

"Two days of fiddling, and then Brennan said he had it figured out and all we had to do was refuel the drive section. He said that if we tried to tow it backward we'd set off all kinds of failsafe systems. Garner, how the hell was I to know—"

"You couldn't. It still doesn't make sense."

Nick ran a hand backward through his white wool crest. "They'd already rigged up a mating plug to match the fuel plug on the Pak ship. Brennan insisted on doing all the work himself, and even he had to use a radiation suit and shield. We moored his own singleship to the tow line, just in case something failed on the way home. That was *my* idea, Garner."

"Uh huh."

"He took off headed back toward Sol. We tried to fly formation with him, but he was putting the ship through maneuvers, testing the control sytems. We kept our distance. Then—he just turned around and headed out into interstellar space."

"You tried to catch him?"

Nick yelped, "What tried? We flew alongside him! I didn't want to make any threatening moves, but he wouldn't communicate, and we were going to run out of fuel. I ordered Dubchek and Gorton to use their drives as weapons if he didn't sheer off."

"What happened?"

"I think he must have turned on his Bussard ramjet field. The electromagnetic effects burned out enough of our equipment to leave us dead in space. We're lucky the drives didn't blow up. A fuel ship finally got to us, and we managed to make some repairs. By that time Brennan was up to ramscoop speed."

"All right."

"How the hell was I to know? We've got his food supply! That bin of roots was almost empty. Was it just a fancy way to commit suicide? Was he afraid of what we'd do with a manned Bussard ramjet ship?"

"I hadn't thought of that. You know, that could be it. Nick, do you remember him mashing out my cigarette?"

Nick chortled. "Sure. He apologized all over the place, but he wouldn't let you smoke. I thought you were going to hit him."

"He's a protector. Whatever he does, it's for our own good." Luke scowled, remembering someone. . .no, that was all he remembered about her. A high school teacher? "He didn't want us to have the Pak ship, or something we could learn from it, or from him."

"Then why did he spend two months out there beyond Pluto? You don't stop halfway with a Bussard ramjet! It costs reserve fuel! And there's nothing at all out there—"

"The cometary belt, they call it. Most comets spend most of their time out there beyond Pluto. It's thin, but there's matter out there. There's a tenth planet too."

"He never went near Persephone."

"But he may have gone near any number of comets."

". . .Right. Okay, he spent two months out there, at

rest as far as our monopole detectors could determine. Last month he started moving again. We followed him that long before we were sure. He's accelerating toward Alpha Centauri. Wunderland."

"How long before he gets there?"

"Oh, twenty years anyway. It's a low thrust drive. But we can warn them, and set things up so that our successors warn them again in fifteen years. Just in case."

"Okay, we can do that. What else? You knew that we dug up the cargo pod."

"That's all we know. The UN can keep secrets too."

"We destroyed the roots and seeds. Nobody really liked the idea, but we did it."

It was a long time before Nick answered, "Good."

"Good or bad, we did it. We haven't had any luck at all understanding the gravity polarizer. If that's what it was. Brennan could have been lying."

"It was a gravity polarizer."

"Just how do you know that?"

"We analyzed the record of the Outsider's course to Mars. His acceleration varies according to local gravitational gradients: not just by thrust but by direction too."

"All right, that'll help. What else can we do?"

"About Brennan, nothing. Eventually he'll starve. Meanwhile we'll always know exactly where he is."

"Or where his monopole source is."

Nick spoke with dwindling patience. "He doesn't have a ship without his monopole package. He doesn't have a food supply, period. He's *dead,* Garner."

"I keep remembering that he's smarter than we are. If he can find a way to hibernate, it would get him to Wunderland. A thriving colony. . .and so what? What does he want with Wunderland?"

"Something we haven't thought of."

"I'll never know what it is. I'll be dead before Brennan reaches Wunderland." Luke sighed. "Poor Outsider. All this way to bring us the roots that would let us lead a normal life."

"His intentions were good. Life is hard on us heroes," Nick said seriously.

INTERLUDE

How to describe a gap of two centuries? Events are the measure of time. A great many things happened in two hundred and twenty years.

The dry corpse of Phssthpok ended in the Smithsonian Institution. There was some discussion as to whether to class it among the hominids. His story was third hand by now, with Brennan unavailable, but his skeleton matched hominid bone structure, bone for bone.

Lucas Garner was dead when the Pak ship passed course midpoint. It did not make turnover. Nick Sohl was watching when its magnetic trace passed Wunderland, two years early and still accelerating toward nowhere. And he wondered.

Olympus Base on Mars was rebuilt to study Phssthpok's cargo pod *in situ,* that being easier than trying to lift it against gravity with the gravity polarizer still going. The study group was reluctant to shut it down until they knew how to restart it. They used a hovering singleship to fuse the dust beneath the base, as protection against martians.

The Belt population increased considerably. Bubble worlds proliferated, some equipped with drives to move them around. Mining was becoming more difficult; the best lodes had been exhausted. Cities spread throughout the larger rocks. A decreasing percentage of Belters flew singleships.

A large ice asteroid impacted on Mars, causing dust storms and minor quakes to trouble Olympus Base.

The interstellar colonies prospered and changed. Jinx developed extensive vacuum industries, where the planet's landscape rises out of the atmosphere at the East End. Society became repressive on Plateau. Wunderland's population expanded and spread thinly across the major continent, so that cities were long in developing. Civilization developed underground on We Made It, to avoid the hurricane winds of summer and winter. Home was settled, and prospered, benefitting from new techniques and from mistakes made on the earlier colony worlds.

Laser beams passed between Earth and the colonies, and occasional ramrobots left the linear accelerator on Juno, carrying cargoes of new knowledge. Of late most of the ramrobot "gifts" were advances in biological engineering, seeds and frozen fertilized eggs. News from the colonies was sparse, though Jinx and Home had excellent communications lasers.

The drug problem on Earth had become a dead issue by Lucas Garner's time. Potential drug addicts tended to become wireheads; the experience was more complete, and current was cheap after the initial expense of the operation. Wireheads bother nobody; the wirehead problem was never serious. By 2340 it had almost solved itself. People had learned to handle it.

Earth's population kept itself stable, by force when necessary.

The gravity polarizer seemed beyond human understanding.

Improved alloplasty—gadgets instead of organ transplants—went a long way toward solving the problem of organ bank shortages. The UN citizenry even voted to remove the death penalty for certain crimes: income tax evasion, illegal advertising. The heavy authority given the ARM, the United Nations police, was relaxed somewhat.

War on a major scale had not happened in some time.

Life within the solar system had become somewhat idyllic. . .

VANDERVECKEN

I   The perversity of the universe tends to a maximum.
II If something can go wrong, it will.
                              —Finagle's First and Second Laws

He woke with the cold burning his nose and cheeks. He woke all at once, and opened his eyes to black night and clear bright stars. He sat upright in vast surprise. This took some effort. He was wrapped like a pupa in his mummy bag.

The shadows of peaks thrust into the starscape. City light glowed far away beyond a lumpy horizon.

He had gone hiking in the Pinnacles that morning, after a week of backpacking. He had gone the full route, through the caves, up miles of narrow trail bordered by manzanita and empty space, up to where crude steps and metal handrails had had to be set into the rock. He had eaten a late lunch up there at the top of everything. Started down in plenty of time, his legs protesting the renewed work. The Pinnacles' strange vertical geology reached up like fingers toward the sky. Then. . .what?

Apparently he was still here, halfway up a mountain, his mummy bag spread on the path.

He did not remember going to sleep.

Concussion? A fall? He snaked an arm from within the mummy bag and felt for bruises. None. He felt fine; he didn't hurt anywhere. The air chilled his arm now, and he wondered. The day had been so *hot*.

And he'd left his backpack in the car. He'd left the car in the Pinnacles parking lot a week ago, and he'd come back to it this morning and left his gear in the trunk, with the mummy bag. How had it gotten up here?

The trails through the Pinnacles were dangerous enough in bright daylight. Elroy Truesdale was not about to negotiate them in darkness. He made a midnight snack from his backpack—which should have been in the car, and which was sitting near his head, covered with dew—and waited for dawn.

At dawn he started down. His feet felt fine, and the empty desolate rockscape was a joyful thing to see. He sang loudly as he negotiated the incredible trails. Nobody screamed at him to shut up. His legs did not ache despite the afternoon's climb. He must be in pretty good shape, he thought. Though only a fool would carry a backpack on these trails, unless it had been wished on him halfway up a mountain.

The sun was well up when he reached the parking lot.

The car was locked tight, as he had left it. He was not whistling now. This made no sense. Some Good Samaritan had found him unconscious on the trail, or stunned him there; had not called for help; had broken into Truesdale's own car and lugged Truesdale's own backpack halfway up a mountain to slide him into his own mummy bag. What the hell? Had someone wanted Truesdale's car, to frame him for some crime? When he opened the trunk he half expected to find a murder victim; but there were not even bloodstains. He was relieved and disappointed.

There was a message spool sitting on his car entertainment set.

He fitted it in and heard it out.

Truesdale, this is Vandervecken. By now you may or may not have realized that four months have vanished from your young life. For this I apologize. It was necessary, and you can afford to lose four months, and I intend to pay a fair price for them. Briefly: you will receive five hundred UN marks per quarter for the rest of your life, provided that you make no attempt to find out who I am.

On your return home you will find a confirming spool from Barrett, Hubbard and Wu, who will supply you with details.

Believe me, you did nothing criminal during the four

*months you can't remember. You did things you would
find interesting, but that's what the money's for.*

*You would find it difficult to learn my identity in any
case. A voice pattern would tell you nothing. Barrett,
Hubbard and Wu know nothing about me. The effort
would be expensive and fruitless, and I hope you won't
make it.*

Elroy did not twitch when acrid smoke curled up from
the message spool. He had half expected that. In any case
he had recognized the voice. His own. He must have made
this tape for. . .Vandervecken. . .during the time he
couldn't remember.

He spoke to the blackened tape. "You wouldn't lie to
yourself, would you, Roy?"

Under what circumstances?

He got out of the car and walked to the Tourist Office
and bought a morning newstape. His set still worked,
though the message spool was a charred lump. He played
the tape for the date. January 9, 2341.

It had been September 8, 2340. He had missed Christ-
mas and New Year's Day and four months of *what?* In
rising fury he lifted the car phone. Who handled kidnappings? The local police, or the ARMs?

He held the phone for a long moment. The he put it
down.

It had come to him that he was not going to call the
police.

While his car flew him back toward San Diego, Elroy
Truesdale writhed in a kind of trap.

He had lost his first and, to date, only wife because of
his reluctance to spend money. She had told him often
enough that it was a character flaw. Nobody else had it.
In a world where nobody starved, a life style was more
important than credit security.

He had not always been like this.

At birth Truesdale had owned a trust fund intended to
keep him, not rich, but comfortable for the rest of his life.

It would have done so; but Truesdale wanted more. At age twenty-five he had convinced his father to turn the money over to him. He wanted to make some investments.

He *would* have been rich, from the way it sounded. But it had been a complicated con. Somewhere on Earth or in the Belt, a man who might or might not be named Lawrence St. John McGee was living in luxury. He couldn't possibly have spent it all, not even on his scale of living.

Possibly Truesdale had overreacted. But he had no real talents; he could not count on *himself* as security. He knew that now. He was a salesman in a shoe store. Before that it had been a service station, trading batteries on passing cars and checking the motors and fans. He was an ordinary man. He kept himself in shape because everybody did; fat and loose muscles were regarded as personal carelessness. He had given up his beard, a pretty good beard, after Lawrence St. John McGee had walked off with his fortune. A working man did not have the time to keep up a good beard. Two thousand a year for life. He could not turn down the money.

Now he was in a trap, walled in by his own character flaws. *Damn* Vandervecken. And he must have cooperated, sold himself out. That had been *his* voice on the message tape.

Wait. There might be no money. . .just a cheap promise to buy "Vandervecken" a few additional hours and send Truesdale a few hundred miles south.

Truesdale called home. There was four months' worth of calls waiting in storage in his phone. He keyed it for *Barrett, Hubbard and Wu,* and waited out the sorting process.

The message was there. He heard it through. It said about what he had expected it to.

He called the Better Business Bureau.

Yes, they had records of Barrett, Hubbard and Wu. It was a reputable firm, as far as they were concerned, specializing in corporate law. He got their number from Information.

Barrett was a smartly dressed woman in middle age. Her manner was competent and brusk. She was reluctant to tell him anything at all, even after he had identified himself.

"All I want to know," he told her, "is whether your firm is sure of your funds. This Vandervecken has promised me five hundred marks quarterly. If he cut off your funds, that would cut *me* off, wouldn't it? Regardless of whether I've abided by the terms of the agreement."

"That's not *true*, Mr. Truesdale," she answered severely. "Mr. Vandervecken has bought you an *annuity*. If you violate the terms of your agreement with him, the annuity passes to, let me see now, to Criminal Rehabilitation Studies for the remainder of your life."

"Oh. And the terms are that I shouldn't try to find out who Mr. Vandervecken is."

"Roughly, yes. It's all spelled out quite fully in a message which—"

"I have it."

He hung up. And pondered. Two thousand a year, for life. And it was real. It was hardly a living, but it would make a nice addition to his salary. Already he had thought of half a dozen ways to use the first few checks. He might try a different job. . .

Two thousand a year. It was an exorbitant price to pay for four months of labor. Most kinds of labor. What had he *done* with those four months?

And how had Vandervecken known it would be enough?

I probably told him myself, Truesdale thought bitterly. Self-betrayal. At least he hadn't lied. Five hundred every three months, to put a touch of luxury in his life . . .and he would wonder for the rest of his life. But he would not go to the police.

He could not remember ever having suffered such a case of mixed emotions.

Presently he began listening to the other messages stored in his phone.

"But you did," said the ARM lieutenant. "You're here." He was a square-jawed, brawny man with eyes that did not believe. A close look into those eyes and you, too, would doubt whatever you had been telling him.

Truesdale shrugged.

"What changed your mind?"

"Money again. I started going through the messages in my phone. There was another message from a different legal firm. Do you know the name *Mrs. Jacob Randall?*"

"No. Wait a minute. Estelle Randall? President of the Struldbrugs' Club until—um."

"She was my great-to-the-fourth grandmother."

"And she died last month. My condolences."

"Thanks. I, I—see, I didn't see Greatly 'Stelle that often. Maybe twice a year, once at her birthday party, once at a christening or whatever. I remember we had lunch together a few days after I found out I'd lost all my money. She was mad. Oh, boy. She offered to refinance me, but I turned her down."

"Pride? It could happen to anyone. Lawrence St. John McGee practices an old and polished profession."

"I know."

"She was the oldest woman in the world."

"I know." The presidency of the Struldbrugs' Club went to the oldest living member. It was an honorary title; the Acting President usually did the work. "She was a hundred and seventy-three when I was born. The thing is, none of us ever expected her to *die*. I suppose that sounds silly?"

"No. How many people die at two hundred and ten?"

"Then I played that tape from Becket and Hollingsbrooke and she was dead! And I've inherited about half a million marks, out of a fortune that must be unbelievable. She's got enough great-to-the-Nth grandchildren to take over any nation in the world. You should have seen the birthday parties."

"I see." The ARM's eyes looked deep into him. "So you don't need Vandervecken's money now. Two thousand a year is peanuts now."

"And the son of a bitch made me miss her birthday."

The ARM leaned back. "You tell a strange story. I

never heard of any kind of amnesia that left no memory at all."

"I haven't either. It was as if I went to sleep and woke up four months later."

"But you don't even remember going to sleep."

"That's right."

"A stun gun could do that. . . Well, we'll put you under deep hypnosis and see what we come up with. I don't suppose you have any objections? You'll have to file some permission forms."

"Fine."

"You, ah, may not like what we find out."

"I know." Truesdale was already bracing himself against what he could find out. *The voice had been his own.* What had he been afraid to remember about himself?

"If you committed any crime during that period you can't remember, you may have to pay the penalty. It's not that useful an alibi."

"I'll risk it."

"Okay."

"You think I'm faking this?"

"The thought crossed my mind. We'll find out."

"Okay, snap out of it," said a Voice. And Truesdale snapped out of it like a man awakened too suddenly, dreams dying in his mind.

The Voice was Doctor Michaela Shorter, a broad-shouldered black woman in a loose blue business jumper. She said, "How do you feel?"

"Fine," said Truesdale. "What luck?"

"It's very peculiar. You not only don't remember anything during those four months; you didn't even sense time passing. You didn't dream."

The ARM lieutenant was off to the side, where Truesdale didn't notice him until he spoke. "Do you know of any drugs that would do that?"

The woman shook her head.

"Doctor Shorter is an expert at forensic medicine," the

lieutenant said to Truesdale. "It sounds like somebody's thought of something new." To Doctor Shorter he said, "It could be something really new. Would you do some computer work?"

"I did," she said shortly. "Anyway, no drug could be that selective. It's as if he'd been stunned asleep, then put in frozen storage for four months. Except that he'd show medical signs of thawing: cell ruptures from ice crystalization and like that." She looked sharply at Truesdale. "Don't let my voice put you under again."

"I wasn't." Truesdale stood up. "Whatever was done to me, it would take a laboratory, wouldn't it? If it was *that* new. That'll narrow the search a bit, won't it?"

"It should," said Doctor Shorter. "I'd look for a by-product of genetic research. Something that decomposes RNA."

The ARM lieutenant growled, "You'd think snatching you off a mountain would leave some traces too, but it didn't. A car would have been spotted by radar. Vandervecken must have had you carried down to the parking lot on a stretcher, around oh four hundred, when there wouldn't be anyone around."

"That'd be goddam dangerous, on those paths."

"I know. Have you got a better answer?"

"Haven't you learned *anything?*"

"The money. Your car stayed in the parking lot because the parking fee was paid in advance. So was your annuity. All from an account registered to the name of Vandervecken. A new account, and it's been closed."

"Figures."

"Does the name mean anything to you?"

"No. Probably Dutch."

The ARM nodded to himself. He stood up. Doctor Shorter was looking impatient to get her examining room back.

Half a million marks was a lot of money. Truesdale played with the idea of telling his boss to go to Hell. . . but, despite tradition, Jeromy Link didn't deserve that kind of treatment. No point in sticking him for an emergency replacement. Truesdale gave Jeromy a month's notice.

Because it was temporary, his job became more pleasant. A shoe clerk. . .but he met some interesting people that way. One day he took a hard look at the machinery that molded shoes around human feet. Remarkable, admirable widgetry. He'd never realized it before.

In his off hours he was planning a sightseeing vacation.

He resumed acquaintance with numberless relatives when Greatly 'Stelle's will was executed. Some had missed him at her funeral and at her last birthday party. Where had he been?

"Damndest thing," said Truesdale—and he had to tell the story half a dozen times that evening. He took a perverse delight in doing so. "Vandervecken" hadn't wanted publicity.

His delight was punctured when a second-cousin-in-law said, "So you were robbed again. You seem to be robbery-prone, Roy."

"Not any more. This time I'm going to get the son of a bitch," said Truesdale.

The day before his backpacking trip began, he stopped in at ARM Headquarters. He had trouble remembering the brawny ARM lieutenant's name. Robinson, that was it. Robinson nodded at him from behind a boomerang desk and said, "Come on in. You enjoying life?"

"Somewhat. How are you making out?" Truesdale took a seat. The office was small but comfortable, with tea and coffee spigots set in the desk.

Robinson leaned back from the desk as if glad of the interruption. "Mostly negatives. We still don't know who kidnapped you. We couldn't trace the money anywhere, but we're sure it didn't come from you." He looked up. "You don't seem surprised."

"I was sure you'd check on me."

"Right. Assume for the moment that someone we'll call Vandervecken has a specific amnesia treatment. He might go around selling it to people who want to commit crimes. . .like murdering a relative for her inheritance."

"I wouldn't do that to Greatly 'Stelle."

"Regardless, you didn't. Vandervecken would have had to pay *you,* and a hefty sum, too. The idea's ridiculous. Other than that, we found two other cases of your type of selective amnesia." There was a computer terminal in the desk. The ARM used it. "First one was a Mary Boethals, who disappeared for four months in 2220. She didn't report it. The ARMs got interested in her because she'd stopped getting treatments for a kidney ailment. It seemed likely she'd got a transplant from an organlegger. But she told a different story, very much like yours, including the annuity.

"Then there was a Charles Mow, disappeared in 2241, came back four months later. He had an annuity too, but it got cut off because of some embezzling in Norn Insurance. It made Mow mad enough to come to us. Naturally the ARMs started looking for other cases, but they didn't find any. And that was it for a hundred years. Until you showed up."

"And my annuity's been cut off."

"Tough. Now, in those two previous cases the money was to go to prosthetics research. There wasn't any criminal rehabilitation a hundred years ago. They all went into the organ banks."

"Yah."

"Otherwise the cases were all quite similar. So it looks like we're looking for a struldbrug. The time fits: the earliest case was a hundred and twenty years ago. The name Vandervecken fits. The interest in prosthetics fits."

Truesdale thought about it. There were not that many struldbrugs around. Minimum age for admission to that most exclusive of clubs had been frozen at one hundred and eighty-one. "Any specific suspects?"

"If there were, I couldn't tell you. But, no. Mrs. Randall definitely died of natural causes, and she definitely wasn't Vandervecken. If she had some connection with him, we haven't been able to find it."

"Have you checked with the Belt?"

Robinson looked at him narrowly. "No. Why?"

"Just a thought." Distance in time equals distance in space?

"Well, we can ask. They might have had similar cases. Personally, I don't know where to go from here. We don't know why it was done, and we don't know how."

There wasn't room in all of Earth's national and international parks for the potential backpackers alive in the year 2341. The waiting list for the Amazon jungle was two years long. Other parks had similar lists.

Elroy Truesdale carried a backpack through London, Paris, Rome, Madrid, Morocco, Cairo. He rode supersonic trains between the cities. He ate in restaurants, carrying credit cards rather than dehydrated foods. This was something he had planned for a long time, but he had not had the money.

He saw the pyramids, the Eiffel Tower, and Tower of London, the Leaning Tower—which had been propped up. He saw the Valley of the Fallen. He walked Roman roads in a dozen nations.

Everywhere there were other backpackers. At night they camped in places set aside for them by the individual cities, usually old parking garages or abandoned freeways. They would pool their lightweight stoves to form a campfire and sit around it teaching each other songs. When he tired of them Truesdale would stay at a hotel.

He wore out disposable hiking socks at a furious rate, and bought new ones from dispensers in the campspots. His legs became hard as wood.

A month of this, and he was not finished. Something was driving him to see all of Earth. A cancellation got him into the Australian outback, probably the least popular of the national parks. He spent a week there. He needed the silence and the room.

Then on to Sydney, and a girl with a Belter haircut.

Her back was to him. He saw a pony's tail of bobbing hair, black and wavy and almost long enough to reach her waist. Most of her scalp was bare and as darkly tanned as the rest of her, on either side of a two-inch-wide crest.

Twenty years ago it wouldn't have jarred. There had been a fad for the Belter crest. But it had passed, and now she was like an echo from long ago. . .or far away? She was tall as a Belter, but with musculature far better developed. She was alone; she had not joined the campfire congregation at the other end of this, the eighth floor of a ten-story parking garage.

Inexpert singing echoed between the concrete roof and floor. *I was born about ten thousand years from now. . . When we land upon the Moon I'll show them how. . .*

A real Belter? Backpacking?

Truesdale picked his way to her through a maze of mummy bags. He said, "Excuse me. Are you a Belter?"

She turned. "Yes. What of it?"

Her eyes were brown. Her face was lovely in a fashion that was all planes and angles, and it held no welcome. She would react badly to a pass. Maybe she didn't like flatlanders; certainly she was too tired for games.

Truesdale said, "I want to tell a story to a Belter."

She shrugged her eyebrows: an irritated gesture. "Why not go to the Belt?"

"I'd never get there tonight," he said reasonably.

"All right, go ahead."

Truesdale told her of the kidnapping on the Pinnacles. He was getting glib at it. He told it fast. Already he was sorry he had not simply gone to sleep.

She listened with uneasy patience, then said, "Why tell me?"

"Well, there were two other cases of this kind of kidnapping, both a long time ago. I wondered if anything like it has happened in the Belt."

"I don't know. There may be records in the goldskin files."

"Thanks," said Truesdale, and went away.

He lay in his sleeping bag, eyes closed, arms crossed on his breast. Tomorrow. . .Brasilia? They were still singing:

*Why, I once signed on with Amra, and I damn near
     lost my skin,*

*For the blood it flowed like water when the fighting
     did begin.*

*I'm the only tar who's e'er jumped ship from Vander-
     vecken's crew—*

Truesdale's eyes snapped open.

*And that's about the strangest thing a man will ever
     do.*

He'd been looking in the wrong place.

Backpackers tended to wake with the dawn. Some preferred to find an all-night restaurant for breakfast; others
made their own. Truesdale was cooking freeze-dried eggs
when the girl walked up.

"Remember me? My name's Alice Jordan."

"Roy Truesdale. Have some eggs."

"Thanks." She passed him a packet, which he mixed
with water and poured in with the rest. She was different this morning: rested, younger-looking, less formidable.

"I started remembering things last night. Cases like
yours. They really do exist. I'm a goldskin myself, and I
heard about them, but I never bothered to look up details."

"You're a goldskin?" A cop? Come to that, she was
his size; she'd have the muscle to handle any Belter.

"I've also been a smuggler," she said a bit defensively.
"One day I decided the Belt needed the income more
than the smugglers."

"Maybe I'll have to go to the Belt after all," he said
lightly. Thinking: *Or talk Robinson into sending for the
files.* The eggs were ready. He served them into the cups
all backpackers carried at their belts.

She said, "Tell me more about the Vandervecken case."

"Not much more to tell. I wish I could forget about it."
It hadn't been out of his mind in more than a month.
He'd been robbed.

"Did you go to the police right away?"

"No."

"That's what I remembered. The Snatcher picks his victims from the main Belt, holds them for four months or so, then bribes them. Most of the time the bribe is big enough. I suppose it wasn't in your case."

"Almost." He was *not* going to tell a stranger about Greatly 'Stelle. "But if most of them take the bribes, how do you find out about them?"

"Well, it's not that easy to hide a disappearing ship. Mostly the ships disappear from the main Belt, then reappear four months on in their orbits. But if telescopes don't find them during the four months, someone may ask questions."

They poured the remnants of eggs out of their frictionless cups and filled them with coffee powder and boiling water.

"There are several cases of this kind, and they're all unsolved," she said. "Some Belters think it's the Outsider, taking samples."

"Outsider?"

"The first alien humanity will ever meet."

"Like the Sea Statue? Or that alien that landed on Mars during—"

"No, no," she said impatiently. "The Sea Statue was dug up on Earth's own continental shelf. It was there for over a billion years. As for the Pak, it was a branch of humanity, as far as anyone can tell. No, we're still waiting for the real Outsider."

"And you think he's taking samples to see if we're ready for civilization. When we are, he'll come."

"I haven't said I believed it myself."

"Do you?"

"I don't know. I thought it was a charming story, and a little scary. It never occurred to me that he might be sampling flatlanders too."

He laughed. "Thanks."

"No offense."

"I go to Brasilia from here," he said. It was not quite an offer.

"I rest up. One day on, one day off. I'm strong for a

Belter, but I can't just keep going day after day." She hesitated. "That's why I don't travel with anyone. I've had offers, but I'd hate to think I was slowing someone down."

"I see."

She got up. So did Truesdale. He had the impression that she towered over him, but that was illusion.

He said, "Where are you stationed? Ceres?"

"Vesta. 'Bye."

" 'Bye."

He trekked Brasilia and Sao Paulo and Rio de Janiero. He saw Chichen Itza and grooved on Peruvian cooking. He came to Washington, D.C., with the theft of four months of his life still itching in his brain.

The center of Washington was under a weather dome. They wouldn't let him in with a backpack. Washington was a business city: it governed a respectable section of the planet Earth.

He went directly to the Smithsonian Institution.

The Sea Statue was a mirror-surfaced, not quite humanoid figure. It stood on its great splayed feet with both three-fingered hands upraised as against a threat. Despite the ages it had lain at the bottom of the sea, it showed no signs of corrosion. It looked like the product of some advanced civilization. . .and it was; it was a pressure suit with emergency stasis field facilities, and the thing inside was very dangerous. Once it had gotten loose.

The Pak was an ancient, tired mummy. Its face was hard and inhuman, expressionless. Its head was twisted at an odd angle, and its arms were lax at its sides, unraised against what had crushed its throat. Truesdale read its story in the guidebook, and felt pity. It had come so far to save us all. . .

So: there were *things* out there. The universe was deep enough to hold all manner of things. If something was sampling humanity, the only questions were: why would he bother? And why would he bother to put them back?

No, there was more. Itchy questions: why go to Earth for flatlanders? Couples of sufficient wealth spent their honeymoons on Titan, beneath the huge ringed wonder of Saturn. Surely it would be easy to hijack a honeymoon special. And why pick Belters from the main Belt? Enough of them still went out to mine the outer reaches.

He had a glimmering then, but it wouldn't come clear. He filed it away. . .

There was a trek along the Mississippi, and some climbing in the Rockies. He broke his leg there and had to be flown to a nearby arcology city built into a jagged canyon. A doctor set his leg and used regrowth treatments. Afterward he flew home. He'd had enough.

The San Diego Police had no new information on Lawrence St. John McGee. They were used to seeing Truesdale, and in fact were getting a little tired of him. It was becoming clear to Truesdale that they did not ever expect to find McGee and Truesdale's money.

"He had more than enough to buy a face and fingertip transplant," an officer had told him once. Now they just made soothing noises, and waited until he went away. It had been a year since he last dropped in.

Truesdale went to ARM Headquarters. He took a taxi rather than a slidewalk; his leg still hurt him

"We're working on it," Robinson told him. "A case this strange doesn't get forgotten. In fact—well, never mind."

"What?"

The ARM grinned suddenly. "It's got no real connection. I asked the basement computer for other unsolved crimes with a technologically advanced base, no time limit. I got some weirdies. You ever hear of the duplicate Stonehenge?"

"Sure. I was there, a month and a half ago."

"Aren't they amazing? Some clown put up that duplicate in a single night. Next morning there were two Stonehenges. You can't tell the difference except by position: the duplicate is a few hundred yards further north. There are even the same initials carved in the duplicate."

Truesdale was nodding. "I know. That's got to be the most expensive practical joke ever pulled."

"We don't really know which is the real Stonehenge, either. Suppose the joker moved both Stonghenges? He had the power to move all the rocks in the duplicate. All he had to do was move the rocks in the real Stonehenge and put the duplicate in its place."

"Don't tell anyone."

The ARM laughed.

"Did you get anything from the Belt?"

Robinson lost his smile. "Yah. Half a dozen known cases, kidnapping and amnesia, and all unsolved. I still think we're looking for a struldbrug."

All unsolved. It boded ill for Truesdale's case.

"An old struldbrug," said the ARM. "Someone who was already old enough a hundred and twenty years ago, to think he'd learned enough to solve the problems of humanity. Or maybe to write a definitive book on human progress. So he started taking samples."

"And he's still at it?"

"Or a grandson took over the business." Robinson sighed. "Don't worry about it. We'll get him."

"Sure. You've only had a hundred and twenty years."

"Don't noodge," said Robinson.

And that did it.

The center of goldskin police activity was the center of government: Ceres. Police headquarters on Pallas, Juno, Vesta, and Astraea were redundant, in a sense, but very necessary. Five asteroids would cover the main Belt. It had happened that they were all on the same side of the sun at the same time; but it was rare.

Vesta was the smallest of the five. Her cities were on the surface, under four big double domes.

Thrice in history a dome had been holed. It was not the kind of event that would be forgotten. All of Vesta's buildings were pressure-tight. Several had airlock tubes that led out through the dome.

Alice Jordan entered the Waring City police airlock

after a routine smuggler patrol. There were two chambers, and then a hallway lined with pressure suits. She doffed her own suit and hung it. The chest bore a flourescent she-dragon, breathing fire.

She reported to her superior, Vinnie Garcia. "No luck."

Vinnie grinned at her. She was dark and willowy, her fingers long and slender: far more the Belter stereotype than Alice Jordan. "You had some luck on Earth."

"Finagle's Jest I did. You have my report." Alice had gone to Earth in hope of solving a growing social problem. A flatlander sin—wireheading, the practice of running current into the center of the brain—had been spreading through the Belt. Unfortunately Earth's solution had been to wait it out. In three hundred years it would solve itself . . .but that was hardly satisfactory to Alice Jordan.

"That's not what I meant. You made a conquest." Vinnie paused. "There's a flatlander waiting for you in your office."

"A flatlander?" She had shared a bed with one man on Earth, to nobody's satisfaction. Gravity, and lack of practice. He'd been polite about it, but they had not seen each other again.

She stood up. "Do you need me for anything else?"

"Nope. Have fun," said Vinnie.

He tried to stand up when she came in. He botched it a bit in the low gravity, but managed to get his feet to the floor and keep the rest of him upright. "Hello. Roy Truesdale," he said, before she could fumble for the name.

"Welcome to Vesta," she said. "So you came after all. Still hunting for the Snatcher?"

"Yes."

She took a seat behind her desk. "Tell me about it. Did you finish the backpacking trip?"

He nodded. "I think the Rockies were the best, and there's no trouble getting in. You ought to try it. The Rockies aren't a national park, but not many people want to build there either."

"I'll try it, if I ever get to Earth again."

"I saw the other Outsiders. . .I know, they aren't really Outsiders, but sure as hell, they're *alien*. If the real Outsider is like those. . ."

"You'd rather think Vandervecken is human."

"I guess I would."

"You're putting a lot of effort into finding him." She considered the idea that Truesdale had come chasing a certain Belter woman. A flattering thought. . .

"The law didn't seem to be getting anywhere," he said. "Worse than that. It looks like they've been hunting Vandervecken or someone like him for a hundred and twenty *years*. I got mad and signed up for a ship to Vesta. I was going to find Vandervecken myself. That's a hassle, you know?"

"I know. Too many flatlanders want to see the asteroids. We have to restrict them."

"I had to wait three months for crash couch space. I still wasn't sure I wanted to go. After all, I could always cancel. . . Then something else happened." Truesdale's jaw clamped in retrospective anger.

"Lawrence St. John McGee. He took me for just about everything I owned, ten years ago. A swindle."

"It happens. I'm sorry."

"They caught him. He was calling himself Ellery Jones from St. Louis. He was running a whole new game, in Topeka, Kansas, but someone tipped off the marks and they got him. He had new fingerprints, new retina prints, a new face. They had to do a brain wave analysis before they were sure it was him. I may even get some of my money back."

She smiled. "Why, that's wonderful!"

"Vandervecken tipped him. It was another bribe."

"Are you sure? Did he use that name?"

"No. Damn him for playing games with my head! He must have decided I was hunting him because he robbed me. He took four months of my life. He threw me Lawrence St. John McGee, so I should stop worrying about my missing four months."

"You don't like being that predictable."

"No. I do not." He wasn't looking at her. His hands were closed hard on the arms of her guest chair. Muscles bunched and swelled in his arms when he did that. Some Belters affected to hold flatlander muscles in contempt. . .

She said, "Vandervecken may be too big for us."

His response was interesting. "Now you're talking. What have you found out?"

"Well. . .I've been hunting Vandervecken too. You know that there have been other disappearances."

"Yah."

Her desk, like Robinson's, had a computer terminal in it. She used it. "Half a dozen names. And dates: 2150, 2191, 2230, 2250, 2270, 2331. You can see our records go back further than yours. I talked to this Lawrence Jannifer, the latest one, but he can't remember anything more than you can. He was taking a fast orbit to the lead Trojans with some small machine parts, when. . .blackout. Next thing he knew he was in orbit around Hector." She smiled. "He didn't take it the way you did. He's just glad he was put back."

"Are any of the others alive and available?"

"Dandridge Sukarno and Norma Stier, disappeared 2270 and 2230, respectively. They wouldn't give me the local time of day. They took their fees and that's that. We traced the fees to two different names—George Olduvai and C. Cretemaster—and no faces to go with the names."

"You have been busy."

She shrugged. "A lot of goldskins get interested in the Snatcher at one time or another. Vinnie sort of puts up with it."

"It sounds like he takes a sample every ten years. Alternating between Earth and Belt." Truesdale whistled uneasily. He was remembering those dates. "Twenty-one fifty is almost two hundred years ago. No wonder he called himself Vandervecken."

She looked at him sharply. "Is there some significance—?"

"Vandervecken was the captain of the Flying Dutchman. I looked it up. You know the Flying Dutchman legend?"

"No."

"There used to be commercial sailing ships—sailing on the ocean, by wind power. Vandervecken was trying to round the Cape of Good Hope during a heavy storm. He swore a blasphemous oath that he would round the Cape if he had to beat against the wind until the last day. In stormy weather passing ships can still see him, still trying to round the Cape. Sometimes he stops ships and asks them to take letters to home."

Her laugh was shaky. "Letters to *who?*"

"The Wandering Jew, maybe. There are variations. One says Vandervecken murdered his wife and sailed away from the police. One says there was a murder on board. Writers seem to like this legend. It turns up in novels, and there was an old flat movie, and an even older opera, and—have you heard that old song the back-packers sing around the campfires? *I'm the only tar that e'er jumped ship from Vandervecken's crew. . ."*

"The Bragging Song."

"All the legends have that one thing in common: an immortal man sailing under a curse, forever."

Alice Jordan's eyes went big and round.

"What is it?" he asked.

"Jack Brennan."

". . .Brennan. I remember. The man who ate the roots aboard the Pak ship. Jack Brennan. He's supposed to be dead."

"Supposed to be." She was looking down at her desk. Gradually her eyes focused on coils of printout. "Roy, I've got to get some work done. Where are you staying, the Palace?"

"Sure, it's the only hotel in Waring City."

"I'll pick you up there, eighteen hundred. You'll need a guide to the restaurants anyway."

For a monopoly, the Palace was an excellent hotel. Human service was spotty, but the machinery—bathroom facilities, cleaning widgetry, waiters—all ran to perfection. Belters seemed to treat their machines as if their lives depended on them.

The east wall was three meters from the dome itself, and featured picture windows guarded by big rectangular screens that swung automatically to shut out raw sunlight. The screens were open now. Truesdale looked out through a wall of glass, over the shallow bulge of the Anderson City dome, past a horizon so jagged and close that he felt he was on a mountain peak. But the stars were not this vivid from any mountain on Earth. He saw the universe, close enough to touch.

And the room was costing him plenty. He was going to have to learn to spend money again without wincing.

He took a shower. It was fun. The shower delivered great slow volumes of hot water that tended to stay on his body as if jellied. There were side jets, and a needle spray. A far cry from the old days, he supposed, when the deep cavity that now housed Anderson City had been carved by the extensive, expensive mining of hydrate-bearing rock. But fusion was cheap, and water once made could be distilled over and over, indefinitely.

When he left the shower he found that there had been a delivery. The information terminal beside his desk had delivered several books' worth of information, printing it into a book the size of the San Diego telephone book, with pages that could be wiped after the departure of a guest. Alice Jordan must have sent this. He leafed through it until he found Nicholas Sohl's memoirs, and started there. The section on the Pak ship was near the end.

There was a chill on him when he finished. Nicholas Sohl, once First Speaker for the Belt. . .not a fool. *The thing to remember,* Sohl had written, *is that he's brighter than we are. Maybe he's thought of something I haven't.*

But how bright would a man have to be to make up for the lack of a food source?

He read on. . .

Alice Jordan arrived ten minutes early. At the door she glanced past him at the information terminal. "You got it. Good. How far did you get?"

"Nick Sohl's memoirs. A textbook on the physiology of the Pak. I skimmed Graves's book on evolution. He claims a dozen plants that could have been imported from the Pak world."

"You're a flatlander. What do you think?"

"I'm not a biologist. And I skipped the proceedings of Olympus Base. I don't really care why a gravity polarizer doesn't work yet."

She sat down on the edge of the bed. She was wearing loose slacks and a blouse: not dressed for dinner, in Truesdale's view. But he hadn't expected skirts in Vesta's gravity.

She said, "I think it's Brennan."

"So do I."

"But he's *got* to be dead. He didn't have a food source."

"He had his own singleship on a tow line. Even two hundred years ago, a singleship kitchen would feed him for a long time, wouldn't it? It was the roots he was missing. Maybe he had a few he took from the cargo pod, and there were more aboard the Pak ship. But when he ate those he'd be finished."

"But you still think he's alive. So do I. Let's hear your reasons."

Truesdale took a minute to get his thoughts organized. "The Flying Dutchman. Vandervecken. A man immortalized by a curse. It fits too well."

She nodded. "What else?"

"Oh, the kidnappings. . .and the fact that he puts us back. Even with the chance that he'll get caught, he puts us back. He's too considerate for an alien and he's too powerful for a human. What's left?"

"Brennan."

"Then there's the duplicate Stonehenge." He had to tell her about that. "I've been thinking about it ever since you mentioned Brennan. You know what it sounds like to me? Brennan had plenty of time with the gravity polarizer in the Pak cargo pod. He must have solved the principle, and improved it into a gravity generator. Then he had to play games with it."

"Games. Right again. This superintelligence must have been like a new toy to him."

"He may have pulled some other practical jokes."

"Yes," she said with too much emphasis.

"What? Another practical joke?"

Alice laughed. "Ever hear of the Mahmed Asteroid? It was in those excerpts I sent you."

"I guess I didn't get to it."

"An asteroid a couple of miles in diameter, mainly ice. The Belt telescopes spotted it fairly early, in. . .2183, I think. It was still outside Jupiter's orbit. Mahmed was the first man to land on it. He was also the man who plotted its orbit and found out that it was going to hit Mars."

"Did it?"

"Yah. It probably could have been stopped, even with the technology of the day, but I suppose nobody was really interested. It was going to hit well away from Olympus Base. They did carve off a hefty chunk of ice and move it into a new orbit. Nearly pure water, valuable stuff."

"I don't see what this has to do with—"

"It killed the martians. Every martian on the planet, as far as we can tell. The water vapor content of the atmosphere went way up."

"Oh," said Truesdale. "Genocide. Some practical joke."

"I told you, Vandervecken may be too big for us."

"Yah." From a recorded voice on a self-destructing spool, Vandervecken had grown in all dimensions. Now he was two hundred and twenty years long, and the realm of his activities blanketed the solar system. In physical strength he had grown too. The Brennan-monster could have slung an unconscious Elroy Truesdale over his shoulder and carried him down off the Pinnacles. "He's big, all right. And we're the only ones who know it. What do we do now?"

"Let's get dinner," she said.

"You know what I mean."

"I know what you mean," Alice said gently. "But let's get dinner."

The top of the Palace Hotel was a four-sided dome that showed two views of reality. For the east and west quadrants looked out on Vesta, but the north and south quadrants were holograph projections of some mountainous part of Earth. "It's a looped tape, several days long," Alice told him. "Taken from a car cruising at ground level. This looks like morning in Switzerland."

"It does," he agreed. The vodka martini was hitting him hard. He'd skipped lunch, and now his belly was a yawning vacuum. "Tell me about Belter foods."

"Well, the Palace is mainly french flatlander cooking."

"I'd like to try Belter cooking. Tomorrow?"

"Honestly, Roy, I got spoiled on Earth. I'll take you to a Belter place tomorrow, but I don't think you'll find any new taste thrills. Food's too expensive here to do much experimental cooking."

"Too bad." He glanced at the menu on a waiter's chest, and recoiled. "Ye gods. The prices!"

"This is as expensive as it gets. At the other end is dole yeast, which is free—"

"Free?"

"—and barely worth it. If you're down and out it'll keep you fed, and it practically grows itself. Normal Belter cooking is almost vegetarian except for chicken and eggs. We grow chickens in most of the larger domes. Beef and pork we have to grow in the bubble-formed worlds, and seafood—well, we have to ship it up. Some comes freeze-dried; that's cheaper."

They punched their orders into a waiter's keyboard. On Earth a restaurant this expensive would at least have featured human waiters. . .but Roy somehow couldn't imagine a Belter playing the role of waiter.

The steaks Diane were too small, the vegetables varied and plentiful. Alice tore in with a gusto he admired. "I missed this," she said. "On Earth I had to take up backpacking to work off all I was eating."

Roy put his fork down. "I can't figure out what he *ate.*"

"Drop it for awhile."

"All right. Tell me about yourself."

She told him about a childhood in Confinement Asteroid, and the thick basement windows from which she could see the stars: stars that hadn't meant anything to her until her first trip outside. The years of training in flying spacecraft—not mandatory, but your friends would think you were funny if you dropped out. Her first smuggling run, and the goldskin pilot who hung on her course like a leech, laughing at her out of her com screen. Three years hauling foodstuffs and hydroponics machinery to the Trojans before she'd tried it again, and then it had been the same laughing face, and when she'd bitched about it he'd lectured her on economics all the way to Hector.

They were down to coffee (freeze-dried) and brandy (a Belt product, and excellent). He told her about the cousins and the part-cousins and the generations of uncles and part-uncles and great-uncles and -aunts to match, all spread across the world, so that there were relatives anywhere he chose to go. He told her about Greatly 'Stelle.

She said, "So he was right."

He knew just what she meant. "I wouldn't have gone to the law. I couldn't have turned down the money. Alice, he thinks of the whole human race that way. On wires. And he's the only one who can see the wires."

Alice's face was almost a snarl. "I won't *let* a man think of me that way."

"And he takes samples. To see how we're doing, where we're going. I suppose his next step is a selective breeding project."

"All right, what's our next move?"

"I don't know." He sipped at his brandy. Wonderful stuff; it seemed to turn to vapor in his mouth. The Belt ought to export it. It'd be cheap in fuel: all downhill.

She said, "We've got three choices, I think. First is to tell everything we know, first to Vinnie, then to any newstape producer that'll listen."

"Will they listen?"

"Oh—" she waved a negligent hand. "They'll publish, I think. It's a new slant on things. But we don't have any proof. We've got a theory, and it's got a gaping hole in it, and that's *all* we've got."

"What did he eat?"

"Right."

"Well, we can try it."

Alice thumbed a call button. When the waiter slid over in a whisper of air, she punched for two more brandies. She said, "Then what?"

". . .Yah."

"People would listen, and talk it over, and wonder. And nothing would happen. And gradually it would all blow over. Brennan would just wait it out, as long as it takes: a hundred years, a thousand. . ."

"We'd never know. We'd be yelling into a vacuum."

"All right. Second choice is for us to drop it now."

"No."

"Agreed. Third choice is to go after him. With a Belt police fleet, if they'd back us. Otherwise, alone."

He thought about it, sipping brandy. "Go where?"

"All right, let's think about that." Alice leaned back with her eyes half-closed. "He headed out toward inter-stellar space. He stopped in the cometary belt, well be-yond Pluto's orbit, for a couple of months—came to a dead stop, which must have cost him plenty in fuel—then went on."

"His *ship* went on. If he's here now, he must have sent the Pak drive section on without him. That leaves him with the Pak control cabin and a Belt singleship."

"And fuel. All the fuel he wants, from the maneuvering reserve tanks in the drive section. They were filled before he took off."

"All right. We assume he found a way to grow the roots for food. Maybe he took some seeds from the cargo pod before he left Mars. What does he need now that he doesn't have?"

"A home. A base. Building materials."

"Could he have mined the comets for those?"

"Maybe. For gasses and chemicals, anyway."

"All right. I've been thinking about this too," said

Truesdale. "When you speak so glibly of the cometary belt, do you think you're talking about a ring of rocks like the asteroid belt? The cometary belt is a region of convenience." He spoke with some care. The brandy was getting to his tongue. If he mangled some complicated word she would only laugh. "It's where the comets slow up and hover and fall back toward the sun. It's ten to twenty times the volume of the solar system, and most of the solar system is in a plane anyway. There's hydrogen in most of the compounds in a comet's tail, isn't there? So Brennan's got no fuel problem. He could be anywhere in that shell by now, and somewhere else tomorrow. Where do we look?"

She watched him narrowly. "You're giving up?"

"I'm tempted. It's not that he's too big for me. He's too small. His hiding place is too mucking big."

"There is another possibility," she said. "Persephone."

Persephone. And how the hell had he forgotten that there was a tenth planet? Still— "Persephone's a gas giant, isn't it?"

"I don't know for sure, but I suppose so. It was detected by its mass, its influence on the orbits of comets. But the atmosphere could be frozen. He could hover until he'd burned a hole through the frozen layers, then land." She leaned forward across the table. Her eyes were intense, and deep brown. "Roy, he had to get metals from *somewhere*. He built some kind of gravity generator, didn't he? And he must have done some experimenting to get it. Metal. Lots of metal."

"From a comet head, maybe?"

"I don't think so."

Truesdale shook his head. "He couldn't mine Persephone. A planet that big has to be a gas giant—with a molten core. It'll heat itself; it'll have a gaseous atmosphere. He couldn't land in it. The pressure would be, well, *Jovian*."

"A moon, then! Maybe Persephone's got a moon!"

". . .Why the hell not? Why shouldn't any random gas giant have a *dozen* moons?"

"He spent two months at rest, making sure he could

live out there. He must have located Persephone and studied it with his telescopes. When he was sure it had moons, that was when he cut loose from the Pak drive section. Otherwise he'd have come home and turned himself in."

"That sounds right. He may have been growing tree-of-life too. . . .He might not still be there."

"He'd have left traces. We're talking about a *moon* now. There'd be a scar where he landed a fusion drive, and big gaping scars where he dug his mines, and buildings he'd have to abandon, and *heat*. He could cover up some of the damage, but not the heat, not on some little moon way the hell beyond Pluto. It would have gone into the environment, and fouled up superfluid effects, and vaporized some of the ices."

"We'd have proof," said Truesdale. "Holograph pictures. At worst we'd have holos of the scars he left on Persephone's moon. Not just a half-cocked theory."

"And at best?" She grinned. "We'd meet the Brennan-monster face to face."

"Have at him!"

"Right on." Alice raised her brandy. They clinked the blown glass snifters carefully, and drank.

The fear of falling brought him half awake, and the familiar sensations of a hangover did the rest. He sat up on a bed like a pink cloud: Alice's bed. They'd come here last night, perhaps to celebrate or to seal a bargain, perhaps just because they liked each other.

No headache. Good brandy leaves a hangover, but not a headache.

It had been one of the better nights.

Alice wasn't there. Gone to work? No, he could hear her in the kitchen. He padded into the kitchen on bare feet. She was frying pancakes in the nude.

He asked, "Did we really mean it?"

"Now you get to taste Belter cooking," she said. She handed him a plate with a stack of pancakes, and when he grabbed it wrong they bounced and floated, just like in the advertisements. He managed to catch them, but the stack came down skewed.

They tasted like pancakes: good pancakes, but pancakes. Maybe you had to include the nudity of the cook to make it Belter cooking. He poured imitation maple syrup, and made a mental note: send Alice some bottles of Vermont maple syrup, if she stayed in the Belt, if he ever reached Earth alive.

He asked again. "Did we really mean it?"

She gave him a cup and a jar of freeze-dried coffee with an Earth brand. "Let's find out about Persephone first. Then we can decide."

"I can do that myself, at the hotel. Route you the information the way you sent it to me yesterday. Save you some work."

"Good idea. Then I can brace Vinnie."

"I'm wondering if a goldskin fleet would let me come along."

She sat in his lap—feather-lightly, but a lot of girl, as much girl as a man could need. She looked him in the eyes. "Which way are you hoping?"

He thought about it. "I'll come if your superiors let me. But I'll put it to you straight: if I can set the goldskins on Vandervecken's tail, I've proved that he can't manipulate me. As long as Vandervecken knows it, that's all I care about."

"I. . .suppose that's fair enough."

They left the apartment together. Alice's apartment was part of what seemed a cliff dwelling, apartments carved into a wall of the deep hydrate-mining scar that was Alderson City. They took a tube train back to Waring, and parted there.

PERSEPHONE: First discovered by mathematical analysis of perturbations in the orbits of certain known comets, 1972. First sighted 1984. Persephone is retrograde, in an orbit tilted sixty-one degrees to the ecliptic. Mass is somewhat less than Saturn.

Possible first exploratory visit to Persephone was by

Alan Jacob Mion, in 2094. Mion's claim has been cast into doubt by the lack of photographic evidence (his films were damaged by radiation, as was Mion himself; he had stripped shielding from his ship to save fuel) and by Mion's claim that Persephone has a moon.

A more formal exploratory expedition was launched in 2170. Persephone was reported to have no moons and an atmosphere typical of gas giant worlds, rich in hydrogen compounds. The planet's atmosphere would be worth scoop-mining if the planet itself were as available as Jupiter. There have been no further expeditions.

Damn, thought Truesdale. No moons.

He wondered if Brennan could have scoop-mined Persephone's cold chemical gasses. With what, his cupped hands? And for what? He couldn't have found metals that way. . .and it didn't matter; he'd have left no scars in the clouds.

He located the report of the 2170 expedition and read it. With a little more trouble he found a condensed interview between Alan Jacob Mion and a reporter for *Spectrum News*. He was a boastful, flamboyant type, the kind of man who would take a year off to orbit a tenth planet, just to say he was the first. Not a careful observer. Perhaps his "moon" had been a comet head cruising past Persephone on a slow parabola.

He used his information terminal to send the material off to Police Headquarters.

Alice came back about 1800. "Vinnie didn't buy it," she said wearily.

"I don't blame her. No moons. All our beautiful logic, and no mucking moon." He had spent the day trying to play tourist in a city that wasn't designed for tourists. Waring was a working city.

"She wouldn't have gone for it even if there'd been a moon. She said. . .well, I'm not sure she wasn't right." Alice's weariness was not a thing of gravity. She did not drop sagging onto the bed. Her posture was straight, her head high. But in her eyes and her voice. . . "In the first place, this is all hypothetical, she said. Which is true. In the second place, if it *were* true, what would we be sending a poor, helpless goldskin fleet into? In the third place, this Snatcher business has been adequately explained as cases of the Far Look."

"I didn't get that."

"The Far Look. Self-hypnosis. A Belter spends too long staring into infinity. Sometimes he wakes up in orbit around his destination without remembering anything after his takeoff. In fact, Vinnie *showed* me the report on Norma Stier. Remember her? Disappeared 2230—"

"Right."

"She was on course during that four months she was supposed to be missing. The films in her ship prove it."

"But the *bribes*. The Snatcher *bribes* the people he kidnaps."

"We've got evidence of a couple of bribes. But they could be explained away. People using the Snatcher story to hide profits from a smuggling run—or something dirtier." She smiled. "Or Vandervecken doctored the films on Norma Stier's ship. I believe in the Snatcher, myself."

"Hell, yes!"

"But Vinnie makes a telling point. What are we going up against with a miserable Belt police fleet? Brennan had to get his metal from somewhere. If he mined Persephone's moon, he must have moved it afterward!"

"Uh?"

"That didn't occur to you?"

"No."

"It's not that startling. What are we talking about, a mass the size of Ganymede, or a little ball of rock like Vesta? Asteroids have been moved before."

"Right. . .and he had unlimited hydrogen fuel, and he already had his gravity generator, and we're already assuming he moved the Mahmed Asteroid. But he couldn't have moved it far. Any metallic chunk we find out there is going to be Persephone's moon, right? And he wouldn't have moved it unless it was pretty telling evidence against him."

"You're still going up against him?"

Truesdale took a deep breath. "Yah. I'll need your help to pick my equipment."

"I'm coming with you."

"Good."

"I was afraid I'd have to drop it," she said. "I don't have the money to finance anything like this, and you didn't seem. . .eager enough, and Vinnie just about convinced me it's a wild goose chase anyway. Roy, suppose it is?"

"It'll still make a nice little honeymoon trip. And we'll be the only humans alive who've seen the tenth planet. I suppose we can sell the equipment again when we get back?"

They got down to technical discussions.

It was going to cost.

Brennan. . .

. . .what can one say about Brennan? He will always make maximum use of his environment to achieve his ends. Knowing his environment, knowing his motives, one could predict his actions exactly.

But his mind. What goes on in his mind?

His chosen career—the career that has chosen him for its life's work—is accomplished largely by waiting. Long ago he was prepared. Now he waits and watches, and sometimes he adds refinements to his preparations. He has his hobbies. The solar system is one of these.

Sometimes he takes samples. Otherwise he watches the moving lights of fusion drives with his eccentric substitute for a telescope. He catches fragments of news and entertainment broadcasts with sophisticated noise filtering equipment. Earth provides most of these fragments. The Belt communicates via lasers, and they are not aimed at Brennan.

Civilization goes on. Brennan watches.

In a news broadcast he learns of the death of Estelle Randall.

This raises an interesting possibility. Brennan begins to watch for a fusion light source moving toward Persephone.

Roy wasn't sure what had wakened him. He lay quiet in the web hammock, feeling the ship alive around him.

The vibration of the drive was feel rather than sound. Two days of that, and he couldn't sense it without concentrating. The sensation had not changed—he thought.

Alice was beside him in the other hammock. Her eyes were open, her mouth faintly frowning.

That scared him. "What is it?"

"I don't know. Suit up."

He grimaced. *Suit up*—she'd had him climbing in and out of that damn emergency suit for six hours of the first day. It was a man-shaped clear plastic bag with a zipper that ran from chin to knees, forking at the crotch. You could get into it in an instant, and it took another instant to plug that thick air-and-water tube into the ship's life-system; but he'd caught the zipper a couple of times and got language one does not expect from one's sex partner regardless of previous experience. "From now on you wear nothing but a jock strap," she'd ordered. "And you wear that all the time. *Nothing* gets caught in that zipper." The last couple of hours she was throwing the suit at him from behind, a crumpled ball he had to shake out and get into in ten seconds. When he could do it with a blindfold, she was satisfied.

"It's your first move," she'd said. "Always. Anything happens, *get into that suit.*"

He snatched the suit without looking, slid feet and hands and head in and zipped it two-handed and plugged into the wall. Another instant to pull the shoulder pack out of its recess, slip it on, pull the plug and plug it into *that.* Stored air filled his suit, tasting tasteless. Alice was still faster; she was ahead of him, swarming up the ladder.

She was in the pilot's chair when he came through the hatch. "Nice going," she said without looking around.

"What's happening?"

"The drive's functioning perfectly. We're doing one gee exactly, still lined up for Persephone."

"Okay." He relaxed. He moved toward the other chair, stumbling slightly.

She looked around. "Don't you feel it?"

"Feel what?"

"Maybe it's me. I feel. . .light."

Now he felt it too. "But we're registering one gee."

"Yah."

He made an intuitive leap. "Check our course."

She threw him an odd look, then nodded and went to work.

He couldn't help. He had spent part of the first day and all of the next using learning tapes; he now had a good classroom education in how to fly, maintain, and repair a Belt cargo spacecraft. But Alice knew the instruments. He left her to it.

He felt it when the change came: a little more weight settling on his shoulders, a faint creaking in the fabric of the ship. He saw the fear in her eyes, and he said nothing.

Some time later she said, "We are no longer moving toward Persephone."

"Ah." He felt cold fear within him.

"How did you know?" she asked.

"I guessed. But it makes sense. Brennan's got generated gravity; we've been assuming that. If we were in a strong gravitational field, there might be a tidal effect."

"Oh. Well, that's what's happened. It didn't register on the autopilot, of course. Which means I'll have to get our new course by triangulation. It's for sure we're going wide of Persephone."

"What can we do about it?"

"Nothing."

He didn't believe her. They'd planned it all in such vast detail. "Nothing?"

She turned around in her seat. "You may remember that

we were going to blast up to a peak velocity of fifty-six hundred miles per second, then coast. We've got enough fuel to do that twice, once going, once coming."

"Sure." Two hundred and fifty-six hours accelerating, the same decelerating, about a hundred hours coasting. And if they had to use some fuel exploring, they'd come back at lower peak velocity. He ought to remember. They'd worked out dozens of possibilities. They'd taken a cargo ship to carry the extra fuel, lasers to cut away the empty cargo hold if things *really* went wrong and they had to save the weight. And the lasers would double as weapons.

All the planning, and now what? He'd sensed it then, and said nothing. He sensed it now, before she finished speaking—

"We're moving at about twenty-two thousand miles per second now. I haven't got it exactly—that'll take *hours*—but as it stands we've got almost enough fuel to bring us to a complete stop."

"Out in the cometary belt?"

"Out in the ass end of nowhere, right."

—that there was something dreadfully wrong in making plans against Brennan. Brennan was beyond planning.

His mind planned anyway. There were old stories. . . men had survived emergencies in space. . .Apollo Thirteen, and the voyage of Four Gee Jennison, and Eric the Cyborg. . . "We could blast laterally to reach Persephone, then whip around the planet in a hyperbola. At least it'd send us back into the solar system."

"We might have enough fuel for that. I'll do a course analysis. Meanwhile—" She played with the controls.

The feel of gravity slowly died away.

The vibration of the drive was gone. It left a silence in his head.

Elroy Truesdale is less predictable than Brennan. Of the several choices that face him now, one is clearly best; but how can Brennan count on his following it? Breeders often don't. Worse, he may have a companion aboard that big ship. Female and Belter: Truesdale is at least that predictable. But how can Brennan predict the whims of a girl he never met?

It's like that with Truesdale's weaponry. Lasers, of course. Lasers are too useful as an all-purpose tool to leave behind. He'd pick lasers, and one other weapon. Grenades, bullets, sonic stunners, plastic explosive? There are about four good choices. One best choice, except that Brennan might anticipate it. Truesdale's logical move is to flip a coin, twice. Brennan knows that he is bright enough to realize it.

So he flipped a coin twice before takeoff. Which way did it fall, Brennan? Brennan laughs inside his head, though his face does not move. When Truesdale is clever, Brennan is pleased.

And what will he do now? Brennan mulls the point. Fortunately it does not matter. Nothing Truesdale can do will take him out of range of Brennan's oddball telescope. . .the same instrument he used to alter Truesdale's course. Brennan turns to other things. In a few days. . .

"If we didn't have to worry about Brennan, I know just what we'd be doing," said Alice. "We'd be decelerating, and blasting out a help call. In a few months some-one would mount an expedition and pick us up."

They were in Roy's hammock, loosely moored against free fall. They had spent more and more time in the hammocks these last few days. They slept more. They had sex more often, for love or for reassurance or to end the occasional snappish quarrels, or because there was noth-ing constructive to be done.

"Why should anyone come for us?" Roy asked. "If we were damn fools enough to come—"

"Money. Rescue fees. It would cost us everything we own, of course."

"Oh."

"Including the ship. Which would you rather be, Roy? Broke or dead?"

"Broke," he said immediately. "But I'd rather not have

the choice. And I don't. You're the Captain, as per agreement. What are we going to do, Captain?"

Alice shifted against him, and reached around him to tickle the small of his back with her fingernails. "I don't know. What do you want to do, my loyal crew?"

"Count on Brennan. But I hate it."

"Do you think he'll put you back twice?"

"Brennan's got a pretty good record for. . .humanitarianism. When I turned down his bribe it went to Criminal Rehabilitation Studies. Before that it was going to medical research in prosthetics and alloplasty."

"I don't see the connection."

"You wouldn't. Belter. On Earth there was this *thing* going with organ banks. Everyone wanted to live forever, I guess, and the easiest way to get enough transplants for all the sick people was to use condemned criminals. They were imposing the death penalty for anything and everything, including too many traffic violations. That was when Brennan was plowing money into other kinds of medical research."

"We never had that problem," Alice said with dignity, "because we *decided* not to. We never turned our criminals into donors."

"Granted. You got through that period on pure moral fiber."

"I'm serious."

"We got through it because medical research found better ways of doing things. Brennan was backing that research. Now we've got live felons again, and they've got to be returned to society somehow."

"And Brennan's backing that. And this is the same soft-hearted Snatcher who's bound to put us back on Earth if we don't do anything in our own behalf."

"You asked my opinion, my Captain. You have no reason to treat my answer as mutiny."

"At ease, my loyal crew. I just—" Her hand clenched into a fist. He felt it against his back. "—don't mucking like to depend on someone—"

"Neither do I."

"—someone with as much arrogance as the Brennan-monster. Maybe he really does see us as animals. Maybe he just—threw us away because we were coming to bother him."

"Maybe."

"I still haven't seen anything ahead of us."

"Well, wherever we're going, we're going a hell of a lot faster than we planned."

She laughed. Her fingernails drew circles on the small of his back.

There was something ahead of them. It was invisible to telescope and radar, but it registered, barely, on the mass detector. It might have been a stray comet, or a flaw in the mass detector, or—something else.

They had been falling for six days. Now they were 7×10^9 miles from Sol—as far as Persephone. Now the mass indicator showed a tiny, distinct image. It was smaller than any moon a gas giant ought to have. But matter was so thin out here—almost as thin as interstellar space—that by long odds they should have been falling toward nothing at all.

They thought it was Brennan. They took hope, and fear. And the telescope showed nothing.

He wasn't sure what had wakened him. He listened to the silence, he looked about him in the half-light. . .

Alice was sagging forward against the restraining straps around her hammock, hanging toward the ship's nose. As was he.

He had learned his lesson well. He had his pressure suit in hand before he released the straps. He clutched them as an anchor and donned the suit one-handed. The pull was a few pounds, no more. Alice was ahead of him again, drifting down the ladder toward the nose.

The mass detector was going crazy. Beyond the porthole was a wilderness of fixed stars.

"I can't do a course estimate out here," said Alice. "There aren't any reference points. It was bad enough back there, two days out from Sol."

"Okay."

She slammed a fist into the porthole glass. "It's *not* okay. I can't find out where we *are*. What does he *want* with us?"

"Easy, easy. *We* came to *him*."

"I can do a Doppler shift on the sun. At least it'll give us our radial velocity. I can't do that with Persephone, it's too goddamn *dim*—" She turned away suddenly, her face convulsed.

"Take it easy, Captain."

She was crying. When he put his arms around her she beat gently on his shoulders with her fists. "I don't *like* this. I *hate* depending on someone—" She sobbed rackingly.

She had more responsibility than he. More stress.

And—he knew it was true—she couldn't make herself depend on anyone. Within his big family Roy had always had someone to run to in an emergency. He'd felt sorry for anyone who didn't have such a failsafe in his life.

Love was an interdependence kind of thing, he thought. What he and Alice had wouldn't ever quite be love. Too bad.

—Which was a silly thing to be thinking while they waited the whim of Brennan, or the Snatcher, or Vandervecken, or whatever was out there: a flimsy chain of reasoning, and something that moved spacecraft about like toys on a nursery floor. And Alice, who had her head buried in his shoulder as if trying to blot out the world, still had them anchored to a wall by one hand. He hadn't thought of it.

She felt him stiffen and turned too. A moment she looked, then moved to the telescope controls.

It looked like a distant asteroid.

It was not where the mass indicator had been pointing, but behind that point. When Alice threw the image on the screen, Roy couldn't believe his eyes. It was like a sunlit landscape in fairyland, all grass and trees and growing things, and a few small buildings in soft organic shapes; but it was as if a piece of such a landscape had been picked up and molded by the hands of a playful topologist.

It was small, much too small to hold the film of atmosphere he could see around it or the blue pond gleaming across one side. A modeling-clay donut with depressions and bulges on its surface, and a small grass-green sphere floating in the hole, and a single tree growing out of the sphere. He could see the sphere quite clearly. It must have been huge.

And the near side of the structure was all bathed in sunlight. Where was the sunlight coming from?

"We're coming up on it." Alice was tense, but there were no tears in her voice. She'd recovered fast.

"What do we do now? Land ourselves, or wait for him to land us?"

"I'd better warm up the drive," she said. "His gravity generator might kick up storms in that artificial atmosphere."

He didn't ask, *How do you know?* She was guessing, of course. He said, "Weapons?"

Her hands paused on the keys. "He wouldn't—I don't know."

He pondered the question. Thus he lost his chance.

When he woke he thought he was on Earth. Bright sunlight, blue sky. the tickling of grass against his back and legs, the touch and sound and smell of a cool and pollinated breeze. . .had he been abandoned in another national park, then? He rolled on his side and saw Brennan.

Brennan sat on the grass, hugging his knobby knees, watching him. Brennan was naked but for a long vest. The vest was all pockets: big pockets, little pockets, loops for tools, pockets on pockets and within pockets; and most of the pockets were full. He must have been carrying his own weight in widgetry.

Where the vest didn't cover him, Brennan's skin was all loose brown wrinkles like soft leather. He looked like the Pak mummy in the Smithsonian, but he was bigger and even uglier. The bulge of chin and forehead marred the smooth lines of the Pak head. His eyes were brown and thoughtful, and human.

He said, "Hello, Roy."

Roy sat up convulsively. There was Alice, on her back, eyes closed. She still wore her pressure suit, but the hood was open. There was the ship, resting belly-down on. . .on. . .

Vertigo.

"She'll be all right," Brennan was saying. His voice was dry, faintly alien. "So will you. I didn't want you coming out with weapons blazing. This ecosystem isn't easy to maintain."

Roy looked again. Uphill across a rounded green slope, to where an impossible mass floated ready to fall on them. A grass-covered spheroid with a single gigantic tree growing out of one side. The ship rested beside its trunk. It should have fallen too.

Alice Jordan sat up. Roy wondered if she'd panic. . . but she studied the Brennan-monster for a moment, then said, "So we were right."

"Pretty close," Brennan agreed. "You wouldn't have found anything at Persephone, though."

"And now we're caught," she said bitterly.

"No. You're guests."

Her expression didn't change.

"You think I'm playing euphemisms. I'm not. When I leave here I'm going to give you this place. My work here is almost finished. I'll have to instruct you in how not to kill yourselves by pushing the wrong buttons, and I'll give you a deed to Kobold. We'll have time for that."

Give? Roy thought of being marooned out here, unreachably far from home. A pleasant enough prison. Did Brennan think he was setting up a new Garden of Eden? But Brennan was still speaking—

"I have my own ship, of course. I'll leave you yours. You intelligently saved the fuel. You should become very rich from this, Roy. You too, Miss."

"Alice Jordan," she said. She was taking it well, but she didn't seem to know what to do with her hands. They fluttered.

"Call me Jack, or Brennan, or the Brennan-monster.

I'm not sure I'm still entitled to the name I was born with."

Roy said one word. "Why?"

Brennan understood. "Because my job here is over. What do you think I've been doing out here for two hundred and twenty years?"

"Using generated gravity as an art form," said Alice.

"That too. Mainly I've been watching for high-energy lithium radicals in Saggitarius." He looked at them through the mask of his face. "I'm not being cryptic. I'm trying to explain so you won't be so nervous. I've had a purpose out here. Over the past few weeks I've found what I was looking for. Now I'll be leaving. I never dreamed they'd take so long."

"Who?"

"The Pak. Let's see, you must have studied the Phssthpok incident in detail, or you wouldn't have gotten this far. Did you think to ask yourselves what the childless protectors of Pak would do after Phssthpok was gone?"

Clearly they hadn't.

"I did. Phssthpok established a space industry on Pak. He found out how to grow tree-of-life in the worlds of the galactic arms. He built a ship, and it worked for as far as any Pak could detect it. Now what?

"All those childless protectors seeking a mission in life. A space industry to build ships designed for one job. Something could happen to Phssthpok, you know. An accident. Or he might lose the will to live, halfway here."

Roy saw it then. "They'd send another ship."

"That they would. Even if he got here, Phssthpok could use some help searching a volume thirty light years in radius. Whoever followed Phssthpok wouldn't aim directly for Sol; Phssthpok would have searched Sol by the time he got here. He would aim to the side, away from Phssthpok's obvious area of search. I figured that would give me a few extra years," said Brennan. "I thought they'd send another ship almost immediately. I was afraid I wouldn't be ready."

"Why would it take them so long?"

"I don't know." Brennan made it sound like an admission of guilt. "A heavier cargo pod, maybe. Breeders in suspended animation, in case we died out over two and a half million years."

Alice said, "You said you'd been watching—"

"Yah. A sun doesn't burn fuel quite like a Bussard ramjet. There's a constriction and a hell of a lot of heat, then the gas expands into space while it's still fusing. A Bussard ramjet will put out a lot of funny chemicals: high-energy hydrogen and helium, lithium radicals, some borates, even lithium hydride, which is generally an impossible chemical. In deceleration mode those all go out in a high-energy stream at nearly lightspeed.

"Phssthpok's ship worked that way, and I didn't expect they'd fool with his design. Not just because it worked, but because it was the best design they could get. When you're as bright as a Pak, there's only one right answer for a given set of tools. I wonder if something happened to their technology after Phssthpok left. Something like a war." He pondered. "Anyway, I've found funny chemicals in Saggitarius. Something's coming."

Roy dreaded to ask. "How many ships?"

"One, of course. I haven't actually found the image, but they'd have sent the second ship off as soon as they built it. Why wait? And maybe another ship behind it, and another behind that. I'll search them out from here, while I've still got my quote telescope unquote."

"Then what?"

"Then I'll destroy as many ships as there are."

"Just like that?"

"I keep getting that reaction," Brennan said with some bitterness. "Look: If a Pak knew what the human race was like, he'd try to exterminate us. What am I supposed to do? Send him a message, ask for truce? That information alone would tell him enough."

Alice said, "You might convince him you were Phssthpok."

"I probably could at that. Then what? He'd stop eating, of course. But first he'd want to deliver his ship. He'd never believe we've already developed the technology to make artificial monopoles, and his ship is the second of its kind in this system, and we might need the thalium oxide too."

"Um."

"Um," Brennan mimicked her. "Do you think I like the idea of murdering someone who came thirty-one thousand light years to save us from ourselves? I've been thinking this through for a long time. There's no other answer. But don't let that stop you." Brennan stood up. "Think it through. While you're at it, you might as well explore Kobold too. You'll own it eventually. All of the dangerous things are behind doors. Have a ball, swim where you find water, play golf if you like. But don't eat anything, and don't open any doors. Roy, tell her about the Bluebeard legend." Brennan pointed over a low hill. "That way, and through the garden, and you come to my laboratory. I'll be there when you want me. Take your time." And he went, not strolling, but running.

They looked at each other.

Alice said, "Do you think he really meant it?"

"I'd like to," said Roy. "Generated gravity. And this place. *Kobold*. With gravity generators we could move it into the solar system, maybe, and set it up as a disneyland."

"What did he mean about—Bluebeard?"

"He meant, 'Really don't open any doors.' "

"Oh."

Given an unlimited choice of direction, they chose to follow Brennan over the hill. They did not catch sight of him again. Kobold had the sharply curved horizon of any small asteroid, at least from the outer curve of the toroid.

But they found the garden. Here were fruit trees and nut trees and vegetable patches in all stages of bloom. Roy pulled up a carrot, and it brought back a memory: he and some cousins, all about ten years old, walking with Greatly 'Stelle in the small vegetable garden on her estate. They'd pulled carrots, and washed them under a faucet. . .

He dropped the carrot without tasting it. He and Alice walked beneath the orange trees without touching them. In fairyland one does not lightly ignore the command of the resident warlock. . .especially as Roy was not sure that Brennan understood the power of the temptation to disobey.

A squirrel darted into a tree as they came near. A rabbit looked at them from a row of beets.

"It reminds me of Confinement Asteroid," said Alice.

"It reminds me of California," said Roy. "Except for the way the gravity bends around. I wonder if I've been here before."

She looked at him sharply. "Do you remember anything?"

"Not a thing. It's all strange. Brennan never mentioned the kidnappings at all, did he?"

"No. He. . .may think he doesn't have to. We must have it all figured out, because we're *here*. If Brennan thinks in pure logic, then he'd just be covering old ground, as if we've already talked it all out."

Beyond the garden they could see the topmost tower of a medieval castle, almost on its side from this perspective. Brennan's laboratory, no doubt. They looked, then turned away.

The land grew wilder, became a stretch of California chaparral. They saw a fox, ground squirrels, even a feral cat. The place was lousy with wildlife: like a park, except for the way it *bent*.

On the inner curve of the toroid they stood beneath the grassy sphere, looking up at their ship. The great tree pointed its branches at them. "I could almost reach those branches," said Roy. "I could climb down."

"Never mind. Look there." She pointed around the curve of the donut.

Where she pointed was a flowing stream, and a waterfall that fell *up* out of the middle, fell from the major section of Kobold to the grassy sphere.

"Yah. We could get to the ship, if we wanted to take that fall."

"Brennan has to have a way to get from here to there."

"He did say, *Swim in any water you find.*"

"But I can't swim. You'd have to do it," said Alice.

"Okay. Come on."

The water was icy cold at first. Sunlight glittered blind-ingly off the water. . .and Roy wondered again. The sun was hot and bright overhead. But they'd have *seen* an atomic generator that size.

Alice looked down at him from the bank. "Are you sure you want to do this?"

"Pretty sure." He laughed partly because he was shiv-ering. "If I get in trouble, get Brennan. What do you want from the ship?"

"Clothes." She was naked under the transparent pres-sure suit. "I kept wanting to cover myself with my hands."

"From *Brennan?*"

"I know, Brennan's sexless. Still."

He asked, "Weapons?"

"No point." She hesitated. "I tried to think of some way to check what Brennan's been telling us. There aren't any instruments on the ship that would do it. Still. . .you might try pointing the solar storm warning toward Saggi-tarius."

Roy swam toward the waterfall. There was none of the sound of wild water. It could not be as dangerous as it . . .ought to be.

Something brushed his ankle. He twitched and looked down. Silver flashed away from him through the water. A fish had brushed his leg. That had never happened to him before.

He came to where water was falling up. He rested, treading water, letting it draw him in. There was a moment of disorientation, and then. . .

. . .he was in a smoothly flowing stream. Alice stood watching him with concern. She stood horizontally out from the side of a sheer cliff.

Currents around his feet made him wonder. He ducked under, into turbulence, and came out the other side of the stream, headed back. He ducked again, and rode the current to where it emptied onto the green ball in a kid-ney-shaped pond. The ship was just a few yards away.

He pulled himself out of the water, laughing and blowing. A stream that flowed two ways through the air!

The ship's solar storm warning showed no sign of a disturbance in Saggitarius. It proved nothing. He didn't know how much activity it took to set the instrument off.

He stowed clothing for both of them in another pressure suit, and added a couple of handmeals because he was hungry. He brought them back in the sealed suit. He had never looked at the weapons.

There was a Möbius strip forty feet across and six feet broad, made of some silvery metal, suspended almost horizontally in the air with part of the edge embedded in bare dirt. They studied it for awhile, and then Alice. . . tried it.

Gravity was vertical to the surface. She walked around the outside, negotiated the twist upside down, and came back along the inside. She jumped down with her arms raised for applause.

There was a miniature golf course. It looked absurdly easy, but Roy borrowed a putter from a rack and tried it anyway. He got several shocks. The ball drew strange curves in the air, sometimes bounced higher than it had fallen, and once it came back at his head as hard as he had hit it. He stuck with it long enough to realize that the gravity fields were changing from minute to minute, and then he gave up.

They found a lily pond studded with water sculptures, gentle shapes that rose and flowed out of the surface. By far the most detailed shape was a large sculptured head in the center of the pond. It changed shape as they watched, from the hard face and swelling skull of the Brennan-monster to—

"I think that must be Brennan too," said Alice.

—to a square face with deep-set eyes, and straight hair in a Belter strip cut, and a brooding look, as if the man remembered some ancient wrong. The lips curved in a sudden smile, and the face began to melt. . .

Kobold had turned. It was dusk in that region when they returned to the castle.

It stood up out of a rise of ground, a structure of rough-hewn dark stone blocks, with windows that were vertical slits, and a great wooden door built for giants. "Franken-stein's castle," said Roy. "Brennan still has a sense of humor. We might just bear that in mind."

"Meaning his story could be a put-on."

Roy shrugged. *What can we do about it?*

It took two hands to turn the knob of the great door, and both of them pushing to open it.

Vertigo.

They stood at the edge of a vast open space. All through it was a maze of stairways and landings and more stairways. Through open doors they could glimpse gardens. There were faceless dummies, a score of them, climbing up and climbing down and standing on the landings and walking into the gardens. . .

. . .but they stood at all angles. Two-thirds of the land-ings were vertical. Likewise the gardens. Dummies stood unconcerned on vertical landings; two dummies climbed a flight of stairs in the same direction, one going up, one down. . .

Brennan's voice boomed, echoing, from somewhere above them. "Hi! Come on up. Do you recognize it?"

Neither of them answered.

"It's Esher's *Relativity*. It's the only copied work on all of Kobold. I thought about doing *The Madonna of Port Lligat,* but there wasn't room."

"Jesus," Roy whispered. Then he shouted, "Had you thought of setting up a *Madonna of Port Lligat* at Port Lligat?"

"Sure!" came the cheerful bellow. "But it would have scared a lot of people. I didn't want to make that many waves. I shouldn't even have done that duplicate Stone-henge."

"We've not only found Vandervecken," Sally whis-pered. "We've found Finagle Himself!" Roy laughed.

"Come on up!" Brennan bellowed. "It'll save shouting. Don't worry about the gravity. It adjusts."

They were exhausted when they reached the top of the tower. "Esher's *Relativity*" ended in a spiral stair, and that seemed to go on and on, past slits of windows designed for archery fire.

The room at the top was dark, and open to the sky. By Brennan's whim its roof and sides seemed smashed away, as by rocks fired from ballistas. But the sky was not the sky of Earth. Suns glared there, hellishly bright, fearfully close.

Brennan turned from his controls—a wall of instruments six feet tall and twelve feet long, prickly with lights and levers and dials. In the dim light of the suns he looked like some ancient mad scientist, bald and disfigured, pursuing knowledge at any cost to himself and the world.

Alice was still staring at the altered sky. But Roy bowed low and said, "Merlin, the king commands thy presence."

Brennan snapped, "Tell the old buzzard I can't make him any more gold till the lead shipments arrive from Northumberland! Meanwhile, how do you like my telescope?"

Alice said, "The whole *sky?*"

"Lie down, Alice. You'll strain your neck in that position. It's a gravity lens." He read their puzzlement. "You know that a gravity field bends light? Good. I can make a field that warps light into a focus. It's lenticular, shaped like a red blood platelet. That's how I get my sunlight. Sol seen through a gravity lens, with a scattering component to give me blue sky. One fringe benefit is that the lens scatters light going the other way, so you can't see Kobold until you're right on top of it."

Roy looked up at the suns burning close. "That's quite an effect."

"That's Saggitarius, the direction of the galactic hub. I still haven't found that goddamn ship, but it makes for pretty lights, doesn't it?" Brennan touched a control and the sky slid past them, as within some faster-than-light craft moving through a globular cluster.

Roy said, "What happens when you find him?"

"I told you that. I've played it out a hundred times in my head. It's as if I've lived it all before, in all possible ways. My ship's a duplicate of the one Phssthpok used, except for some refinements. I can get up to three gravities with the ram alone, and I've got two hundred years' worth of weaponry developments in the cargo pod."

"I still think—"

"I know you do. It's partly my doing that you haven't had a war in so long. So you've grown soft, and it makes you more likable, bless you. But this is a war situation."

"But is it?"

"What do you know about the Pak?"

Roy didn't answer.

"There's a Pak ship coming. If the Pak in question ever finds out the truth about us he'll try to exterminate us. He may succeed. I'm telling you this, dammit! I'm the only man who's ever met a Pak. I'm the only man who could ever understand one."

Roy bristled. The arrogance of him! "Then where is he, O All-Knowing Brennan?"

Another might have hesitated in embarrassment. Not Brennan. "I don't know yet."

"Where should he be?"

"On his way to Alpha Centaurus. From the strength of the signal—" Brennan manipulated something, and the sky surged past them in streaks of light. Roy blinked, fighting vertigo.

The stars jarred to a halt. "There. In the middle."

"Is that where your funny chemicals are coming from?"

"More or less. It's not exactly a point-source."

"Why Alpha Centaurus?"

"Because Phssthpok would have gone almost in the opposite direction. Most of the nearby yellow dwarf suns are all to one side of Sol. The Centaurus suns are an exception."

"So this second Pak would look around the Centaurus system, and if he didn't find Wunderland he'd head on away from Sol."

"That was my best guess. But," said Brennan, "the direction of his exhaust shows him coming dead on. Now I have to assume he's been watching for Phssthpok to leave here. I did send Phssthpok's ship off toward Wunderland. I have to assume it didn't fool him. If Phssthpok hasn't left here, he may have found what he was looking for. So Pak number two is coming here."

"And where would he be now?"

The sky surged again. Bright suns backed by tiny suns, dim-lit gas and dust clouds, a panorama of the universe flowed past and lurched to a stop. "There."

"I don't see him."

"I don't either."

"So you haven't found him. Do you still claim to understand the Pak?"

"I do." Brennan didn't hesitate. In all the time he knew him, Roy Truesdale only saw him hesitate once. "If they're doing something unexpected it's because of a change in their environment."

Unexpectedly Alice spoke. "Could there be a lot of ships?"

"No. Why would the Pak send us a fleet?"

"I don't know. But they'd be further away than you'd guess from the density of your funny chemicals. Harder to find," she said. She was cross-legged on the floor, with her head thrown back to see the stars. Brennan didn't seem to be listening—he was working the telescope controls—but she went on. "The exhaust would be more blurred. And if they were further away they'd be moving faster, wouldn't they? You'd get higher velocity particles."

"Not if they were carrying more cargo," said Brennan. "That would slow them." The sky surged toward them, and blurred. "But it's so damn unlikely! There's only one assumption that would fit. Please bear with me; this takes a lot of fiddling, getting these fields just right." The starfield half-cleared, then blurred again. "I'd have had to do this eventually anyway. Then we can all stop worrying."

The blur of the sky condensed into hard white points. Now there were no giant suns in the field of view.

But there were a couple of hundred blue points all the same size, tiny, set wide apart in what Roy gradually realized was a hexagonal array.

"I just didn't believe it," said Brennan. "It was too much coincidence."

"It is. It's a whole fleet!" Roy felt horror and the beginnings of panic. A fleet of Pak, coming here—and Brennan, the Protector of Man, hadn't anticipated it.

He'd trusted Brennan.

"There must be more," said Brennan. "Further in toward the galactic core. Too far to see with my instruments. A second wave. Maybe a third."

"These aren't *enough?*"

"They aren't enough," Brennan agreed. "Don't you understand? Something's happened to the galactic core. It's the only thing that could bring this many ships this far. That implies that they've evacuated the Pak world. I don't see enough ships to do it, not even with the wars that must have been fought, with each protector trying to get his descendants on the first ships."

Little blue lights against a sky of too-bright stars. All that, from little blue lights?

Alice rubbed her neck. "What could have happened?"

"Any kind of thing. Black holes wandering through the core suns, picking up more and more mass, maybe wandering too near Pak. Or some kind of space-born life. Or the galactic core could be exploding in a rash of supernovae. It's happened in other galaxies. What burns me is that it had to happen now!"

"Can't you think of any other explanation?"

"None that fits. And it's not quite as coincidental as it sounds," Brennan said wearily. "Phssthpok built the best astronomical system in millennia, to chart his course as far as he could. After he left they must have looked around and found—something. Supernovae in a dense cluster of older suns. Stars disappearing. Places where light was warped. It's still a Finagle's Coincidence. I just didn't believe it."

"Maybe you didn't want to," said Alice.

"You can believe that!"

"Why here? Why come to us?"

"To the only known habitable world outside the galactic core? Besides that, we've had time to find them some others."

"Yah."

Brennan turned to look at them. "Are you hungry? I am."

Deep within the eye-twisting maze of "Esher's *Relativity*" was a miniature kitchen. It was a landing from one viewpoint, but from another it was a wall, and the wall held cookwear closets and a sink and a pair of ovens and a pull-down platform with burners in it. Raw materials had been dumped near the wall: a squash, a canteloupe, two rabbits whose necks were broken, carrots, celery, handfuls of spices.

"Let's see how fast we can produce," said Brennan. He became a many-armed blur. Roy and Alice stood back from his flashing hands. One held a knife, and it moved in silver streaks, so that carrots became rolling discs and the rabbits seemed simply to fall apart.

Roy felt disoriented, cut off from reality. Those little blue lights above the tower room had no intuitive connection with a fleet of superbeings bent on exterminating mankind. This pleasant domestic scene didn't help. While a knife-wielding alien prepared his dinner, Roy Truesdale looked through the great castle door at a landscape tilted on its side.

Alice said, "That food is all from outside, isn't it? Why didn't you want us to eat anything?"

"Well, there's always the chance that tree-of-life virus has gotten to something. Cooking kills it, and there's precious little chance it can live in anything anyway unless I've spread thalium oxide through the soil." Brennan did not look up or interrupt his work. "I had a Finagle's Puzzle facing me when I cut loose from Earth. There was food, but what I needed was the virus in the tree-of-life roots. I tried to grow it in various things: apples, pomegranates—" He looked up then, to see if they'd catch the reference. "I got a varient that would grow in a yam. That was when I knew I could survive out here."

Brennan had arranged rabbit and vegetables as for a still-life painting. He put the pot in the oven. "My kitchen had all kinds of freeze-dried produce. I used to like to eat well, luckily. Later I got seeds from Earth. I was never in danger; I could always just go home. But I didn't like what was going to happen to civilization if I did." He turned. "Dinner in fifteen minutes."

She asked, "Weren't you lonely?"

"Yah." Brennan pulled a table out of the floor. It was not memory plastic extruding itself, but a thick slab of wood, heavy enough to require Brennan's own muscles. A look back at Alice may have told him that she expected more of an answer. "Look, I'd have been lonely anywhere. You know that."

"No, I don't. You'd have been welcome."

Brennan seemed to go off at a tangent. "Roy, you've been here before. You guessed that?"

Roy nodded.

"How did I wipe out just that section of your memory?"

"I don't know. Nobody knows." Roy tensed inside himself.

"Simplest thing in the world. Just after I stunned you, I took a recording of your brain. Your complete memory. Before I left you in the Pinnacles I wiped your mind completely, then played the recording into it. It's more complex than that—the process involves memory RNA, and very complex electrical fields—but I don't have to select the memories I want to remove."

Roy's voice came out faint. "Brennan, that's horrible."

"Why? Because for awhile you were a mindless animal? I wasn't going to leave you that way. I've done this twenty times now, and never had an accident."

Roy shuddered. "You don't understand. There was a *me* that spent four months with you. He's gone. You murdered him."

"You're beginning to understand."

Roy looked him in the eye. "You were right. You're different. You'd be lonely anywhere."

Brennan set the table. He held chairs for his guests, moving with the smooth lack of haste that marks a perfect headwaiter. He served, taking half the food for himself, then sat down and ate with the efficiency of a wolf. He was neat, but he finished long before they did. There was now a noticeable bulge beneath his sternum.

"Emergencies make me hungry," he said. "And now I'd like to excuse myself. It's not polite, but there's a war to fight." And he left, sprinting like a roadrunner.

For the next few days Roy and Alice felt like unwanted guests of a perfect host. They didn't see Brennan much. When they glimpsed him across the landscape of Kobold he would be moving at a dead run. He would stop to ask them how they were enjoying themselves, tell them of something they might have missed, then be off again—at a dead run.

Or they would find him in the laboratory making ever-finer adjustments in his "telescope." There was only one ship in the field now, seen against a background of red dwarfs and interstellar dust clouds: a blus fusion flame, blue-shifted yellow helium light, sparkling around the edges.

He would talk to them, but without interrupting his work. "It's the Phssthpok configuration," he told them with evident satisfaction. "They didn't mess with a good thing. See the black dot in the center of the flame? Cargo pod comes first during deceleration. And it's a bigger cargo pod than Phssthpok was carrying, and the ships are moving slower than his · did at that distance. They aren't *that* close to the speed of light. They won't be here for a hundred and seventy-two or -three years."

"Good."

"Good for me, or it should be. Cargo pod first, and breeders in the cargo pod in frozen sleep. A vulnerable configuration, wouldn't you say?"

"Not at odds of two hundred and thirty to one."

"I'm not crazy, Roy. I'm not going to attack them myself. I'm going for help."

"Where?"

"Wunderland. It's closest."

"What? No. Earth is closest."

Brennan looked around. "Are you crazy? I'm not even going to *warn* Earth. Earth and the Belt are eighty percent of humanity, including all my descendants. Their best chance is to miss the fight. If some other world does the fighting, and loses, the Pak may still miss Earth for awhile."

"So you're using the Wunderlanders as a decoy. Are you going to tell them?"

"Don't be silly."

They toured Kobold, and tried to keep out of Brennan's way. He would come on them unexpectedly, jogging around a boulder or out of a grove of trees, eternally hurried or eternally keeping himself in fighting trim; he never said which. Always he wore that vest. He didn't need modesty, he didn't need protection from the elements, but he needed the pockets. For all Roy knew the vest held protection too: a fold-up pressure suit, say, in one of the larger pockets.

Once he found them near one of the rounded huts. He led them into an airlock, and showed them something beyond the glass inner wall.

Floating within a great rock-walled cavity: a silvery sphere, eight feet across, polished to a mirror brightness.

"Takes a damn finicky gravity field to keep it there," said Brennan. "It's mostly neutronium."

Roy whistled. Alice said, "Wouldn't it be unstable? It's too small."

"Sure it would, if it weren't in a stasis field. I made it under pressure, then got the stasis field around it before it could blow up in my face. Now there's more matter on top of it. Would you believe a surface gravity of eight million gees?"

"I guess I would." Neutronium was as dense as matter could get: neutrons packed edge to edge under pressures greater than those at the centers of most stars. Only a hypermass would be denser, and a hypermass would not be matter any more: just a gravitational point-source.

"I thought of leaving it here as a decoy, in case a Pak ship got past me. Now there are too many. I can't leave Kobold for them to find. It would be a dead giveaway."

"You're going to wreck Kobold?"

"I have to."

Sometimes they did their own cooking—avoiding the potatoes and yams, as per Brennan's instructions. Sometimes he cooked for them. His blinding speed never seemed hurried, but he never stayed to talk after he had finished eating. He was gaining weight, but it seemed to be all muscle, and the great knobby joints still gave him the look of a skeleton.

He was unfailingly polite. He never talked down to them.

"He treats us like kittens," said Alice. "He's busy, but he sees to it we're fed and sometimes he stops to scratch our ears."

"Not his fault. We can't do anything to help. I wish there were something—"

"Me too." She lay on the grass in the warm sunlight, which had taken on an odd color. Brennan had taken the scattering component out of the gravity lens that showed the sun. The light interfered with his seeing. The sky was black now. The sun was bigger and dimmer; it would not burn out a human eye.

He had stopped Kobold's rotation to make it easier to adjust the multiple gravity fields. Now there was always wind. It whistled through the permanent night around Brennan's laboratory; it cooled the noonday heat on this side of the grassy sphere. The plants had not yet started to die, but they would.

"A hundred and seventy years. We'll never even know how it ended," said Alice.

"We could live that long."

"I suppose."

"Brennan must have more tree-of-life virus than he needs." When she shuddered, he laughed.

She sat up. "We'll have to be leaving soon."

"Look."

There was a bobbing head in the waterfall. An arm emerged and waved to them. Presently Brennan swam to them across the pond, his arms whirling like propellers.

"I have to swim like crazy," he said. "I'm heavier than water. How're you making out?"

"Okay. How goes the war?"

"Tolerably." Brennan held up a handful of spools in a sealed plastic bag. "Star maps. I'm about ready to leave. If I could think of a great new weapon to take along, I'd spend up to a year making it. As is, there's only final inspection."

"We've got weapons in the ship. You can have them," said Roy.

"Sold, with thanks. What'd you bring?"

"Hand lasers and rifles."

"Well, they can't mass very much. Thanks." Brennan turned back to the pond.

"Hey!"

Brennan turned. "What?"

"Could you use any other kind of help?" He felt silly asking.

Brennan looked at him for a long moment. "Yes," he said. "Remember, you asked."

"Right," Roy said firmly. By now that *What have I gotten myself into now?* sensation was a familiar one.

"I'd like you to come along."

Roy stopped breathing.

Alice spoke. "Brennan? If you really need the help, I volunteer too."

"Sorry, Alice. I can't use you."

She bridled. "Did I mention that I'm a trained goldskin? Trained in weapons, spacecraft, and pursuit."

"You're also pregnant."

Brennan, infinitely adaptable himself, had the knack of

dropping bombs into a conversation without seeming to realize it. Sally lost her breath. "I am?"

"Should I have been more tactful? My dear, you may expect a blessed event—"

"How do you know?"

"The hormones have made some obvious changes. Look, this can't be a total shock. You must have skipped—"

"—skipped my last shot," she finished for him. "I know. I was thinking about having a child, but that was before all this Vandervecken business came up, and after that. . .well, Roy, there was only you. I thought all flat-landers. . ."

"No, I'm cleared to have a child. Where do you think new flatlanders come from? I'd have told you, but it never. . ."

"Well, stop looking so flustered." She stood up and put her arms around him. "I'm proud. Have you got that through your thick head?"

"Me too." He smiled, forcing it a bit. Of *course* he wanted to be a father. But— "But what do we do now?"

She looked troubled, but didn't answer.

This was rapidly getting out of hand. Brennan had dropped too many bombs at once. Roy closed his eyes tight, as if that would help. When he opened them Brennan and Alice were still watching him.

Alice was pregnant.

Little blue lights.

"I, I, I'll go," he told them. "I'm not running out on you, love," he added quickly and urgently. His hands had closed too tightly on her shoulders. "We're bringing a child into the world. The same world which, by an odd coincidence, is now the target for t-t-two hundred and thirty—"

"I've located the second wave," said Brennan.

"Dammit! I didn't need to hear that!"

Alice put a hand across his mouth. "I understand, my loyal crew. I think you're right."

And the air was full of the smell of burning bridges.

They stood beneath the branches of the single huge tree, watching. Brennan was occupied with a portable control set taken from his vest. Roy only watched.

The two-hundred-year-old singleship looked like a short insect with a long stinger, the cargo webs spread like diaphanous wings, the stinger tipped with actinic light. The sound of it was a shrill scream. Brennan had spent a full day teaching Alice how to use the ship, care for it, repair it. Roy would not have guessed that a day would be enough, but if Brennan was satisfied. . . And she was doing well. She went straight up, then turned smoothly into what had been the sun.

Roy felt a twitchy urgency, a sense that if he didn't do something now, right now, he was committed for life. But the moment was long past. He only watched.

The sun looked odd now. Brennan had fiddled with the gravity lens, turning it into a launching system for the singleship. As Roy watched the sun shifted a bit left, dimming, to catch the singleship dead center.

She was gone.

"She won't have any trouble," said Brennan. "She should make a good thing out of that ship. It's not just a relic. It's got historical significance, and I made some interesting changes in—"

"Sure," said Roy. He saw that the grass was dying and the leaves on the tree were turning yellow. Brennan had drained the pond; it was a shallow sea of mud. Kobold had already lost its magic.

Brennan slapped him on the shoulder. "Come on." He walked out into what had been a pond. Roy followed, wincing. The cool mud squished between his toes.

Brennan stooped, reached deep into the sludge, and lifted. A metal door came up with a sucking sound. An airlock door.

It was all happening very fast now. The airlock led into a cramped control room, with two crash chairs and a three hundred and sixty degree wraparound vision screen over a control board like that of any spacecraft. Brennan said, "Use straps if you want. If we foul up now we're all dead anyway."

"Shouldn't I know something—"

"No. You can inspect the vehicle to your heart's content after we're under way. Hell, you'll have a year at it."

"Why so hurried?"

Brennan looked sideways at him. "Have a heart, Roy. I've been sitting out here for longer than your Greatly 'Stelle was alive." He activated the vision screen.

They floated within the hole in Kobold's donut.

Brennan stabbed a button.

Kobold receded violently. "I'm giving us a running start," Brennan said. "We'll get root two times the velocity."

"Good."

Kobold slowed, stopped, then came up like a wargod's fist. Roy yelped. He couldn't help it. They were through the hole in an instant, and black space ahead.

Roy turned his chair for a rear view, but Kobold was already gone. Sol was a star among stars.

"Let's magnify that," said Brennan. Sol became much larger—the view expanding over a rectangular section of the vision screen—and there was Kobold, receding. The magnification jumped again, and Kobold filled the screen.

Brennan pushed a red button.

Kobold began to crumple in on itself, as if an invisible hand were wadding it up. Rock churned and began to glow yellow-hot. Roy felt queasy in his soul and in his belly. It was as if someone had bombed Disneyland.

He said, "What did you do?"

"Shut down the gravity generators. I couldn't leave it out here for the Pak to find. The longer it takes them to find artifacts around Sol, the better off we are." Kobold was all yellow-hot and melted, and tiny. "In a few minutes it'll all be plated across that eight foot ball of neutronium. When it cools it'll be practically unfindable."

Now Kobold was a blinding white point.

"What happens next?"

"For a year and two months and six days, nothing. Want to inspect the ship?"

"Nothing?"

"By which I mean that we won't be doing any accelerating for that long. Look." Brennan's fingers flashed over the control panel. The vision screen obeyed, showing a tridee map of Sol and her neighborhood out to twenty-five light years.

"We're here, at Sol. We're on our way to *here*. That point is just between Alpha Centaurus and Van Maanen's Star. When we fire up the Pak ship we'll be heading directly into the Pak fleet. They won't be able to get our velocity toward them without knowing our exhaust velocity, and they won't know our transverse component at all. They'll have to assume I'm coming from Van Maanen's Star to Alpha Centaurus. I don't want to lead them back to Sol."

"That makes sense," Roy admitted reluctantly.

"Let's take that tour," said Brennan. "Later we can go into detail. I want you able to fly this ship if anything happens to me."

The *Flying Dutchman,* Brennan called it. Though there were ships within it, it was hardly a ship. "If you wanted to be picky about it, I could claim we're sailing," Brennan said cheerfully. "There are tides, and photon winds, and shoals of dust that could chew us up."

"But you did all our steering at takeoff."

"Sure, but I could spin us a light-sail if I had to. I don't want to. It would make us more visible."

The *Flying Dutchman* was a matrix of rock, mostly hollow. Three great hollows held the components of a Pak-style Bussard ramjet ship. Brennan called it *Protector*. Another had been enlarged to house Roy Truesdale's cargo ship. Other hollows were rooms.

There was a hydroponics garden. "This is off limits," said Brennan. "Tree-of-life. Don't ever go in here."

There was an exercise room. Brennan spent some time

showing Roy how to adjust the machines for a breeder's muscles. Gravity was almost zero aboard the *Flying Dutchman*. They would both have to exercise.

There was a machine shop.

There was a telescope: big, but conventional. "I don't want to use gravity generators from now on. I want us to look like a rock. Later we'll look like a Pak ship."

Roy thought that was unnecessary. "It'll be half of a hundred and seventy-three years before the Pak find any trace of what we're doing now."

"Maybe."

And there was *Protector*.

For the first several weeks of the voyage they did little besides train Roy Truesdale to use that ship. He was drilled in the differences between Phssthpok's ship and Brennan's. "I don't know how long we'll want to keep up the camouflage," Brennan told him. "Maybe for keeps. Maybe never. It depends."

So Brennan turned the control pod into a training room by hooking sensors to the control systems and monitoring the inputs from outside. Roy learned to maintain a constant point nine two gee. He learned to feather the fields to smear the exhaust a bit. Phssthpok's drive had not been as precisely tuned as Brennan's, due to its thirty-one thousand light year voyage.

The control pod was much bigger than Roy had expected. "Phssthpok didn't have this much room, did he?"

"Nope. Phssthpok had to carry food and air and recycling equipment for something like a thousand years. I don't. We'll still be crowded. . .but we'll be entertained. Phssthpok didn't have our computer technology either, or didn't use it."

"I wonder why."

"A Pak wouldn't see the point of taking a machine to think for him. He thinks too well already. . .and likes it too much, for that matter."

The inside of the teardrop-shaped cargo pod was nothing like that of the alien ship that had come plowing into the solar system two centuries ago. Its cargo was death. It could sprout heavy attitude jets and fight itself. Its long

axis was an X-ray laser. A thick tube parallel to the laser
would generate a directed magnetic field. "It should foul
up the fields in a monopole-based Bussard ramjet. Of
course that might not hurt him enough unless your tim-
ing was right." When Roy had learned how to use it—
and that took time; he knew little about field theory—
Brennan started drilling him on *when*.

That was the point at which Roy rebelled.

The past two months hadn't been particularly pleasant.
Roy was back in school, the only student of a full-time
teacher who could not be snowed or evaded. He didn't
like being a child again. He missed the open spaces of
Earth. He missed Alice. Hell, he missed *women*. And it
was going to go on for five years!

Five years, and the rest of his life on Wunderland. He
didn't know that much about Wunderland, but he knew
that its population was small and thinly spread, its technology just adequate. A pastoral paradise, perhaps; a nice
place to spend one's life. . .until Brennan arrived. Then
Wunderland would go on a war footing.

"The Pak fleet is a hundred and seventy-three years
away," he pointed out now. "We'll be at Wunderland in
five years. What makes you think you need a gunner?
What am I doing here, anyway?"

Brennan took a handhold at the rim of a fusion bomb's
rocket nozzle. "You could say I've learned some humil-
ity. I thought of looking for a Pak fleet, long ago, but I
didn't. The probability was just too low. Well, I've
stopped taking chances."

"What chances? We know where the Pak fleet is."

"I didn't want to worry you. It's a long shot."

"Worry me! I'm *bored!*"

"All right, let's go back a bit," said Brennan. "We
know where the first fleet is, and how big it is. The
second fleet wasn't launched for another three-hundred-
odd years. All I've found of it is a patchy source of those
same chemical exhausts, off center to the first fleet and
moving a bit faster. They wouldn't follow directly behind
the first fleet. It'd be eating up too much of their fuel."

"How big?"

"Smaller. Order of a hundred and fifty ships, assuming they didn't change the design, which they may have. I can't tell."

"Is there a third fleet?"

"If there is, I'll never detect it. They had to go out for new resources to build the second fleet. They may have had to mine worlds in nearby systems and build the ships there. How long would it take them to build a third fleet? If it's there, it's too far away for me. But the point is that there had to be a *last* fleet."

"So what?"

"I'm suggesting that when the last fleet left—the second or the third or the fourth, it doesn't matter—some protectors stayed behind. We assume they were the ones without breeder descendants. They stayed behind partly to save room on the ships, and partly because they might do some good on Pak."

"On an empty world? How?"

"They could build a scout fleet."

It was not the first time Roy had worried about Brennan's sanity. The changes in his physiology, plus twenty-two decades alone. . .but if Brennan were insane, he might be too bright to give it away.

Gently Roy pointed out, "But your scout fleet would be at least five hundred years behind the rest."

"Sounds silly, does it? But they're free to experiment. They don't have to use a proven design, because they're only risking themselves. They don't need a cargo pod. They could take three gravities forever, I think; I know I could. That cuts down on their supply weight, because the trip takes less time. With the breeders gone they can do all kinds of things. . .like making new metal mines by setting up eruptions in the crust of Pak."

"You've got quite an imagination."

"Thank you. What I'm getting at is that they could plan to pass the first wave of refugee ships about where the Pak telescopes aren't good enough to scout the territory any further. From there on they lead the fleet. Still bored?"

"No. You're daydreaming, though. They might never

have built these hypothetical ships. Whatever sent them scurrying out of the galactic core might have caught the scouts."

"Hell, it could have caught the third wave and brushed the second. Or the scout ships might have blown up. Or—lest you miss the point of all this—they could be arriving now."

"You haven't found them?"

"What, with a whole sky to search? They wouldn't just come down our throats; they'd converge on Sol from random directions. I would, if I were doing it. Remember what they're expecting to find: a world of Pak protectors running a civilization two hundred years old. That's enough time to build up a virgin world, starting with a population of. . .oh, thirty million breeders of all ages would have given Phssthpok about three million newly changed protectors. The scouts wouldn't want to give away the position of their fleet."

"Uh huh."

"There is something I can do, but it'll take a few days of work to make the tools. First I'm going to make sure you can fight this ship. Let's go back to the lifesystem pod."

A directed magnetic field would churn the interstellar plasma as it was guided into a Bussard ramjet. As a weapon it might be made to guide the plasma flow across the ship itself. The gunner would have to vary his shots, or an enemy pilot could compensate for the weapon's effect. If the local hydrogen density were uneven, that would hurt him. If the plasma were dense enough locally, the enemy could not even turn off his drive without being cremated. Part of the purpose of the ram fields was to shield the ship from the gamma ray particles it was burning for fuel.

"Hit him near a star, if you get the choice," said Brennan. "And don't let him do that to you."

The laser was surer death, if it hit a ship. But an enemy ship would be at least light-seconds away at the start of a battle. It would make a small, elusive target, its image delayed seconds or minutes. The thousand mile wings of a ram field would be easier to hit.

The guided bombs were many and varied. Some were simple fusion bombs. Others would throw bursts of hot plasma through a ram field, or carbon vapor to produce sudden surges in the burn rate, or half a ton of pressurized radon gas in a stasis field. Simple death or complicated. Some were mere decoys, silvered balloons.

Roy learned.

The wreck of Kobold was almost three months behind them, and Roy was at war. Lately he had come to enjoy these simulated battles, but he wasn't enjoying this one. Brennan was throwing everything at him. The Pak scouts had used a three gee drive until they crossed his wake, and then Wham! Six gees and closing. Some of his missiles were going wild; the scouts were doing something to the guidance. The pair dodged his laser with such ease that he'd turned the damn thing off. They'd used lasers on *him,* firing not only at his ship but at the field constriction behind him where hydrogen atoms met and fused, so that *Protector* surged unevenly and he had to worry for the generator mountings. They threw bombs at unreasonable velocities, probably through a linear accelerator. He had to dodge in slow random curves. *Protector* was not what you'd call maneuverable.

Three days he'd been in the lifesystem module, eating and drinking there and using pep pills instead of sleep. Playing Brennan's game. He was mad clean through. Within ships he could infer only from instruments, he imagined hard faces like Brennan's.

Two scouts closing from behind, and finally he hit one with the directed magnetic field and watched its ram field flare and dissipate.

That was when he realized that there were two *pairs* of ships in tandem. Damn Brennan anyway! He'd hit a lead ship, but the trailing ship was still there. . .and slowing. Somehow the loss of the lead ship had slowed it. Roy concentrated on the second team, which was still closing.

He tried a turn. Two ships linked should be less ma-

neuverable than one. . .and an hour later he knew that
they were. He'd turned only a fraction of a minute of arc,
but they had turned less. He could keep up his dodging
and still turn inside them.

He tried some of his weaponry on the lone ship behind
him.

Then half his weapons board was red, and he had to
guess what had exploded in the trailing pod. Probably
that idiot projector: he'd been trying to punch a hole in
the lone ship's ram field. He bet his ship he was right,
and gambled further that the explosion had wrecked his
laser, which might otherwise have been of some use. He
fired a flurry of bombs from the side of the cargo pod opposite the explosion. The lead ship of the remaining pair
flared and died.

That left two, each the trailing ship of a pair, making
less than his own acceleration. He dithered a bit, then
ran for it. He continued to dodge missiles and laser beams.

The scouts fell away. He watched them dwindling. . .
and then one wasn't dwindling. . .and it finally dawned on
him that that one had picked up acceleration somehow
and was coming up from behind at something like eight
gees.

Roy's first impulse was to scream, "Brennan! What are
you trying to pull?"

He'd done that before. This time he restrained it. Because he'd guessed the answer: the second ship was
burning *Protector's* own exhaust! Never mind how: that
was it, that was why they moved in tandem.

He dropped two half-tons of radon with the drives dis-
connected.

Radon has a short half-life: it *has* to be kept in stasis.
The generator was outside the bomb shell, and was partly
soft iron. The enemy's ram field tore it apart. A minute
later the radon was in the constriction, and incredible
things were happening: radon fusing to transuranian elements, then fissioning immediately. The constriction exploded. The ram field sparkled like a department store
Xmas tree gone manic. The Pak ship flared into a small
white point, fading.

The last Pak ship was far behind.

Coming out of it was a slow process. Roy had to keep telling himself: this isn't real, this is only pretend. He jumped violently when Brennan's alien head poked through the twing.

Then he shouted, "What the hell was that about him burning my exhaust?"

"I just knew you'd bring that up," said Brennan. "I'll tell you in detail, but first let's talk about the battle."

"Screw the battle!"

"You did well," said Brennan. "There isn't much left of your weapons pod, but that's okay if you don't meet any more scouts. You don't have reserve fuel to get into orbit around Wunderland; you used too much. But you can abandon *Protector* and land with the cargo ship."

"That's nice. That's very reassuring. Now tell me how a Pak scout can burn my own exhaust and come tearing up my tailpipe!"

"It's one possible configuration. In fact, it's the one I'm about to start looking for, because it'd be easy to find. I can show you better with diagrams."

Roy had calmed down a bit when they reached the *Flying Dutchman's* control room. He had also started to shake. Three days in *Protector's* control chair had left him exhausted.

Brennan looked at him thoughtfully. "Want to put this off?"

"No."

"Okay, I'll make it quick. Let's look at what your ram field does. It picks up interstellar hydrogen in a path three thousand miles across. It sweeps it in via magnetic fields, pinches it together hard enough and long enough to produce some fusion. What comes out is helium and some leftover hydrogen and some higher-order fusion products."

"Right."

"It's also a hot, fairly tight stream. Eventually it'll spread out into nothing, like any rocket exhaust. But suppose a ship were following you, *here*." Brennan made pictures on the screen: two tiny ships, the second following a hundred miles behind the first. He spread a wide cone before the lead ship, converging it almost to a point behind the ship. A needle shape with the ship in its point—the ship's protective shield—brought the incoming hydrogen into a ring shaped constriction.

"You're collecting the fuel for him. His ram field is only a hundred miles across—" Brennan drew a much narrower cone. "—and it gives him finer control over his fuel flow. It's already hot and dense. It burns better, in higher-order fusion. The exhaust would be rich in beryllium.

"It's just one of the things those last remaining Pak might have tried. The lead ship would be nothing but a ram: no onboard fuel, no insystem motor, no cargo. It would have to be towed up to ramscoop speed. The following ship is heavier, but it gets more thrust."

"You think that's what's coming at us?"

"Maybe. There are other ways to work it. Two ships, independent, held together by a gravity generator. In a pinch they could split up. Or the lead ship might be the ship proper, with the hind ship only an afterburner. Either way, I can find them. They'll produce beryllium frequencies like a neon sign on the sky. All I've got to do is build the detector."

"Need help?"

"Eventually. Go to sleep. We'll try another dry run in a month or so."

Roy stopped in the doorway. "That long?"

"Just to keep you on your toes. You're as ready as you'll ever be. Only, be more careful with that electromagnetic projector. When you wake up I'll show you what the Pak scouts did to it."

"What *you* did to it."

"What they would have done. Go to sleep."

Brennan was in the machine shop for three days. If he slept he slept there. He skipped meals there. Whatever he was doing filled the machine shop with constant racket and sent a humming vibration through the rock of the *Flying Dutchman.*

Roy read a couple of old novels stored in the computer. He floated through bare rock caverns and corridors, and was oppressed by the sensation of being underground. He worked himself to exhaustion in the exercise room. Free fall had cost him some muscle tone. Have to do something about that.

He researched Wunderland and found about what he expected. Gee: 61%. Population: 1,024,000. Colonized area: 3,000,000 square miles. Largest town: München, population: 800. Farewell, city life. Come to that, München would probably look like New York to him by the time he got there.

There was a time on the fourth day when he found the machine shop quiet and Brennan apparently asleep. He was about to leave when Brennan opened his eyes and started talking.

"You depend too much on those long, slow turns," he said. "The way to dodge Pak weaponry is to vary your thrust. Keep opening and closing the constriction in the ram field. When they throw something like a laser pulse into the constriction, open it. Nothing's going to fuse if you don't squeeze the plasma tight enough."

Roy wasn't flustered. He was getting used to Brennan's habit of resuming a subject that may have been broken off days ago. He said, "That last ship could have done that when I threw radon at him."

"Sure, if he did it fast enough. At good ramscoop velocities the shit should be in the constriction before he knows it's reached the ram field, especially as you didn't put any rocket thrust on it. That was good thinking, Roy. Memo for you: don't ever follow a ship that's running. There are too many things he can throw into your ram field. Hopefully we'll be doing the running in any battle."

Roy remembered what he had come for. "You're two days past dinnertime. I thought I'd—"

"Not hungry. My prism's in the oven, and I've got to wait for it to cool."

"I could bring—"

"No thanks."

"Any significance?"

"Didn't I tell you I was predictable? If there aren't any Pak scouts in the vicinity, you could just as well go on to Wunderland alone. Most of what I know about the Pak is stored in the computer. When a protector feels not needed, he doesn't eat."

"So you're kind of hoping we find Pak scouts."

Brennan laughed: a credible chuckle, though his mouth didn't move. His face wasn't hard, exactly; it was like wrinkled leather. It was his mouth that was like hard shell. Too much of human expression is in the mouth.

On the evening of the same day he came out towing three hundred pounds of machinery, of which a big, solid crystal prism was a prominent part. He wouldn't let Roy help tow it, but they set it up together at the focus of the *Flying Dutchman's* telescope. Roy brought him a sandwich then, and made him eat it. The Jewish mother role irritated him, but so did the thought of going on to Wunderland alone.

Brennan was gone when Roy came looking for him, around mid-afternoon of the fifth day. Roy found him in the one room from which he was forbidden, the hydroponics garden. Brennan was moving down the side of an open tank, consuming sweet potatoes one after another.

The prism threw a rainbow spectrum across a white surface. Brennan pointed to a bright green line. "Beryllium light, blue-shifted," he said. "And the helium lines are up in the violet. Ordinarily beryllium is in the infrared."

"Blue-shifted." Any school child knew what that meant. "He's coming down our throats."

"Maybe not. He's coming toward us, but maybe not dead on. We're only a couple of light-weeks out from Sol, and he's a light-year away, and I think he's decelerating. I'll have to check to see if we're getting his exhaust. But I think he's headed for Sol."

"Brennan, that's worse."

"It's just as bad as it can get. We'll know in a month. He'll have moved by then. We'll have some paralax on him."

"A month! But—"

"Just a minute. Calm down. How far can he go in a month? He's way below lightspeed; we're probably going faster than he is. A month won't cost us much—and I've got to know how many there are, and where they are, and where they're going. And I've got to build something."

"What?"

"A widget. Something I dreamed up after we found the Pak fleet, when I saw that there might be Pak scouts around. The designs are in the computer."

Roy did not fear loneliness. He feared its opposite. Brennan was an odd companion, and *Protector* was going to be cramped when they finally left the *Flying Dutchman*. For a week or so Roy stayed away from the observatory, consciously savoring his alone-ness. In the empty exercise room he hovered in midair, swinging his arms and legs in wide circles. Later he would want to remember the room. Even this half-hollowed ball of rock was too small for a man who would rather be climbing a mountain.

Once he suggested another dry run. Brennan's models of the Pak scouts would be more accurate now. But Brennan wasn't having any. "You know as much as you're ever going to about fighting Pak. Does that scare you?"

"Hell, yes."

"Glad to hear it."

One day Brennan wasn't in the laboratory. Roy went looking for him. The longer it took the more stubborn he got; but Brennan didn't seem to be anywhere aboard.

He finally asked himself, "How would Brennan handle this? Logic. If he's not inside, then he's outside. What's outside that he might need?"

Right. Vacuum, and access to the surface.

The tree, the grass, the mud of the pond bottom were all freeze-dried and dead. The stars were bright and eerie, and more real than they had seemed on a vision screen. Roy could see them as a battlefield: the unseen worlds as territories to be fought over, the gas shells around stars as death traps for an unwary warrior.

He spotted Brennan's torch.

Brennan was working in vacuum, building. . .something. His redesigned pressure suit seemed both alien and anachronistic, and the chest design was a detail from Dali: a Madonna and Child, very beautiful. A torn loaf of bread floated within the window in the Child's torso, and he looked down at it with an adult, thoughtful gaze.

"Don't come too close," Brennan said into his suit mike. "I had plenty of time to fiddle with this ball of rock while I was shaping Kobold. There are deposits of pure elements under all this landscaping."

"What are you making?"

"Something that should collapse a polarized gravity generator at a distance. If generated gravity is what they're using to hold their ships in tandem, they'll have to polarize it to make it work over those distances. We know they know how to do it. They'll put the generator on the trailing ship, because that's the ship that's producing enough excess power to maintain the field."

"Suppose they're using something else?"

"So I waste a month. But I won't believe they're using cables. In deceleration mode even a Pak cable won't stand up to the exhaust from the trailing ship. I might believe they loaded everything on the trailing ship and used the lead ship purely as a stripped Bussard ramjet— a compressor. But they'd lose power and maneuverability.

"I've been trying to design a Pak scout ship myself. It isn't easy, because I don't know what they've got. The worst thing I can think of from our viewpoint is two independent ships with heavy, versatile ram field generators. That way if you lost a couple of lead ships in a battle, you could link the trailing ships, and vice versa."

"Yah."

"But I don't believe it. The more widgetry they put into each ship, the fewer ships they wind up with. I think they'd compromise. The lead ship is a Bussard ramjet, built to fight, but not too different from ours. It's the trailing ship that's versatile, with the oversized adjustable ram field generator. You could link two trailing ships, but not two lead ships. The lead ships are more vulnerable anyway. You saw that."

"Then these scouts are tougher than what I fought."

"And there are three of them."

"Three."

"They're coming in a cone, through—you remember that map of the space around Sol? There's a region that's almost all red dwarfs, and they're coming through that. I think the idea is to map an escape route for the fleet, in case something goes wrong at Sol. Otherwise they'll see to it that Sol is clean, then go on to other yellow dwarf stars. At the moment they're all about a light year from Sol and about eight light-months apart."

Roy looked up. Where within the battlefield—? He found Sol easily, but he couldn't remember the direction of the first scout. He shivered in his suit, though it was far more comfortable than it had ever been. Brennan had been tinkering with it.

"There could be more."

"I doubt it," said Brennan. "I didn't find any more beryllium traces at any frequency shift."

"Suppose they came in ones instead of twos. They'd show as ordinary Bussard ships."

"I don't believe it. Look, they need to be able to *see* each other. If a scout disappears, the others want to know it."

"All right. Now we've got to keep them away from Sol. How about using ourselves as a decoy?"

"Right."

That absent-minded monosyllable was disconcerting. It happened every so often, this implication that Brennan had already thought it through, in every detail, long ago. When he didn't say any more, Roy asked, "Anything I can do to help?"

"No. I've got to finish this. Improve your mind. Brush

up on local astronomy; it's our battle map. Look up Home. We're not going to Wunderland now. We're going to Home, if we get the choice."

"How come?"

"Let's say I'm planning to make a right angle turn in deep space. Home's the easiest target after that. They've also got a good industrial civilization."

HOME: Epsilon Indi 2, second of five planets in a system which also includes 200 asteroids randomly distributed in charted orbits. Gravity: 1.08 Diameter: 8800 miles. Rotation: 23 hours 10 minutes. Year: 181 days. Atmosphere: 23% oxygen, 76% nitrogen, 1% nontoxic trace gasses. Sea level pressure: 11 pounds/square inch.

One moon, diameter: 1200 miles, gravity: .2, surface composition: roughly lunar.

Discovery reported 2094, via ramrobot exploration probe. Settled 2189, by a combination of slowboats and ramrobots...

Settling Home had been made easier by two new techniques. The slowboats had carried sixty colonists each, in stasis. Sixty colonists would have filled three or four slowboats a century earlier. And, though no living thing could survive travel in a ramrobot, it had proved possible to ship fuel to the slowboats via ramrobot. An older technique was used extensively: colony supplies were shipped via ramrobot to orbit about Home, saving room aboard the slowboats. Rams that failed on the way would fail in time for replacements to be sent.

The original colonists had planned to call their new world Flatland. Perhaps it amused them to think of themselves and their descendants as flatlanders. Once on Home they had changed their minds: a belated attack of patriotism.

Population: 3,200,000. Colonized area: 6,000,000 square miles. Principal cities... Roy spent some time memorizing the maps. Cities and towns had tended to form in the forks of rivers. The farming communities were all near the sea. Home had sea life but little land life, and farming of any kind required a complete ecology; but sea life was used extensively for fertilizer.

There were extensive mining industries, all confined to Home itself.

Communication with Earth formed a principal industry, which tended to produce other industries at a steady rate.

Three million. . . A population of three million at this date meant a heavy birthrate, even if initially augmented by bottle-grown babies and later by more colony ships. Roy hadn't thought of that aspect of moving to a colony world. There was a pride in being the father of many children. . .a pride that would have less meaning on Home, where you didn't have to prove genius or invent the wheel or something just to get the license. Still. . .he would have children on two worlds.

Still, Home would probably change for the worse when Brennan put it on a war footing. War was never fun, and —Roy ought to know—this kind of interstellar war was going to be long and slow. What kind of mind did it take to plan a hundred and seventy-three years in advance?

The thing Brennan was building was slightly taller than he was, heavy and cylindrical. He had moved it near one of the great doors beneath which the components of *Protector* waited.

"I want to be damn sure I can get adequate polarization of the field," he told Roy. "Otherwise the whole of *Protector* could wind up falling into it."

"Like Kobold, huh? Can you do it?"

"I think so. The Pak did it. . .we assume. If *I* can't do it I'll have to assume they're holding their ships in tandem some other way."

"Where's it going to ride?"

"I'll string it behind the weapons pod. And your cargo ship behind the lifesystem. We'll look somewhat strung out. It won't surprise the Pak any that I've fiddled with the design of the ship. They would, given the tools and raw materials."

"What makes you think they don't have them?"

"I don't think that," said Brennan. "I keep wondering what they'll build for me once they know what I've got."

One day he was back in the observatory. "All finished," he said briskly. "I can get the polarized gravity field I need. Which means a Pak could get it, which means they're probably using it."

"Then we're ready for takeoff. *Finally.*"

"As soon as I know what the Pak scouts are doing. Twelve hours, I promise."

In the 'scope screen the Pak scouts showed as tiny green lights, a good distance from each other, and measurably closer to Sol. Brennan seemed to know just where to find them, but then he'd been observing them for two months. "Still making three gravities," he said. "They'll be at rest when they reach Sol. I've been right about them so far. Let's see how far I can carry it."

"Isn't it about time you told me what you've got in mind?"

"Right. We're leaving the *Flying Dutchman,* now. The hell with convincing them I'm coming from Van Maanen's Star. They're seeing us from the wrong angle anyway. I'll take off for Wunderland at one point aught eight gee, hold for a month or so, then boost to two gee and start my turn away from them. If they spot me in that time, they'll turn after me, if I can make them think I'm dangerous enough."

"Why," he started to ask, before he remembered that one point aught eight was the surface gravity of Home.

"I don't want them to think I'm a Pak. Not now. They're more likely to chase an alien capable of building or stealing a Pak ship. And I don't want to use Earth gravity. It'd be a giveaway."

"Okay, but now they'll think you came from Home. Do you want that?"

"I think I do."

Home wasn't getting much choice about entering the war. Roy sighed. Who was? He said, "What if two of them go on to Sol and the other comes after us?"

"That's the beauty of it. They're still eight light-months apart. Each of them has to make his turn eight months before he sees the others make theirs. Turning back could cost them another year and a half. By then they may just decide I'm too dangerous to get away." Brennan looked up from the screen. "You don't share my enthusiasm."

"Brennan, it'll be two bloody years before you even know if they've turned after you. One year for them to spot you, one year before you see them make the turn."

"Not quite two years. Close enough." Brennan's eyes were dark beneath their shelf of bone. "Just how much boredom can you stand?"

"I don't know."

"I can make you a stasis field capsule, using two of the radon bombs."

Ye gods, a reprieve! "Hey, that's good. But you'd have to throw away the radon, wouldn't you?"

"Hell, no. I wouldn't *do* it. I'll just move two of the bombs up into the lifesystem and rig a metal shell between the generators."

Conscience smote him. "Look, do you feel the same way I do? About waiting, I mean. We could take turns on watch."

"Come off it. I could wait for Judgment Day without unfolding my hands, if I had a reason."

Roy laughed. The constant delays had really been getting to him.

The stasis box was a soft iron cylinder seven feet long, welded to the shells of two radon bombs to give a total length of fourteen feet. They'd had to run it through the door linking the kitchen and the exercise room.

It fitted Roy like a coffin. It felt like a coffin. Roy's teeth clamped shut, holding words back, as he waited for Brennan to shut the curved hatch.

It made a very solid sound.

Are you sure this will work?

Idiot. Home was settled this way. Of course it'll work. Brennan would've thought he was a fool.

He waited in darkness. He imagined Brennan finishing

the welding, testing currents and circuitry and so forth before linking the switch. Then—he wouldn't sense time passing. When the door opened would he foolishly ask, "Didn't it work?"

Gravity dropped suddenly on him from above. Roy hit the floor and stayed there. He grunted in shock and surprise. No need to ask: *Protector* was in flight, making three gravities easy.

The hatch swung back. Brennan caught him under the armpits and lifted. His hands were hard as hatchet blades. He half walked, half carried Roy to a crash chair. He shifted his grip to Roy's belt and slowly lowered him into the crash chair.

"I'm not a cripple," Roy grunted.

Brennan reclined Roy's chair. "You'll feel like one." He lowered himself into the other chair with the same care. "They bit. They're coming after me. We've been doing two point one six gee for two years now. I kept it that low because I was afraid they'd think I could outrun them."

"Can you? How are they doing?"

"I'll show you." Brennan played with the keyboard, and a starscape filled the screen. "This is two years action telescoped into ten minutes. You'll see it better that way. Can you spot the Pak ships?"

"Yah." Three green dots, visibly elongated, visibly moving. Presently a brilliant white light—Sol—drifted on from stage left.

"I got some paralax on them while they were making the turn. Low acceleration, but a fast turn, about the same turning radius as ours. I think the individual ships must have turned separately. Now they're back in tandem, coming at us at five and a half gee."

"You guessed that almost on the nose."

"Remember, I spent several days with Phssthpok as my mentor. I figured a healthy Pak could take three gee forever, and six gee for five years, which would kill him. They knew their limits and designed for 'em."

Three green stars drifted toward Sol. Presently, one by one, they went out and came on again. Now their color was dimmer, yellower. Roy tried to sit up against his own weight, but Brennan's hand pushed him back. "This is where they switched to acceleration mode."

Roy watched for another minute, but nothing happened, except that the green stars brightened slightly.

"This is where we stand now. Those images are about a light-year away. The ships themselves would be two light-months closer, assuming they've been chasing us at constant acceleration. In a few months we'll know whether any of them turned back. Otherwise the lead pair would reach us in about fourteen months ship's time, except that at some point they'll go into deceleration mode and see if they can hurt us with the backblast, which means it'll take a little longer."

"Fourteen months."

"Ship's time. We're doing relativistic speeds. We'll cover a lot more distance than that."

Roy shook his head. "It comes to me that you woke me just a bit early."

"Not really. I can't think of anything they could do to me over this distance, but I'm not certain they haven't thought of something. I want you awake and fully recovered if something happens to me. And I want these bombs back in the weapons pod."

"It sounds unlikely. What could they do to you that wouldn't kill me too?"

"*All* right, I had another reason for waking you. I could have rigged you a stasis box right after we left Kobold. Why didn't I?"

Roy felt tired. Gravity pulling blood from his brain? "I had to be trained. Trained to fight this ship."

"And are you in condition to fight? Like a pile of wet noodles you are! When things start happening I want you able to move."

He did feel like a pile of wet noodles. Hell. "All right. Shall we—?"

"No chance. For today you just lie there. Tomorrow we'll walk you around a bit. Pretend you've been sick." Brennan glanced sideways at him. "Don't take it so hard. Let me show you something."

Roy had forgotten that this was Phssthpok's own control module, with a hull that could be made transparent at will. It startled him when the wall went invisible. Then he looked.

They were moving *that* fast. The stars behind were red-shifted to black. Ahead, above, they were violet-white. And from the zenith they swept back like a rainbow: violet, blue, green, yellow, orange, red, in expanding rings. The effect was total; all of *Protector*'s interior partitions had turned transparent too.

"No man has ever seen this before you," said Brennan, "unless you count me a man." He pointed. "There. That's Epsilon Indi."

"It's off to the side."

"We're not headed for it directly. I told you, I'm planning to make a right angle turn in space. There's only one place I can do it."

"Can we beat the scouts there?"

"Barely ahead of the second ship, I think. We'll have to fight the first one."

Roy slept ten hours a day. Twice a day he took long walks, from the control room around the exercise room and back, an extra lap each day. Brennan walked with him, ready to reach out. He could kill himself if he fell wrong.

It *felt* like he'd been sick. He didn't like it.

One day they threw the ram field constriction wide open, and—in free fall, protected from the oncoming gamma rays by the scintillating dome of the inner ram field—they moved the radon bombs back to their nests in the weapons pod. For those two hours Roy had his strength back, and he gloried in it. Then he was back in two point one six gee, a four-hundred-pound weakling.

With Brennan's help he worked out a calendar of events for the longest war on record:

> 33,000 BC: *Phssthpok departs Pak.*
> 32,800 BC: *First emigration wave departs Pak.*
> 32,500 BC: *Second emigration wave.*
> X: *Pak scouts.*

> *2125 AD: Phssthpok arrives Sol. Brennan turns protector.*
>
> *2340 AD: Kidnap of Truesdale.*
>
> *2341 AD, October: Discovery of Pak fleet.*
>
> *2341 AD, November: Departure of Flying Dutchman. Destruction of Kobold.*
>
> *2342 AD, May: Discovery of Pak scouts.*
>
> *2342 AD, July: Truesdale in stasis. Departure of Protector.*

At this point relativity would begin to screw up the dating. Roy decided to go by ship's time, given that he would have to live through it.

> *2344 AD, April: Pak ships sighted altering course.*
>
> *2344 AD, July: Truesdale out of stasis.*
>
> *HYPOTHETICAL*
>
> *2345 AD, September: Meet first Pak ships.*
>
> *2346 AD, March: Right angle turn (?) Lose Pak scouts.*
>
> *2350 AD: Arrive Home. Adjust calendars.*

Roy studied Home. Over many decades there had been considerable message laser traffic between Earth and Home. There were travelogues and biographies and novels and studies of the native life. Brennan had already read it all; at his reading speed he hadn't needed anything like his two years head start.

The novels had an odd flavor, a nest of unspoken assumptions that he couldn't quite pin down, until he asked Brennan about it.

Brennan had an eidetic memory and a fine grasp of subtleties. "Partly it's a Belter thing," he told Roy. "They know they're in an artificial environment, and they feel protective toward it. This bit in *The Shortest Day,* where Ingram gets shot for walking on the grass—that's a direct steal from something that happened early in Home history. You'll see it in Livermore's biography. As for their burial customs, that's probably left over from the early days. Remember, the first hundred people who died on Home knew each other like you knew your brother. Anyone's death was important in those days, to everyone in the world."

"Yah, when you put it like that. . .and they've got more room, too. They don't need crematoriums."

"Good point. There's endless useless land, useless until it's fertilized somehow. The bigger the graveyard grows, the more it shows the human conquest of Home. Especially when trees and grass start growing where nothing ever grew before."

Roy thought the idea over, and decided he liked it. How could you lose? Until the Pak arrived.

"These Homers don't seem particularly warlike," he said. "We're going to have to get them on a war footing before the Pak scouts find Home. Somehow."

But Brennan wouldn't talk about that. "All our information is ten to a hundred years old. I don't know enough about Home as it is now. We don't know how the politics have gone. I've got some ideas. . .but mainly we'll be playing it by ear." He slapped Roy on the back: a sensation like being hit by a sackful of walnuts. "Cheer up. We may never get there at all."

Brennan was a wordy bastard when he had the time. More: he was making a clear effort to keep Roy entertained. Perhaps he was entertaining himself as well. It was all very well to talk of a Pak spending eight hundred years sitting in a crash couch; but Brennan had been raised human.

They played games, using analog programs set up in the computer. Brennan always won at chess, checkers, Scrabble and the like. But gin and dominoes were games hard to learn, easy to master. They stuck to those. Brennan still won more than his share, perhaps because he could read Roy's face.

They held long discussions on philosophy and politics and the paths mankind was taking. They read a great deal. Brennan had stockpiled material on all the inhabited worlds, not just Home and Wunderland. Once he said, "I was never sure where I might wind up steering a crippled ship in search of breathing-air and a chance at repair facilities. I'm still not sure."

Over many months Roy began exercising more and sleeping less. He was strong now; he no longer felt like a cripple. His muscles were harder than they had ever been in his life.

And the Pak ships came steadily closer.

Through the clear twing they were invisible, black in a black sky. They were still too distant, and not all of their output was visible light. But they showed under magnification: the sparkling of hysteresis in the wide wings of the ram field, and in the center the small steady light of the drive.

Ten months after Roy had emerged from the stasis box, the light of the leading pair went out. Minutes later it came on again, but it was dim and flickering.

"They've gone into deceleration mode," said Brennan.

In an hour the enemy's drive was producing a steady glow, the red of blue-shifted beryllium emission.

"I'll have to start my turn too," said Brennan.

"You *want* to fight them?"

"That first pair, anyway. And if I turn now it'll give us a better window."

"Window?"

"For that right-angle turn."

"Listen, you can either explain that right-angle turn business or stop bringing it up."

Brennan chuckled. "I have to keep you interested somehow, don't I?"

"What are you planning? Close orbit around a black hole?"

"My compliments. That's a good guess. I've found a nonrotating neutron star. . .almost nonrotating. I wouldn't dare dive into the radiating gas shell around a pulsar, but this beast seems to have a long rotation period and no gas envelope at all. And it's nonluminous. It must be an old one. The scouts'll have trouble finding it, and I can chart a hyperbola through the gravity field that'll take us straight to Home."

Casual as Brennan sounded, that sounded dangerous. And the Pak scouts moved steadily closer. Four months later the first pair of ships was naked-eye visible, a blue-green point alone in a black sky.

They watched it grow. Its drive flame made wiggly

lines on Brennan's instruments. "Not too bad," said Brennan. "Of course you'd be dead if you went outside for awhile."

"Yah."

"I wonder if he's close enough to try the gravity widget."

Roy watched, but did not understand, as Brennan played his control board. Brennan had never showed him how to use that particular weapon. It was too delicate, too intuitive. But two days later the bluegreen light went out.

"Got him," Brennan said with evident satisfaction. "Got the hind ship, anyway. He probably fell into his own black hole."

"Is that what your widget does? Collapse somebody else's gravity generator into a hypermass?"

"That's what it's supposed to do. But let's just see." He used the spectroscope. "Right. Helium lines only. Hind ship gone, lead ship coming on at about one gee. He'll be passing me sooner than he expected. He's got two choices now. Run or ram. I think he'll try to ram—so to speak."

"He'll try to throw his ram field across us. That'd kill us, wouldn't it?"

"Yes. Him too. Well—" Brennan dropped some missiles, then started a turn.

Two days later the lead ship was gone. Brennan swung *Protector* back on course. It had all seemed very like one of Brennan's dry runs, except that it took even longer.

The next pass was different.

It was six months before the remaining Pak came close; but one day they were naked-eye visible, two wan yellow dots in the blackness astern. Their speed had dropped to not much above *Protector*'s own.

From an initial separation of eight light-months the scout pairs had converged over the years, until they were nearly side by side, thirty light-hours behind *Protector*.

"Time to try the gravity widget again," said Brennan.

While Brennan played with the controls, Roy looked up at two yellow eyes glowing beyond the black shadow of the drive section. Intellectually he knew that he would see nothing for two and a half days. . .

And he was wrong. The flare came from below, lighting the interior of the lifesystem sphere. Brennan moved instantly, stabbing out with a stiff forefinger.

For a moment afterward, then, Brennan hovered wire-tense over the dials. Then he was himself again. "Reflexes still in order," he said.

"What happened?"

"They did it. They built a gravity widget like mine. My own widget collapsed into a hypermass, and the hypermass started eating its way up the cable. If I hadn't blown the cable in time it would have absorbed the weapons pod. The energy release would have killed us." Brennan opened the keyboard panel and began closing control elements down against future need. "Now we'll have to beat them to the neutron star. If they maintain their deceleration, we will."

"What are they likely to throw at us in the meantime?"

"Lasers for sure. They need heavy lasers anyway, to communicate with the main fleets. I'm going to opaque the twing." He did. Now they were locked inside a gray shell, the scouts showing only in the telescope screen. "Other than that. . .we're *all* in a bad way for throwing bombs. We're all decelerating. My missiles would be like going uphill; they couldn't reach them at this distance. They can reach me, but their bombs are going in the wrong direction. They'll go right through the ram field from behind."

"Good."

"Sure. Unless they're accurate enough to hit the ship itself. Well, we'll see."

The lasers came in two beams of searing green light, and *Protector* was blind aft. Part of *Protector*'s skin boiled away frighteningly. The underskin was mirror-surfaced.

"That won't hurt us until they get a lot closer," said

Brennan. But he worried about missiles. He began dodging at random, and life became uncomfortable as Brennan played with *Protector's* acceleration.

A cluster of small masses approached them. Brennan opened the ram field constriction wide, and they watched the explosions in relative comfort, though some of them shook the ship. Roy watched almost without fear. He was bothered by the growing feeling that Brennan and the Pak protectors were playing an elaborate game whose rules they both understood perfectly: a game like the space war games played by computer programmers. Brennan had known that he would get the first ships, that the others would ruin his widget, that in matching courses for a proper duel they would slow too far to catch him by the time they discovered the neutron star ahead. . .

A day out from the neutron star, one of the green war beams went out. "They finally saw it," said Brennan. "They're lining up for the pass. Otherwise they could wind up being flung off in opposite directions."

"They're awfully close," said Roy. They were, in a relative sense: they were four light-hours behind *Protector,* closer than Sol is to Pluto. "And you can't dodge much, can you? It'd foul our course past the star."

"Let me get this done," Brennan mumbled, and Roy shut up.

The thrust dropped easily to half a gee. *Protector* swung left, and the lifesystem pod swung oddly at the end of its cable.

Then Brennan turned the ram field off entirely. "There's a bit of a gas shell," he explained. "Now don't bug me for awhile."

Protector was in free fall, a sitting duck.

Eight hours later there were missiles. The scouts must have fired as soon as they saw the sparkle of *Protector's* ram field go out. Brennan dodged, using the insystem drive. The missiles he'd thrown at the scouts had no apparent effect: the hellish green light from the lead ship continued to bathe *Protector.*

"He's cut his ram field," Brennan said presently. "He'll have to cut his laser too, when he runs out of battery power." He looked at Roy for the first time in hours. "Get some sleep. You're half dead now. What'll you be like when we round the star?"

"All dead," Roy sighed. He reclined his chair. "Wake me up if he hits us, will you? I'd hate to miss anything."

Brennan didn't answer.

Three hours away, the neutron star was still invisible ahead of them. Brennan said, "Ready?"

"Ready." Roy was suited up, floating with one hand on the jamb of the airlock. There was still sleep in his eyes. His dreams had been fearsome.

"Go."

Roy went. The lock would pass only one man. He was at work when Brennan came through. Brennan had cut this close, to reduce radiation exposure from the neutron star's thin gas envelope, and to reduce the time the Pak had to blast away at unprotected men.

They detached the cable that led to the drive section, then used it to reel the drive section close, coiling the cable as it came. It was thick and heavy. They stowed it against the stern of the drive section.

They did the same with the cable that towed the weapons pod. Roy worked his two-gravity muscles with adrenalin flooding his system. He was well aware of the radiation sleeting through his body. This was war. . .but with something missing. He could not hate the Pak. He did not understand them well enough. If Brennan could hate them, he could have caught it from Brennan; but Brennan didn't. No matter that he called it war. What he was playing was high stakes poker.

Now the three main sections of *Protector* floated end to end. Roy boarded the Belt cargo ship for the first time in years. As he took his place at the controls, green light flooded the cabin. He dropped the sun screens fast.

Brennan came through the airlock shouting, "Foxed 'em! If they'd done that half an hour ago we'd have been cooked."

"I thought they'd used up their stored power."

"No, that would have been stupid, but they must be pretty low. They thought I'd wait to the last second before I took the ships apart. They don't know what I am yet!" he exulted. "And they don't know I have help. All right, we've got about an hour before we have to go outside. Get us lined up."

Roy used attitude jets to put the Belt ship fourth in line, behind *Protector's* weapons pod. It felt good to be handling controls, to be doing something constructive in Brennan's war. Through the sun screens the components of *Protector* glared green as hell. They were already drifting apart in the reaching tides of the mass ahead.

"Have you named that star yet?"

"No," said Brennan.

"You discovered it. You have the right."

"I'll call it Phssthpok's Star, then. Bear ye witness. I think we owe him that."

NAME: Phssthpok's Star. Later renamed BVS-1, by the Institute of Knowledge on Jinx.
CLASSIFICATION: Neutron star.
MASS: 1.3 times mass of Sol.
COMPOSITION: Eleven miles diameter of neutronium, topped by half a mile of collapsed matter, topped by perhaps twelve feet of normal matter.
SURFACE GRAVITY: 1.7×10^{11} G, Earth standard.
REMARKS: First nonradiating neutron star ever discovered. Atypical compared with many known pulsars; but stars of the BVS type would be difficult to find as compared with pulsars. BVS-1 may have started life as a pulsar, with a radiating gas shell, one hundred million to a billion years ago; then transferred its rotation to the gas shell, dissipating it in the process.

They were going to go past Phssthpok's Star damn fast.

The four sections of *Protector* fell separately. Even the Pak cable would not have held them together. Worse: the tidal effect would have pulled the sections into line with the star's center of mass. The four sections with their snapped cables would have emerged on wildly different orbits.

This way the self-maneuvering cargo ship could be used to link the other sections after perihelion. But he and Brennan could not ride it out here. The Belt ship's cabin was in the nose of the ship, too far from the center of mass.

Roy knew this intellectually. Before they left the ship he could *feel* it.

Protector had been three receding green dots before the Pak laser finally went out. Then they were invisible. And the neutron star was a dull red point ahead. Roy felt its tides pulling him forward against the crash webbing.

"Go," said Brennan.

Roy released the webbing. He stood up on the clear plastic of the nose port, then climbed along the wall. The rungs were made for climbing in the other direction. Maneuvering himself into the airlock was difficult. Minutes from now it would have been impossible. More minutes, and the tides would have crushed him against the nose port, a beetle beneath a heel.

The hull was smooth, without handholds. He couldn't wait here. He hung from the jamb, then dropped.

The ship fell away. He saw a tiny humanoid figure crouched in the airlock. Then four tiny flashes. Brennan had one of the high-velocity rifles. He was firing at the Pak.

Roy could feel the tides now, the whisper of a tug inside his body. His feet came down to the red dot ahead.

Brennan had dropped after him. He was using backpac jets.

The tug inside was stronger. Gentle hands at his head and feet were trying to pull him apart. The red dot was yellowing, brightening, coming up at him like a fiery bowling ball.

He thought about it for a good hour. Brennan had intimidated him to that extent. He thought it through backward and forward, and then he told Brennan he was crazy.

They were linked by three yards of line. The line was taut, though the neutron star was a tiny red dot behind them. And Brennan still had the gun.

"I'm not doubting your professional opinion," said Brennan. "But what symptom was it that tipped you off?"

"That gun. Why did you shoot at the Pak ship?"

"I want it wrecked."

"But you couldn't *hit* it. You were aiming right at it. I saw you. The star's gravity must have pulled the bullets off course."

"You think about it. If I'm really off my nut, you'd be justified in taking command."

"Not necessarily. Sometimes crazy is better than stupid. What I'm really afraid of is that shooting at the Pak ships might make sense. Everything else you do makes sense, sooner or later. If that makes sense I'm gonna quit."

Brennan was hunting for the cargo ship with a pair of binoculars. He said, "Don't do that. Treat it as a puzzle. If I'm not crazy, why did I fire at a Pak ship?"

"Dammit. The muzzle velocity isn't anything *like* good enough. . . How long have I got?"

"Two hours and fifty minutes."

"O-o-oh."

They were back aboard *Protector*'s isolated lifesystem by then, watching the vision screens and—in Brennan's case—a score of instruments besides. The second Pak team fell toward the miniature sun in four sections: a drive section like a two-edged ax, then a pillbox-shaped lifesystem section, then a gap of several hundred miles, then a much bigger drive section and another pillbox. The first pillbox was just passing perihelion when the neutron star flared.

A moment ago magnification had showed it as a dim red globe. Now a small blue-white star showed on its surface. The white spot spread, dimming; it spread across the surface without rising in any kind of cloud. Brennan's counters and needles began to chatter and twitch.

"That should kill him," Brennan said with satisfaction. "Those Pak pilots probably aren't too healthy anyway; they must have picked up a certain amount of radiation over thirty-one thousand light years riding behind a Bussard ramjet."

"I presume that was a bullet?"

"Yah. A steel-jacketed bullet. And we're moving against the spin of the star. I slowed it enough that the magnetic field would pick it up and slow it further, and keep on slowing it until it hit the star's surface. There were some uncertainties. I wasn't sure just when it would hit."

"Very tricky, Captain."

"The trailing ship probably has it worked out too, but there isn't anything he can do about it." Now the flare was a lemon glow across one flank of Phssthpok's Star. Suddenly another white point glowed at one edge. "Even if they worked it out in advance, they couldn't be sure I had the guns. And there's only one course window they can follow me through. Either I dropped something or I didn't. Let's see what the last pair does."

"Let's put *Protector* back together. I think that must be the drive section ahead."

"Right."

They worked for hours. *Protector* was fairly spread across the sky. Roy worked with his shoulders hunched against deadly green light, but it never came. The second pair of Pak scouts was dead.

Midway they stopped to watch events that had happened an hour ago: the third pair of Pak scouts reconnecting their ships in frantic haste, then using precious reserve fuel to accelerate outward from the star. "Thought so," Brennan grunted. "They don't know what kind of variable velocity weapon I've got, and they can't afford to die now. They're the last. And *that* puts them on a course that'll take them way the hell away from us. We'll beat them to Home by at least half a year."

Roy Truesdale was thirty-nine years old when he and Brennan rounded Phssthpok's Star. He was forty-three when they slowed below ram speed outside the Epsilon Indi system.

There were times during those four years when Roy thought he would go mad.

He missed women. It wasn't Alice Jordan he was missing now; he missed *women,* the varied score he had loved and the hundreds he had known slightly and the billions he had not. He missed his mother and his sister and his aunts and his ancestresses all the way back to Greatly 'Stelle.

He missed women and men and children and old people; people to fight with, to talk with, to love, to hate. One entire night he spent crying for all the people of Earth, taking care that Brennan shouldn't hear him; crying not for what the Pak fleet could do to them but just because they weren't here or he wasn't there.

He spent long periods in his room with the door locked. Brennan had put the lock on it, and Brennan could have picked that lock in thirty seconds, or opened the door with a single kick; but it had a psychological effect, and Roy was grateful for it.

He missed the space. On any random beach on Earth you could run down the curve of wet hard sand between sea and shore until there was no strength left in you to do anything but breathe. On Earth you could walk forever. In his locked room aboard *Protector,* no longer hampered by *Protector's* heavy acceleration, Roy paced endlessly between the walls.

Sometimes, alone, he cursed Brennan for using up all of the radon bombs. Otherwise he could have ridden this out in stasis. He wondered if Brennan had done it deliberately, for the company.

Sometimes he cursed Brennan for bringing him at all. A silly act for such an intelligence. At full acceleration *Protector* could have outrun the second and third pairs of scouts, with no need to fight. But three gravities might have injured Roy Truesdale.

He hadn't been that much use during the battles. Had Brennan brought him *only* for company? Or as a kind of mascot? Or—he toyed with another idea. One of Brennan's daughters had been named Estelle, hadn't she? She might have passed the name to her own daughter. Greatly 'Stelle.

That was an angry thought: that he had been brought only because he belonged to the protector's blood line, a living reminder of what Brennan was fighting for, to keep Brennan's interest in the war alive. Because he smelled right. Roy never asked him. He didn't really want to know.

"In a sense you're being subjected to sensory deprivation," Brennan told him once. That was not long before turnover, after they had tried something decidedly kooky: Brennan taking the parts of five experts of varying disciplines and accents, in a six-sided discussion of free will versus determinism. It hadn't worked. They were both trying too hard.

Roy was losing the urge to talk.

"We've got all kinds of entertainment," said Brennan, "but no conversation except mine. There's a limit to how much illusion you can get from me. But let's try something."

Roy didn't ask what he meant. He found out a few days later, when he walked into his room and found himself looking down a mountainside.

Now he spent more time in there than ever. Every so often Brennan would change the environment. The 270° holograph vision tapes had come out of the computer memory, and they were all of worlds other than Earth. After a few false starts he avoided scenes that involved people. The people never noticed Roy; they behaved as if he did not exist. That was bad.

He would sit for hours, staring out into the faintly unearthly landscapes, wishing that he could walk out into them. Too much of that was bad too, and he would have to turn them off.

It was during such a time—with the walls around him nothing but walls—that he began wondering again as to just what Brennan was planning on Home.

The Pak scouts had veered wide during the pass around the neutron star. Now their enormous turning radius had finally aimed them toward Home; but their 5.5 gee acceleration would not compensate for the time they had lost. They were out of the running as far as *Protector* was concerned. And Home would have ten months to prepare for their arrival.

A peaceful people was not that easily persuaded to prepare for all-out defense. It took time to convert factories to make weapons. Just how big a threat was one pair of Pak scouts?

"I'm sure they could destroy a planet," Brennan said judiciously when Roy put it to him. "A planet is a big target, and environmental systems are delicate, and it can't dodge like a Bussard ramjet. Aside from that, a Pak scout was probably *designed* to wreck planets. If it can't do that, what good is it?"

"We'll have less than a year to get ready for them."

"Stop worrying. That's long enough. Home already has message lasers that can reach Earth. That speaks well for their accuracy and their power. We'll use them as cannon. And I've got designs for induced gravity weapons."

"But will they build them? These are peaceful people in a stable society!"

"We'll talk them into it."

Sitting in his room, staring into an empty, stormy seascape, Roy wondered at Brennan's optimism. Had he grown unfamiliar with the way breeders thought? "I've stopped taking chances," Brennan had said once. Well?

There had never been a war on Home. . .according to the tapes of their communications to Earth. Their novels rarely dealt in violence. Once they had used fusion bombs to shape harbors; but then they had the harbors, and now they didn't even have the factories any more.

Had Brennan seen something in their novels—a buried violence—that Roy had not?

One day it occurred to him that there was a solution.

It was a horrifying thought. He never mentioned it to Brennan. He feared that it was evidence of his own madness. He conscientiously resumed his long conversations with Brennan; he tried to take some interest in the very predictable course of the remaining Pak; he offered sug-

gestions for the vision walls of his cubical; he played gin
and dominoes. He exercised. He was turning into a mountain of muscle. Sometimes he awed himself.

"Teach me to fight Pak," he once asked Brennan.

"No way," said Brennan.

"The subject might arise. If a Pak ever wanted to take
a breeder prisoner—"

"All right, come on. I'll show you."

They cleared out the exercise room, and they fought.
In half an hour Brennan "killed" him something like
thirty times, pulling his karate blows with exquisite accuracy. Then he let Roy hit him several times. Roy delivered killing blows with a vicious enthusiasm Brennan
may have found enlightening. Brennan even admitted that
they hurt. But Roy was convinced.

Nonetheless they made the fights part of their program.

There were all kinds of ways to kill time. And the time
passed. Sometimes it crawled, excruciatingly slow; but always it passed.

There was one Jupiter-sized mass in the Epsilon Indi
system. Godzilla, Epsilon Indi V, was out of *Protector*'s
path as they braked in at three thousand miles per second. But Brennan veered a bit to show Roy a wondrous
sight.

They slid past a glittering translucent sphere of ice
crystals. It was Godzilla's Trojan point, and it looked
like a vast Xmas tree ornament; but to Roy it was a
Welcome sign. He began to believe they would make it.

Two days later, at 1000 miles/second, the ram field
was no longer doing anything useful. Brennan turned it
off. "Home in forty-two hours," he said. "I could sky-
dive the sun and use the ram field in the solar wind, but
what the hell. We've got plenty of fuel, and I sense
somehow that you're anxious to get down."

"Oddly enough." Roy wore a hungry grin. "Not that I
haven't enjoyed your company." He had Home in the
telescope screen. Home looked like Earth: deep blue
swirled with the white frosting of clouds, the outlines of

continents almost invisible. He felt a throb in his throat. This past year, his vision walls had showed only scenes from Home.

"Listen," he said, "are we going to wait for the ferries or just go down?"

"I thought I'd put *Protector* in distant orbit and go down with the cargo ship. We may need it to refuel *Protector*. Homers haven't done much with their asteroid resources. They may not have any cargo ships."

"All right. Before you turn on the insystem drive, why don't I just go over to the cargo ship and put it through a countdown?"

Brennan studied him for a moment. It was the kind of considering look that sometimes had Roy thinking he'd made a foolish suggestion. But, "All right. That'll save some time. Call me when you're aboard."

Home was already naked-eye visible, a white star not far from the sun. Roy boarded, stripped off his suit, went to the controls and called Brennan. Shortly *Protector* was again under thrust, backing toward Home at one Home gravity.

Roy started his inspection with the life support systems. All okay. The drive system checked out as far as instruments could tell. Roy worried that the drive tube might have been bent out of alignment by the tidal force of Phssthpok's Star. They had never had a chance to inspect for that. They wouldn't, until the cargo ship cut loose from *Protector*.

There was no landing gear to inspect. He'd land in a harbor; the ship would float.

He put twelve hours into his countdown, then broke for a nap. By now Brennan would have called whatever passed for spaceport facilities on Home. In another twelve hours. . .

Under one Home gravity he slept less, and lightly. He woke in the dim light, remembering his odd suspicions of Brennan. There was a faint smile on his face.

He went over them again. . .expecting to see how ridiculous they were. He'd been a bit paranoid then. Man was not meant to live locked in with a not-quite-human being for six years.

He went over his suspicions again, and they were logical. The idea was still horrid, but he could not find the logical flaw.

That bothered him.

And he still didn't know just what Brennan planned for Home.

He got up and prowled the ship. He found something Alice had stowed aboard, long ago: paints for a pressure suit. There had never been a design on the chest of Roy's suit. He draped the suit across a chair and stood before it, waiting for inspiration. But the inspiration that came to him was a vivid flourescent target.

Sucker. If he was right—but he couldn't be right.

He called Brennan. *Have it out—*

"All okay here," said Brennan. "How're things at your end?"

"Green bird, as far as I can tell without actually flying it."

"Good."

Roy found that he was stupidly trying to read expression in the hard face. "Brennan, something occurred to me a while ago. I never mentioned it—"

" 'Bout two and a half years back? I thought something was bothering you besides the lack of a harem."

"Maybe I'm nuts," said Roy. "Maybe I was nuts then. It hit me that you'd have a lot easier job of talking the Home population into backing your war, if you first—" He almost didn't say it. But of *course* Brennan had *thought* of it. "If you first seeded the planet with tree-of-life."

"That wouldn't be nice."

"No, it wouldn't. But will you *please* explain to me why it isn't logical?"

"It isn't logical," said Brennan. "The crop would take too long to grow."

"Yah," Roy said in a burst of relief. Then, "Yah, but

you kept me out of the hydroponics garden. Wasn't that because some of the virus might get to me?"

"No. It was because the smell would get to you and you'd eat something."

"And the same with the garden on Kobold."

"Right."

"The garden Alice and I wandered through without smelling anything at all."

"You're older now, idiot!" Brennan was losing his temper.

"Yah, of course. Sorry, Brennan. I should have thought of all this—" *Brennan was losing his temper? Brennan?* And—"Dammit, Brennan, I was only a *month* older when you told me never to enter the *Flying Dutchman*'s hydroponics garden!"

"Censor you," said Brennan, and he clicked off.

Roy leaned back in the crash chair. Thick depression was on him. Whatever else he was, Brennan had been a friend and ally. Now—

Now, very suddenly, *Protector* surged under three gravities acceleration. Roy sagged back. His mouth went wide in shock. Then, with all the strength of a now-massive right arm, he reached up to the controls and found a red button.

It was under a guard lock.

The key was in his pocket. Roy dug for it, cursing steadily under his breath. Brennan wanted to immobilize him. It wasn't going to work. He reached up against three gravities of pull, opened the guard, pushed the button.

The cable that linked him to *Protector* blasted free. He was falling.

It took him a full minute to bring the drive up to thrust. He started a ninety degree turn. *Protector* couldn't possibly match the turning radius of the smaller cargo ship. Through the port he watched *Protector*'s drive flame drifting away to the side.

He saw it go out.

Why had Brennan turned off the drive?

Never mind. Next step: the com laser, and warn Home.

Assuming he was right. . .but he dared assume nothing else, now. Brennan could clear himself afterward: turn himself over to spacemen from Home, wearing nothing but a pressure suit, and tell them how Roy had gone mad. Perhaps it would be true.

He swung the com laser toward Home and began tuning it. He knew the frequency he wanted, and the spot. . . if it was on the right side of the planet. What would Brennan be doing now? What *could* he do? *That* was what he would be doing. There was little of free will in a protector. . .and Hell's own weaponry in *Protector*'s weapons pod. He was going to kill Roy Truesdale.

Home seemed to be turning the wrong face. The colony was big, as big as a medium-sized nation, but it had stupidly turned its back! And where was Brennan's killing beam? He *had* to use it.

And *Protector*'s drive was still out. Not trying to chase him down.

Was Brennan still aboard the ship?

Roy saw a possibility then. Irrational, but no time to think: he swarmed out of the crash chair and scrambled down a ladder. The weapons were in the airlock. And the inner door was still open. Roy dashed in, snatched one of the lasers off the wall, and leapt back before the door could close on him.

It hadn't moved.

But if Brennan wasn't aboard *Protector*. . .

Then, irrational as it certainly was, Brennan must be trying to save the situation and Roy Truesdale too. To do that he must board the cargo ship. A feat of impossible heroism. . .but Roy could see him setting *Protector*'s drive to cut off automatically, then dropping out of the airlock toward the cargo ship just as Roy cut the cable. Dropping onto the hull, welding a line before Roy could build up thrust. Then, down the line to the airlock.

Impossible? What was impossible to Brennan? Roy held the gun ready, waiting for the inner airlock door to close.

He had his answer in the roar and flash behind him. In a whistling shriek of breathing-air the Brennan-monster was through the hull side of the cabin toilet, through the toilet door and closing it softly behind him. The door was not hull material; it buckled slightly under the pressure; but it held.

Roy raised the gun.

Brennan threw something. It came too fast to see, and it hit Roy in the upper right arm. The bone shattered like fine crystal. Roy spun half around with the impact, his arm swinging out from his shoulder like something dead. The laser bounced off the wall and back at him.

He fielded it with his left hand and finished his turn.

Brennan was poised like a pitcher on the mound. He held a soft carbon lubrication disc the size of a hockey puck.

Roy shifted his grip on the laser. Why didn't Brennan throw? Now he had the trigger. *Why didn't Brennan throw?* He fired.

Brennan leapt to the side, incredibly fast, but not as fast as light. Roy swung the beam after him. It crossed Brennan's body just below the waist.

Brennan dropped, cut in half.

His arm wasn't hurting him at all, but the sound of Brennan's fall hurt Roy sickeningly in the guts. He looked down at his arm. It dangled, swollen like a melon and running blood where a fragment of bone poked through. He looked back at Brennan.

What was left of Brennan rose up on its hands and came for him.

Roy sagged against the wall. The cabin was going round and round. Shock. He smiled as Brennan came near. He said, "Touché, Monsieur."

Brennan said, "You're hurt."

Things were graying out, losing color. Roy was aware of Brennan ripping his shirt to tie a tourniquet below his shoulder. Brennan talked in a steady monotone, whether or not he expected Roy to hear. "I could have killed you if you weren't a relative. Stupid, stupid. May the ceiling fall on you, Roy. Roy, listen, you've got to live. They might not believe what's in the computer. Roy? Dammit, listen!"

Roy fainted.

He was delirious during most of what followed. He did manage to swing the cargo ship around toward Home, but his technique was sloppy, and he wound up in an escape orbit. The ships that came after him were designed for exploring the inner system. They managed to retrieve him, and Brennan's body, and the computer aboard *Protector*. *Protector* itself they had to abandon.

The injury to his arm seemed sufficient explanation for the state of coma in which they found him. It was some time before they realized that he was sick with something else. By then two of the pilots were down with it.

PROTECTOR

"A chicken is an egg's way of making another egg."
—Samuel Butler.

Every human protector must wake this way. A Pak wakes sentient for the first time. A human protector has human memories. He wakes clear-headed, and remembers, and thinks with a certain amount of embarrassment: *I've been stupid.*

White ceiling, clean coarse sheets over soft mattress. Mobile pastel screens on both sides of me. Window before me; a view of small, twisted trees on a somewhat patchy lawn, all bathed in sunlight that was a bit orange for Earth. Primitive facilities and lots of room: I was in a Home hospital, and I'd been stupid. If Brennan had only —but he shouldn't have had to tell me anything. That close to Home, of course he'd infected himself. In a pinch he need only see to it that he or his corpse reached Home. And he'd let me catch it: same reasoning.

He'd told me most of it. What he'd really been after, out there beyond the edge of the Solar system with his tree-of-life supply left behind on Mars, was a variant of the tree-of-life virus that would grow in an apple or a pomegranate or something. What he'd gotten was a variant that would live in a yam grown with thalium oxide. But somewhere in there, he'd found or created a variety that would grow in a human being.

That was what he'd been planning to seed on Home.

A mean trick to play on a defenseless colony. Such a virus probably would not restrict itself to the right age limit. It would kill anyone who wasn't between—assuming broad limits—forty and sixty. Home would have ended as a world of childless protectors, and Brennan would have had his army.

I got up, and startled a nurse. She was on the other side of a flexible plastic wall. We were sealed in with our infection. There were two rows of beds, and on each a half-changed protector showing signs of starvation. Probably all the proto-protectors on Home were right in this big room. Twenty-six of us.

Now what?

I thought it through, while the nurse was getting a doctor and the doctor was donning a pressure suit. Plenty of time. My thoughts moved so fast! Most problems were not problems long enough to be interesting. I checked Brennan's chain of logic, then started over. For the moment I must believe what Brennan had said about the Pak themselves. There were no inconsistencies in his picture; he'd lied brilliantly, if he'd lied at all, and I couldn't see a motive. I'd observed the Pak ships directly. . .via Brennan's instruments. Well, I could check those by designing the induced gravity generator independently.

A blond young woman came in through a makeshift airlock. I frightened her by being both ugly and mobile. She politely tried to conceal it.

"We need food," I told her. "All of us. I'd be dead now if I hadn't been carrying a lot of superfluous muscle weight when I caught the infection." She nodded and spoke to the nurse via a pen-sized mike.

She gave me a physical. It told her just enough to upset her badly. I should have been dead, or crippled by arthritis, by most of the rules of medicine. I did some calisthenics for her to prove that I was healthy, and held back so that she wouldn't know how healthy. "It's not a crippling disease," I told her. "We'll be able to lead normal lives once the infection has run its course. It only affects our appearance. Or had you noticed?"

She blushed. I watched her debate with herself as to whether to tell me that I had lost all hope of normal sexual relations. She decided I couldn't handle it yet. "You will have to make some adjustments," she said delicately.

"I suppose so."

"This disease, is it from Earth?"

"No, from the Belt, fortunately. Made it a lot easier to control. In fact, we thought it was extinct. If I'd thought there was the slightest chance. . .well."

"I hope you can tell us something about treatment. We haven't been able to cure any of you," she said. "Everything we tried made things worse. Even antibiotics! We lost three of you. The others didn't seem to be getting any worse, so we just left you alone."

"A good thing you stopped before you got to me."

She thought that was callous. Had she but known. I was the only man on Home who had so much as heard the word *Pak*.

I spent the next few days force-feeding the other patients. They would not eat of themselves; there was no taste of tree-of-life root in normal food. They were all near death. Brennan had known what he was doing when he let me put on all that extra muscle weight.

Between times I learned what I could about the industries of Home. I used the hospital library tapes. I set up possible defenses against a Pak attack, using a probable two million breeders—we'd have to set up a dictatorship, there just wasn't time for anything else, and we'd lose some of the population that way—and exactly twenty-six protectors. I set up alternate lines of defense using twenty-four and twenty-two protectors, in case we didn't all make it through transition. But these were just thought-problems. Twenty-six wasn't enough, not nearly enough, not from what I could learn of Home's level of civilization.

When the other patients woke I could put it to them. They knew more of Home. They might get answers different from mine. I waited. There was time. The Pak scouts were nine months away.

I worked out ways to destroy Home, using a Pak scout pair. I redesigned *Protector,* using what we'd learned of Pak scouts since Brennan built *Protector*.

In six days they started waking up. Twenty-four of us. Doctors Martin and Cowles had caught the infection from their patients; they were still changing.

It was a joyful thing, talking to men whose minds matched my own. Poor Brennan. I talked fast, knowing that that and my flatlander accent would make me incomprehensible to any breeder who might be listening. As I talked they moved about the room, testing their muscles and their new bodies; yet I could know that they were missing not a word. When I had finished we spent several hours discussing the situation.

We had to learn if Brennan could have faked the sightings of the Pak fleet and the Pak scouts. We were lucky. Len Bester was a fusion drive repairman; he was able to design an induced gravity generator. He said it would work, and gave us enough theory to convince us, and told us how it could be made to behave. We decided to accept Brennan's gravity telescope, and the Pak fleet. Otherwise there were ways he could have faked what I had seen of the Pak scouts. We would get no more verification of Brennan's story, aside from its internal consistency, which we also verified.

We made our plans accordingly.

We smashed our way through the plastic airlock and swarmed through the hospital. It was all over before the hospital personnel knew what had happened. We confined them until the tree-of-life virus should render them dormant. Many wanted to continue to care for their patients. This we let them do; but we had to destroy all of the medical supplies. There was danger that when people started collapsing with tree-of-life virus, others would screw up their physiology trying to treat them.

The Claytown police presently surrounded the hospital; but by then we could assume that everyone in the hospital was infected. In the night we scattered.

In the days that followed we attacked hospitals, drug stores, the single pharmaceutical plant. We destroyed television stations to slow the spread of news. People would panic if they learned of a new disease that took the minds of its victims and started spreading itself intelligently. They would find the truth no less horrible.

We found panic enough. Home's populace fought us as they would have fought devils out of Hell. Ten of us died that way, trapped and bound not to kill potential protectors.

And six of us were caught trying to save their families, equipping them with pressure suits or pressure tents to keep out the virus, and hiding them where they could. It wasn't necessary to kill them. We confined them until the breeders in question were dead or in transition.

In a week it was over.

In three weeks they started to wake up.

We began building our defenses.

It has seemed only reasonable to novelize this report. So much of it is conjecture. I never knew Lucas Garner, Nick Sohl, Phssthpok, Einar Nilsson et al. You may take Truesdale as true to life, on the theory that I wouldn't lie without a reason. The rest are probably accurate enough.

Still, Brennan said it first: I'm not sure I'm still entitled to the name I was born with. Roy Truesdale was someone else. Roy Truesdale would have died, and expected to die, trying to prevent what I have done to Home.

We have good reason for not beaming this back to human space, not just yet. Brennan was right: the existence of protectors would alter the development of human civilization. Better you should think of Home as a failed colony, wiped out by disease. If the disease should catch more explorers, why, either they will die in transition or they will wake as protectors, look about them, and reach the same conclusions we did. There is little of free will for a protector.

But the Pak fleet remains ahead of us, though the Pak scouts are gone. (That was fun. We set up mock-cities all over Home, just city lights and lines of highways and fusion sources to stand for power plants. It never occurred to the Pak that we might consider Home expendable.) Almost certainly we can wipe out this fleet; but how many followed them? Were the ships of the second fleet redesigned, improved? If we survive that long, we'll have to follow their trail right back into the Core explosion. If we lose one or another battle, why, some survivor will beam this back at every world in human space.

In which case:

Brennan must have hidden flasks of virus, labeled, where they could be found. Check the duplicate Stonehenge. Look for a package orbiting a blob of neutronium. Failing that, the cargo hold from Phssthpok's ship is available on Mars. Check the walls for scrapings of root with dormant tree-of-life virus in them. Failing that, Home is in rotten shape for colonization, but the atmosphere is still thick with tree-of-life virus. Do not convert anyone to protector if he or she has children.

You'll be smarter than they are. You can whip them. But don't wait. If this reaches you, then a Pak fleet that was tough enough to destroy us is following just behind this laser pulse, at near lightspeed. Now move!

Goodbye and good luck. I love you.